TWICE

LIGHTNING HOPKINS BOOK 2

KEITH SOARES

CONTENTS

PART III
SPLIT INFINITY

Bufflegoat Books LLC
© Copyright 2020 Keith Soares. All rights reserved.
First print edition March 26, 2020
ISBN 978-1-7342349-4-7
Original publication date March 26, 2020

Cover Photography: Dave Scavone, Scavone Photography
Model: Stephanie Japec
Other images licensed from iStock by Getty Images

Dedicated to Yasmin and Becky. Sorry your big birthdays, in the year of the coronavirus, are a bit of a mess.

ALSO FROM KEITH SOARES

The Oasis of Filth

Part 1 - The Oasis of Filth

Part 2 - The Hopeless Pastures

Part 3 - From Blood Reborn

—

The Fingers of the Colossus (Ten Short Stories)

—

John Black

For I Could Lift My Finger and Black Out the Sun

If Only Every Moment Was Black and White

And It Arose From the Deepest Black

The Night Is Black, Without a Moon

On a Black Wind Blows Doom

The Black Eye of the Beholder

In the Black Veins of the Earth

Cloak of Black, Mantle of Sorrow

—

Lightning Hopkins

Struck

Twice

NEWSLETTER

Sign Up for Keith Soares's New Releases Newsletter

Get release news and free books, including private giveaways and preview chapters. To join, just visit KeithSoares.com and select the option at the top of the page to get two free books, or go directly to the newsletter sign up form.

facebook.com/KeithSoaresAuthor
twitter.com/ksoares

PREFACE

Alexandria, Virginia
March 17, 2020

Today is St. Patrick's Day, 2020, and normally bars would be over-
flowing with rowdy patrons consuming green beer (or, for the slightly
more enlightened, very dark brown beer with just the right amount
of cream-colored foam on top). This year, however, most folks are
staying home because there's a global pandemic called the coronavirus going around. Hopefully, you're reading this some time in the
future where you've had the luxury of forgetting this coronavirus ever
happened. Hopefully, I'll forget I wrote about this. Because this story
is not a post-apocalyptic tale, it's an urban fantasy with magic and
mystery and a little bit of mayhem. So let's dispense with the doom
talk.

Instead, I'll think back to a trip I took to Paris, less than a year ago.
Getting to know the City of Light, mostly on foot or via the Metro,
gave me the first-hand inspiration to set this story in that historic
town. Walking along the Seine, standing before Sacre Coeur looking
down on most of Paris, taking in an evening meal at a place where

you feel like an old friend... these and many other moments became the backdrop for Lyn Hopkins's second tale. I hope I've done justice to the experience, particularly now since it represents a free-wheeling, traveling lifestyle that, at least for the moment, is beyond our collective grasp.

So, maybe you're reading this in the same global climate in which I wrote it. If so, I hope you have a few hours of distraction from the mess we're in right now. Or maybe you're reading this in a post-virus world. For you, I hope the sun is bright, the days are warm, and your family and friends are close by. For me, the journey to Paris with Lyn and her friends was a welcome change from reality.

Stay well,

Keith Soares
keith@keithsoares.com

PART I

UNHAPPY RETURNS

1

THE ONE THAT GOT AWAY

I'm alone, completely out of charge, and running for my life.

Believe me, I would much rather that none of those things were true. But you know what they say, you can't pick apples from another person's pear tree. Sorry. No one's ever said that.

The crazy thing is this: I don't know why any of those things are true. I don't know why I'm alone — I don't even know where I am, except that it's dark. How I let myself be completely empty of electro-magic? No clue. Oh wait, I do know why I'm running for my life. Because I don't want to die, and Torden is chasing me with about fifty Stickmen and another one of those Mega Golems he makes from spare Stickman parts.

So I'm running, but wow I must be out of shape, because while I expect Stickmen to gain on me, I never thought Torden could. He's two hundred years old, for shit's sake.

You know, it's times like this that I think about reconsidering my life choices, like being too aloof around friends and family. I know somebody like my brother Kevin *means* well, but — I guess I just hate handouts. And as someone who has literally never worked a day in her life, all I get are handouts.

My best friend Mackenzie has my back, generally. I don't usually do too much to shun her or piss her off. Percival, though? That's harder. We're still all new to this boyfriend/girlfriend thing and, I don't know, his affection sometimes feels like another handout. Geez, I am messed up sometimes.

Like now, for example, thinking about all these things that don't exactly matter because — as I believe I have previously stated — I am *running for my life*. Well, those things do still matter. If I was less of an introverted loner, maybe I'd have a friend or two nearby to help out.

As if I just willed them into existence, I suddenly notice two people running ahead of me, hard to make out clearly in the dark. A man and a woman. Is it Pers and Zee? No, definitely not Zee — the hair's all wrong. Zee's hair is all tight curls in a large arc surrounding her head, but this woman has shorter hair. Lighter. Grey? Yeah, and the man's hair is grey, too.

Oh my God.

"Mom? Dad?" I run faster, willing my legs to catch up, to reach them well ahead of Torden and his asshole friends.

My parents — I haven't seen them in so long. Is it really...? Then they stop, they turn, and even in the gloom, I can see those faces, faces I love. My heart wants to burst.

Suddenly, rough hands grab me from both sides. Luckily for me, these are regular human hands, not Stickmen, as *that* particular touch would sponge the electromagic right out of me, and then, parents or not, my time is up. My mother gasps, reaching for my father's hand as Stickmen surround us all but strangely keep back, never coming close enough to touch any of us. More regulars appear, grabbing both of my parents. *Could they be out of charge, too? Kevin told me my parents are electromagicians. We all are.*

Torden strides into the center of the circle created by his Stickmen while the Mega Golem hangs back, towering like a hideous Halloween animatronic, every eye in its multiple heads trained on me. Torden Detonde starts to laugh, a vicious, raspy laugh that chills my blood. Previously, he tried to kill me. Now he's clearly holding back his most dangerous minions. That really doesn't make me feel great about what he might have in store next.

But my parents...

"Mom," I say incredulously. "Dad... how? Where did you come from? Where have you been?" I don't voice my other question: *Why did you leave me?*

Mom looks like she wants to speak but says nothing, like she doesn't have answers for me. She stares at me with a mix of regret and sadness. Dad shares a similar look, also silent.

"Oh, isn't this touching?" Torden asks, clearly not expecting anyone to answer.

So I do. "Why don't you shut the hell up and leave us alone?"

Torden's laugh suddenly stops, but his grin widens. "So feisty, Lyn Hopkins. Or do you still want me to call you *Lightning*?" As if fueled by his words, the Stickmen swirl around us even faster.

"I'd prefer if you'd keep all of my names out of your damned mouth." You may have noticed that Torden and I are not close.

"What's amusing is how much alike you are," Torden continues, ignoring my request. At the moment, he is most definitely in a position to ignore my request. He slowly makes his way to stand in front of my parents, then reaches one hand up to gently stroke my mother's chin. She pulls away in disgust, and my dad lunges forward before the thugs holding his arms restrain him. "You're so much like Marianne, your dear mother. If I recall correctly, they even made that your middle name. Isn't that right, Lyn?"

I say nothing. If I could make electromagic, I would send bolts of lightning into Torden's eye sockets, despite the fact it wouldn't hurt him and would just deplete me. Still, I'd do it for spite. Short of having any charge, I settle for a withering glare. Sadly, it doesn't feel as rewarding.

Torden turns to my father, and I notice at once the similarities and yet huge differences between the two of them. My dad is taller, his button-up shirt neatly pressed. He holds his head above Torden, despite the fact that Torden is holding all the cards. But their skin — something about my father's skin and Torden's looks the same. When Torden told me his age, it never dawned on me that my father might be super-old like him. Now, I wonder. How have I never noticed before?

"You, Jeremy, I will miss," Torden says with a tone I definitely don't like. "I once considered us to be friends." My father, still not speaking, simply shakes his head. I can't tell if it's a rebuttal of the friendship comment or an overall assessment of Torden. I'm leaning toward the latter. "In any event, we have reached the end of such things." Torden nods and steps away from my parents.

Around us, the Stickmen circle closer, and I see both of my parents eye them with dread. I guess even those in the High Order live with the same mortal fear of Stickmen as the rest of us. I suddenly have a very, very bad premonition, and I tug at the two men holding my arms to no avail. I'm an electromagician, but not a body-builder or some kind of super woman. When my electromagic is empty, I'm just an average twenty-three-year-old person. And not a particularly large one at that. But I tug again. If they would just slip up for a second, maybe I could touch one of my parents' hands, maybe that touch would be enough to bring out the well of power I've felt before. The thugs grab at me, squeezing their meaty hands around my arms, and I know it's useless.

"So, Lyn," Torden says. "You may have once been the one that got away, but now I will make you the one who suffers. Now you get to watch your parents become just another of my golems, what you call my *Stickmen*."

"No!" I scream, thrashing but still caught in the grasp of the men holding me.

In seconds, the Stickman horde closes on my parents, and not one but several of the foul things wrap their horrible hands and arms around my mom and dad. Even in death, my parents remain silent, as I watch their electromagic potential sucked away and their bodies reduced to hollow, blackened shells.

I scream again, this time without words, just sound.

And it's enough to wake me up. Well, technically it's enough to wake up the entire plane, Zee and Percival most of all, as they happen to be sitting next to me. We're on a red-eye to the Midwest, trying to get there before a string of nasty looking storms. You know, the kind that fill us up with electromagic power?

"What. The hell. Was that?" Zee says, peering at me from under the cheap eye mask one of the flight attendants gave her.

"S— sorry," I stammer, giving anyone and everyone within eyeshot a weak, apologetic grin.

The same flight attendant who passed out the masks, a prim-looking older woman with her hair in a severe bun atop her head, comes toward us down the aisle. "Everything okay here? Hm?" she asks with an expression that clearly says, *Stop rocking my boat.*

"Yes, I'm fine. Just a nightmare. I'm so sorry."

"Well, we'll be landing in just about two hours." Her tone is as clear as her expression. *Keep it together until then, young lady, got it?*

I nod, still smiling a pathetic smile. With the memory of both my parents being turned into charred, walking monsters fresh in my mind, I know there's very little chance I'll be dozing off again.

2

THE TROUBLE WITH GETTING ZAPPED

Every life can be boiled down to a sentence. So what's mine? *Girl ignores friends for self-interests; loses all due to foolish risks.* Maybe, but it assumes our single-sentence life summaries can have semicolons, and frankly, that seems like cheating. How about this instead? *Girl has much on the outside, has lost much on the inside, fights this conflict and never wins.* Yeah, that's probably more me. And I know my second sentence was basically longer and could have had semicolons, too. Never mind that. Fighting. Not winning. And yes, I mean the wars, not the battles. Winning in the moment is good and all, but winning the whole thing, the big enchilada... Oh my God is that a terribly overused phrase. I apologize.

Anyway, even after flying most of the way across the country, I am alone. Not running for my life this time. Sorry about retelling a dream before, but it seemed, you know, *mentally* relevant. Scary, but true. But yes, I'm alone. Pers and Zee are nearby, but not anywhere I can see them. They may be a mile or two away for all I know. The point is, we're here to get a charge, and despite the times Pers and I have charged up together — yes, we did the two-person-lightning-strike thing again after that first time — we found that it didn't really fill us up as much as going alone.

I think that's fate or some deity confirming my basic instinct to be a loner; even something as simple as getting juiced up properly requires me to be by myself. *Que será, será.*

So, here I am, in a rapidly increasing rain storm, climbing a rather ridiculously steep hill in the woods. It's dark, I'm just about freezing, and I don't know precisely where I am, other than generally in the state of Colorado. I've slipped so many times that I'm covered in a relatively even coating of mud, head to toe. Seriously. It's in my hair. I know, just what you expected from an NYC girl. I need to get higher, somewhere where the approaching lightning will hit *me* and not the damn trees all around.

And of course, as you would expect in this modern era of being *way* too connected, *way* too much of the time, my phone rings. I tug it out of my pocket with a gloved hand.

"Yello," I say, faking a tone of joyful enthusiasm that I definitely am not feeling.

Angry words respond.

It's Kevin.

He's mad because, once again, I used his credit card to buy my plane ticket. Oh, and Zee's. And Percival's. And snacks on the plane for all of us. And our motel rooms — but those were kinda dingy and cheap. I'm gonna stop now. "I'm sorry, I'll never do it again," I say, and even I can hear the lack of conviction in my voice. If I was reading the ingredients from a cereal box, I might have sounded more earnest and convincing. So, not surprising either of us, Kevin doesn't buy it.

"Do you know how many times you've told me that?" he asks.

"One?" I say, again with little to no conviction.

"I'm not kidding, Lyn." As if I thought Kevin, my way-too-uptight brother who's now High Order leader of the New York City electromagician clan would ever *kid*. "How many times do I have to tell you that you have your *own* card, your *own* accounts... your own money!"

Yeah, all that's true, but I don't have to feel comfortable about it. I skirt the subject. "If it's all family money, what difference does it make?"

More angry words.

"Do you know how many times we've had this conversation?" Kevin asks. I start to say *"One?"* but catch myself. "My accounts are handled by an asset portfolio management consultant. All these oddball expenses mess up my taxes —"

Kevin continues to list reasons why this should matter to me, but given that his lead-off was taxes, I can't manage to pay attention. Besides, I slip again, involuntarily forcing a stream of muttered curses from my lips as I hold the phone away momentarily. "Kev, look," I say, on my hands and knees in cold mud. He hates being called *Kev*. "I'm sorry, I'll pay you back or send you a tax exemption form or whatever you want me to do." I look at the sky eagerly, rain drops blurring my vision. "But right now, I gotta go."

Kevin doesn't even use words as he hangs up. Instead he lets out a sort of loud, frustrated sigh and the line goes dead.

I press the hang-up button on my phone's screen, leaving a healthy brown smudge on the glass from the thumb of my glove. Times like these, I wish I didn't need to wear gloves to keep my electronic devices from being zapped, especially when said gloves are like sponges soaking up cold brown water on a muddy Colorado mountainside, but that's just my lot. I push further uphill, seeing a spot up ahead that I think maybe might work. Yes, I'm aware that *maybe might* is not exactly a ringing endorsement. Did I mention it's raining and dark and I have no idea where I am?

I reach the clearing, seeing the wonderful flash of lightning brightening the clouds as they approach from the west. Even better, there's a picnic table in the middle of the open area, so I use the bench like stairs to climb onto the table surface. A front is moving across the mountain range that's supposed to wallop the eastern side, and I'm pretty much at the dividing line between an angry-looking sky and utter weather chaos. Though the picnic table doesn't give me a lot of extra height, every little bit helps. I check my phone's weather app, using the elbow of my hoodie in a somewhat futile attempt to clean the screen. But I see it. The little zig-zag icons approaching the red dot that is me. *Come on, juice!* I toss the phone away into the grass. It's protected in an industrial-grade case, but between all the water and expected high voltage, I figure a little distance is a good idea.

Miraculously, the wait is mere seconds. I do tend to attract lightning, by the way. A wonderfully powerful bolt stabs into me, electrifying my entire body, nearly lifting me off the table. I stand on tiptoes, my arms outstretched as I take in the power. Another bolt, then another strikes me, and I must look like a kid in a candy store, all smiles.

Which is why, when the lightning lets up, I have a lot of explaining to do.

"Oh my God, are you okay?" a bewildered male voice calls out from the darkness to my right. Sheepishly, I turn my head to see a young man and woman peeking out of the zippered flap of a tent, tucked into the woods just beyond the clearing.

Well, shit. I've wandered into a campground, I think. I hesitate for a moment, wondering if I should try the pathetic smile I used on the flight attendant or go with something else.

I go with Plan B.

Stumbling off the picnic table in feigned distress, I flop myself to the ground, getting even more muddy, if such a thing is even possible. I curse about the mud, but not loud enough for the couple to hear. I think.

They run up to me, completely freaked out, like they had seen something really, really terrible happen to me. Which, from their perspective, they did.

"Holy crap, is she dead?" the woman says.

I roll onto my back, and now the rain is spattering my face, but at least I can look up at the not-so-happy campers and offer them my weakest of assurances. "I..." *Pause for dramatic effect.* "I think I'm okay." Slowly, I sit up. The guy offers some assistance, but by the way he barely puts his hand against my back, it's clear he's worried that I am now possibly a dangerous source of electric shock. Of course, I am, but just not in the way he's thinking. "Wow, what a strange thing," I say, shaking my head and smiling. "But really, I'm okay. I — I think I'll just head back down the mountain. I have friends that are waiting. We got separated."

The woman shakes her head, and weirdly I notice the little water droplets cast off her nose, chin, and hair. "No way," she says, putting a concerned hand on my arm. "We've gotta get you to a hospital. You were just hit by lightning — do you even remember it happening?"

Oh crap. Please stop, kind person. I need to run away now. "No, no, that's not necessary." I push my muddy self up to stand, with the couple looking at me all the while like I might explode or expire at any moment. "I'm fine." I try to shove past them, figuring who's going to follow me through the woods in the rain at night? If I can just get some distance... I only succeed in retrieving my phone from the wet grass.

"No, I won't hear of it. We have a car just a short distance away, in the camp lot. We absolutely have to get you to a doctor." She puts her arm around me like a mother duck.

May Day! May Day! I call out, using my special, silent electric communication, hoping one of my friends is nearby. *Zee! Pers! I need some help. People, uh, saw me, and now they're trying to take me to a doctor. We're headed to a campground parking lot. I could really use an intervention right about now, and I hope you're hearing this!*

There is a moment of terrible silence as the couple leads me away, asking if I need anything, if anything hurts. Finally, in my head, I hear that static pop and sigh in relief. At least, I'm relieved until I hear Percival's mocking reply.

My sweet Miss Hopkins, do I need to come to your rescue again?

3

MONEY CHANGES EVERYTHING

I say, "I'm sorry, babe. I leaving you tonight." Then I punch Percival in the arm. It leaves a pretty satisfying splatter of mud on the shoulder of his jacket.

"Come on, Lyn. Just a little joke! And boy are you filthy."

"I'm not amused." I keep walking, right past him, toward the trees.

"What are you two lovebirds spatting about now?" Zee says, stepping out of the forest and into the artificial light of the parking lot. She has a look about her that tells me she picked up a decent charge.

"I don't want to talk about it," I say. "Not here. Let's go back to the car." I give a little *thank you so much for thinking you saved my life!* wave to the campers and turn to walk down the hill. Our rental car is probably two or three miles away. Retrospectively, I wish we had parked in the campground lot. Retrospectively, I wish I had known there *was* a campground. In my head, I say a little prayer that us walking *back* into the woods won't stir up another round of unnecessary sympathy and interaction with the couple, but I know it won't. I made sure.

I'd love to report that the walk down to the car was uneventful, but I think I added at least another quarter inch of mud to the coating all over my body. This, combined with the stifled giggles of my two supposed friends, does not improve my mood. The only good thing, in fact, is that the rain has mostly subsided.

First to reach the car, I grab for the handle. You know when your hand is already slippery and oh, by the way, the car is still locked, and you try to open the door but the handle just kind of mocks you by immediately flapping back against the car? Yeah that. I grumble, audibly.

"Hold on, hold on," Percival says, digging through a pocket for the keys. Even though I rented the car, he drove. Finally, he presses a button and the car lights blink. I go to grab the handle again. "Whoa! Lyn. You're, um, *very* muddy. I know this is only a rental and all, but shouldn't you change first?"

I grumble, audibly, again. Much louder. But the nondescript four-door sedan is rented on my brother's credit card, and he's already mad, so I doubt he would appreciate any tacked-on cleaning fees. Besides, we all brought a change of clothes — kind of a necessity when charge hunting in the rain. I head to the trunk and wait for Percival to pop it. As soon as it opens, I search for the least muddy spot on my pants and scrub my hands furiously there, then grab my spare hoodie and jeans. Zee and Pers are wet and a little dirty, but infuriatingly less than me. They lean against the car as they swap boots for running shoes, while I stand to one side holding my clothes like a sad lost child.

Zee bangs out her boots a couple of times, then tosses them in the trunk, finally noticing me just standing there. Percival looks up, too. "Lyn? What are you waiting for?"

"Get in the car first," I say.

Zee chuckles, affecting a terrible British accent. "The lady doth wish her privacy, good sir knight." I make a pained smirk that clearly informs Zee of how funny she is, and thankfully they both get in the car without another word.

Once they're in, I stand behind the car and rather clumsily strip down to my underwear, tossing my muddy clothes and boots into the trunk with a disgusting *thwop*. As quickly as I can, I pull on the new jeans, but I am soaked through, so it takes some effort. Especially because I'm now standing barefoot on the pavement and manage to step on about a thousand little stabby pebbles. After the jeans, I pull my new hoodie on, and just as I poke my head through, I notice Percival's eyes in the rearview mirror. He's grinning. Obviously he's been watching me.

Percival wiggles his eyebrows — I roll my eyes. He raises one eyebrow — I shoot him a look. *Not. Now.* He looks away, but I can still see those perfect white teeth. Finally, I pull the hoodie down to actually cover myself, shaking my head. My underwear is already soaking into the dry clothes, which is far from a wonderful feeling. Leaning against the car, I quickly tug on socks and shoes before banging the trunk closed. I see Pers watching me again in the mirror and my face turns red, so I quickly head to the passenger side door and drop into my seat, trying not to make eye contact with him or Zee. For her part, Zee already seems to be half asleep in the back seat. Percival starts the car and turns it around in a wide arc to take us back to the road that leads to our dingy hotel. We won't be flying home just yet; more storms are scheduled for tomorrow and the day after. Now I just know where I *won't* be going to get my charge. Another reason for a city girl like me to hate camping.

———

NOT THREE MINUTES into the ride, Zee speaks. She doesn't sit up or even open her eyes, but she speaks. "How'd you get them off your back?"

"Huh?"

"The cute little camper couple back there — you said they wanted to take you to a doctor," she says.

"Forget about it."

Zee suddenly is sitting upright, eyes open. "Oh then it must be something good if you don't want to say it. You told us you'd tell us back in the car. Well, here we are."

"I said I don't want to talk about it, and then I said let's go to the car. They were unrelated statements."

Zee dips her chin and looks up at me in a *bitch, please* kind of way, and I know she won't let up. *Ugh.* "Fine," I mutter. "I gave them money." Percival looks at me so quickly, the car swerves a little.

"What? *You?*" Zee says. "You hate that kind of thing."

"Which is why I said I didn't want to talk about it."

"How much?" Percival asks.

Damn it. "A hundred bucks," I whisper, barely moving my lips.

"Each?" Zee asks, too loud.

I nod.

Do you see why I hate people knowing I have money? Why I shun it and use Kevin's credit card for everything, rather than the one he gave me? Which, by the way, is in an envelope in a drawer at home. I hate carrying it. The only reason I have cash now is because we're traveling. I sense the weird vibes coming from both Pers and Zee, making my grumpiness settle in even more. I know what they're thinking — they don't have two hundred bucks to just hand out to strangers.

Crap. Being an EM makes me a freak in society, having to do crazy shit like stand on a picnic table in the rain to get struck by lightning. Still, it's the lesser of my issues. Being a little rich girl makes everyone look at me sideways. Half want to hate me, and the other half want to use me. I don't want to deal with any of that.

Once we get back to our motel rooms — one for Percival and me, one for Zee — Pers opens the door to our place, giving me a look. Pretty much the same look he gave me when he spied me changing clothes.

"I need to take a shower," I say, brushing past him, in a tone that makes it clear I'll be doing so alone.

4
___

THE NEW NORMAL

Pretty much everything had changed.

Well, I still lived in my parents' ridiculously luxurious townhouse with my older brother, Kevin, and Zee remained in her tiny apartment in the Garment District. But other than those two things, pretty much everything else had changed.

Percival found a new place, which was basically a requirement once a Stickman broke into the basement he was renting in Jersey. Even though the owners never saw the thing, they definitely saw the mess it left behind. Entry to Percival's old place was down some steps on the side of the house, through a rather cheap wooden door with an even cheaper screen door in front. The Stickman ripped both off the hinges. When the homeowners asked Percival what the hell had happened, he couldn't think of a better excuse and said his friend Robin got upset at him and did it. That was far too close to the truth, given that our friend Robin was the Stickman in question, before we put him out of his endless misery. Nonetheless, the homeowners were no longer happy with Pers as their tenant, so they politely but firmly asked him to find a new place. And made him pay for repairs. I offered to help, but I guess he was too proud. Somehow, having my boyfriend reject my money only made it worse that I had it and offered it in the first place.

And yeah, Percival and I are together, and everyone knows it. Well, every EM I know, given that they saw us after all the craziness at Torden's pavilion. Since I know very few people who aren't EMs, that pretty much means everyone. Juliet approves, in a maternal sort of way. That's very sweet of her, and I love her more for it, but it also reminds me that my family has paid her to live in our house to cook and clean for us for who knows how long. Which in turn reminds me of the emptiness where my real mother should be. Not that any of it is Juliet's fault. She's incredible. I probably would have fallen apart years ago if it weren't for her.

But life in general... *that* had most certainly changed. Torden is gone, Rand is gone, the whole damn weirdo pavilion on Orchard Beach is shuttered and abandoned. But that doesn't mean that the EMs who lived there were tossed out. Kevin took over as High Order clan chief of New York City, and he decided to move the base somewhere else. Now here's where obscene amounts of wealth come in handy — Kevin already owned a massive building in Harlem which was underutilized. I discovered that *underutilized* was real estate agent bullshit for *empty*. So that empty building suddenly became full.

We go there, all of us — Pers, Zee, me — from time to time, hoping to fit in some way we never did at Torden's pavilion. While I can't speak for my friends, I can speak for me. It never works. I never feel at home in my brother's clan headquarters. Oh, and I should clarify that Kevin *insists* that I never call it his *clan headquarters*. I admit that's kind of a terrible name; he calls it a community membership center. Right. Because it technically *is* in a community, but membership is *absolutely* required. The general community isn't allowed in, only EMs. And he's thinking about branching out, opening more. *Let's not allow any EM to feel unwanted*, that's what Kevin says, my own brother. So why don't I feel totally comfortable there?

One time, I watched as a nice enough woman who lives nearby stopped in to check on "joining the club." Kevin at least had the foresight to have an EM at the front desk 24/7, and that day it was Mary Tate. She politely informed the woman that membership was, unfortunately, full. Not sure how that's gonna fly if Kev opens ten of these places around town.

To his credit, my brother was able to get most of the EMs from Torden's little group to see the light, or at least supposedly. Though he is the indisputable High Order leader in New York now, he runs things as a sort of mini-democracy, and that gets a lot of fans, even from those who formerly sided with Torden. Perhaps the most popular vote so far was to create a permanent home for The Fuse Box, taking up the entire top floor of the building and open for business six nights a week. It has a bar, some tables, a dance floor, sound booth. Mary Tate was unanimously elected bartender, and Hayden became the DJ, jobs they are actually *paid* for. A bunch of other EMs were hired to do all the additional work of making food, running tables, cleaning up, and filling in when Hayden or Mary Tate take a day off. Percival even DJed one time. I was glad when Hayden came back.

The new Fuse Box charges a small cover, and of course the food and drinks cost money, so I guess my brother has figured out a way to make EM entertainment profitable. It even has a logo on a neon sign, like it's all official, which I guess it is. Best of all, because it isn't housed in some random empty building, the entire club has its own power, coming from the city grid — no EM has to waste a charge to spin tunes or fire up the disco ball. Yes, there is a disco ball. I'd say of all the times I've visited Kevin's new building since it opened, 90 percent of them were to go to The Fuse Box.

Another big change is simply how much time my real life is on display. I mean, I can't exactly date Percival and not have him come to my fancy-pants house, can I? Plus, if we go out, it's kinda stupid for me to make him pay all the time, like it's some required act of chivalry. He works odd jobs, while I have an unlimited expense account. It only makes sense. (I still use Kevin's card, at least in spurts. When he yells at me, I stop, but only for a little while.)

Zee has been on some dates, but nothing serious. The chance lost when Robin died is still too close and painful. Pers and I often ask her to come along with us sometimes, but I can tell that makes her uncomfortable.

And there's that word: uncomfortable. Like how I feel living in a mansion. Like how I feel flaunting a wealth I never did a thing to earn. Like how I feel in the EM community center. No. All those examples are true, but they're just examples. Being uncomfortable is just how I *feel*.

Which means that, still, when things feel overwhelming to me, the fact that I'm a rich girl with electromagic powers in a relationship with a guy who basically has model good looks, and I'm a member of a community where my actions changed everyone's lives... well, I have to disconnect.

I would have flown to Colorado to charge hunt by myself, but Pers is getting to know me too well. When my phone buzzed the alert, he casually leaned over, casually asked if we should go together.

See? That's just the kind of thing that keeps me uncomfortable. Being part of something. It can be too much pressure, too much of a need to do it all right, keep everyone happy. By myself, I have a much lower chance of pissing people off or saying the wrong thing.

And if I'm gonna stay sane in this new normal, I'm gonna need to figure out how to salvage my downtime. I'm going to need to be sneaky about it, hide my intentions, run off and recharge. Figuratively and literally.

I wake up next to Percival in the seedy motel room on the third morning and start to pack before he's up. I think about doing it. I think long and hard about it. I already have my stuff in a bag.

Then he stirs, lifting himself up on his elbows in bed, his curly blond locks falling onto his tanned, shirtless shoulders. He yawns. "Morning, Lynzo. Coffee?" He smiles his perfect smile.

"Pack first," I say. "And don't call me *Lynzo*." I've made this request three mornings in a row and realize with dread that it may be too late. Percival may have chosen a nickname for me.

Do you see why just about *everything* makes me uncomfortable?

5

OPPORTUNITY KNOCKS

The following morning starts much differently. I'm at home, sitting to Kevin's left as Juliet brings us breakfast. She made one of my favorites — steel-cut oats with berries and juice. I hold my gloved hands on both sides of the steaming bowl for a moment, just taking in the warmth. It's early September and the air in the city has just started to turn cool, especially in the morning. I love the colder weather, very possibly because the onset of winter tends to bring on a weird sort of, I don't know, *hibernation* for electro-magicians. Why? Simple. If there are no thunderstorms, there's no way to safely recharge. Not everyone has the money to fly south, and pretty much no one resorts to a wall outlet, unless they want to end up a shell of themselves as an EM junkie. It's not a big deal, though, since an uncharged EM is basically just a regular person. On most occasions, there's no need for one of us to lift ourselves over a building or fire bolts of electricity from our fingertips. A typical NYC EM will bottle up some just-in-case power and leave it that way all winter long. You know, just in case a Stickman jumps out at you, and you need to *move*.

For me, the winter almost makes me believe I'm not a weirdo. Almost.

"Lyn, you know you don't need those, right?" Kevin says, breaking the silence as he lowers his newspaper. Geez, he is so old-school.

I look around, confused. "Need what?"

Kevin pokes a blueberry with his fork and pops it into his mouth, then turns the fork around to point it at my hands. "The gloves. You've worn them forever, and I've never mentioned it because you never wanted to talk about electromagic. Now, you know, since things have changed, well, I just wanted to be sure you know that you don't need them."

I scoff, reaching in my pocket for my phone. "Sure, I do. One wrong touch, and I'll fry this thing."

Kevin pulls out his phone, taps the screen several times, then turns it to face me. It's perfectly fine. At first, I don't register why this is a surprise. After all, I'm an EM and Kevin isn't — well, shit. That's just habitual thinking. Of course, Kevin's an EM. So then what? How's he doing it, not exploding the phone with his power? Come to think of it, Zee, Pers, and the other EMs I know hardly ever wear gloves. I'm an idiot.

"Okay, then teach me, *sensei*. How can you do that?" Yes, my tone is annoyed and a little bitter. Gloves have been a part of me for so, so long. I might feel naked without them.

"Well, you know how you bring *up* your powers, when you want to use them, when your body gets tingly from the flow of electricity? Just do the opposite of that. Instead of bringing it up, tamp it down."

So simple. Of course.

I put my phone on the table and then look at my gloves like they're simultaneously aliens from another planet and my very own skin. And then I start to pull one off. *Tamp it down.* I drop the glove on the table and notice how pale the flesh of my hand is. Not surprising when most of my outdoor activities involve being struck by lightning, not sunbathing.

Slowly, I reach for the phone. *Tamp it down.* I pick up the phone. And a blue-white arc of electricity envelops my hand, surrounding the device. I drop it on the table, watching it expel loose little plumes of smoke.

Shooting Kevin a nasty look, I see his mouth hanging open. "Um. Okay. Well, keep trying. In the meantime, I'll make a call to get you a new phone."

I sigh. "Any other words of wisdom?"

"Sorry, Lyn, really. Maybe you should practice on something cheaper and less important a few times until you get the hang of it."

"Sure, I'll run down to the Cheaper-And-Less-Important phone store after breakfast."

Kevin puts down the paper and huffs. "Come on, it's not so bad. You'll have a new phone tomorrow, I promise. And I'll have them send over a few returns — phones that turn on but maybe have a busted screen or something. You can practice on those."

"Sounds like a fun afternoon."

"Oh! That reminds me. I sent you an email," Kevin says, suddenly excited to change the subject.

"You sent me... an email. When we live in the same house?"

"Yes," he says, completely serious, as if that is a reasonably sane thing to do.

"Oh, well, let me just check it on my phone." I don't even look down, don't even break eye contact.

Kevin sags. "Right. Okay, I sent you and your friends Percival and Mackenzie an email. I want to meet with you at the community center this afternoon. I suggested two o'clock. Does that work for you?"

"Let me just check my calendar on my phone."

He shoots me an exasperated look. "Enough. I said I'd replace the phone. I want you to come down because I have something to discuss with the three of you."

"Am I going to hate it?"

"With you," he says, "who knows?"

———

A FEW MINUTES BEFORE 2PM, Percival parks his car in the small lot behind my brother's building and we all get out. Punctuality is a virtue, so they say, but for us it's pure curiosity that gets us there on time. The ride consists of one question from both Percival and Zee: "What does your brother want?" To which I reply the truth: "How should I know?" The email, which they show me on their phones — insert grumble here — doesn't offer any new information. Between Pers and Zee, the possibilities range from giving us an award for our work in bringing down Torden to being kicked out of the EM community altogether. So that tells you our mutual level of confidence.

Entering, we wave to Laura, an EM I know in passing who happens to be manning the front desk at the moment. She must be expecting us, because she guides us down a hallway to a back office reserved for my brother, and he's waiting there behind a large desk. Typical for my brother, he has a number of folders, a stack of papers, and a laptop, but they look like they've been arranged on the desktop with surgical precision. He nods and gestures for us to sit in three chairs conveniently arranged in front of his desk.

"Thanks for coming, all of you," Kevin says.

"What's with all the formality?" I ask abruptly, before my butt even has two seconds to warm the seat.

My brother smiles and looks at us each, one at a time, slowly. "On the contrary, I suppose I'll dispense with any formalities and simply get to the point. Okay with everyone?"

"Absolutely," Pers says. Zee nods. I just shrug.

"I asked all three of you here — together — because I have a question to ask you as a group. Apologies for the lack of details so far, but what I am going to ask you is something I haven't done — *we* haven't done before. So I wanted to make this a conversation, rather than shoot you an email and hope to get some cohesion from your responses." He looks at us as if he wonders if we're keeping up. I freeze, then finally raise one hand, spinning my finger around in a loop to say *continue...* "Here's my question: would you — all three of you — be interested in working for me? Well, technically you'd be working for the High Order, but I would be your direct supervisor. You'd be paid a salary, of course, and you could choose to live for free in one of the apartments here in the building. If you like, no requirements."

We all stare until Zee pipes up with the question on all of our lips. "Doing *what*?"

Kevin blinks, clears his throat. "Well, that's the tricky part. We'd have to carefully consider what your titles would be, and how we'd present you to the community, but in a nutshell, this: I want all three of you to become our first rank-and-file oversight team, ever."

"Overseeing what?" Zee asks.

"Well, the EM community, of course."

Percival, often discounted in the intelligence department because of his uncanny good looks, gets it first. "You want us to be EM cops?"

Kevin grimaces at the word. "No, not exactly."

"Then describe what you'd like us to do," Pers says.

"I want you to keep an eye on the community and investigate any irregularities. Much like when you discovered what Torden was up to at the pavilion, I want you to use your curiosity, your tenacity, your sense of what's right, to find issues that could negatively affect the community and bring them to light, so that they can be dealt with."

"Yep," Percival says. "Cops."

Kevin sighs. "Look, that's exactly the sort of description that others *won't* like, so while I agree with you that you would have a role similar to police investigators, I'd like to work with you, if you all are interested in the jobs, to come up with a better way to say it."

"Is there something specific you want us to be looking into?" I ask. "Has something happened?"

"Yes and no," Kevin replies. "Nothing urgent or dangerous like the Torden situation. But I have thoughts on what I would like you to be doing if you accept."

"What's the salary? And how long?" Zee says, cutting in. Kevin tells her the number and says the jobs are ours until we don't want them anymore. I see both Pers and Zee's eyebrows raise before they can catch themselves, and I realize it must be a good offer. I'm immediately pissed at myself once more for being such an out-of-touch rich girl, and I even mildly fake surprise at the salary number, so I don't look like such a pampered jerk. Luckily, the others are internally calculating. "We need to talk in private for a few."

"Of course," Kevin says, getting up and leaving us alone in the room.

"Holy shit," Zee says in a hushed whisper like we're being watched. "I would quit my crappy job in a heartbeat for that much money. I don't care about the free apartment — any EM can live here for free — but I could definitely see myself upgrading from my old apartment. I might even move out of the Garment District." I'm silent, as matters of money don't have a huge impact on me, and I really, really don't want to come off horribly in front of my friends. "What do you think, Pers?" Zee asks.

He gets wide-eyed. "I mean, I *might* be able to make that much running jobs —" I never ask Percival about his jobs. I really don't want to know. "— but it would take *a lot* of jobs in a year. And yeah, I don't care to live here. Too weird."

"So..." I add, in a low and unsure voice. "You both want to take the job?" Pers and Zee look at each other, then back to me, and shrug. "What would we call ourselves, then? EM Police sounds terrible."

"I have no idea," Percival says, and Zee nods in agreement.

There's a knock at the door and Kevin sticks his head in. "Need more time?" I shake my head, and he comes back to sit behind his desk. "So, then, do you accept?"

"We can't come up with a decent title," Zee says.

Bobbing his head in agreement, Kevin purses his lips, thinking. "How about simply Special Assistant? It would, by the way, absolutely be a stepping stone to bigger things within the High Order."

Percival grins, pearly whites blazing. "Special Assistant to the High Order? Me? I kinda like that."

"Me, too," Zee says, mirroring Pers's smile. Then they both turn to me. "Lyn? You in?"

"Do I have a choice?" I want to be an official part of the Order about as much as I want another hole in my head.

"Nope," Percival says, flipping blond locks over one ear.

"Then I guess I'm in," I say.

Kevin grins. "It should be easy. And besides, there will be some travel. It'll probably be fun." Then his tone changes. "*Ubi concordia, ibi victoria*," he says solemnly. He loves reciting this High Order mumbo jumbo — it means *Where there is unity, there is victory*, but it's Kevin's tone that stands out. Immediately, the gravity of the situation hits me.

What the hell have I done?

6

BABY BOOMING

"All right, questions," Percival gleefully says to Kevin. "Do we get badges? Uniforms? Is there an EM jail where we get to lock people up?"

Kevin can't help but roll his eyes. "No, no, none of that. I don't want you to *arrest* people, I want you to investigate anything that seems strange."

Personally, I don't think this is the greatest way to begin a dicey new job. I may even already regret saying yes. "What was it you wanted us to look into?" I ask, hoping Pers will take the hint and be quiet.

My brother nods, opening a desk drawer. "First of all, it may be absolutely nothing. A statistical anomaly, if you like." He flops a folder down on the surface of the desk and waits for me to pick it up.

I don't even open it. A single word handwritten on the tab of the folder is enough to pique my interest. "Paris?"

"Yes."

"So, we're traveling right away?" Zee asks. "To France."

"Assuming you're all on board with it, yes," Kevin replies.

Percival interjects. "To do what? What's going on in Paris?"

"There are additional details — people you will need to meet with, addresses, numbers — but the gist is this: there are a lot of EMs being born in Paris this year."

Zee blinks. "That's it? Check up on a bunch of French babies? And you want to pay us a salary for this?"

"Yes, Mackenzie," Kevin says. "But it's more than just a bunch of French babies. Over the years, the High Order has kept quite a lot of records, and during the last several decades, much of this data has been migrated to cloud-based data systems, making it much easier for us to notice things like statistics that are... *unusual*. In fact, this has been the primary focus of my role within the Order for much of my life. And what I've discovered is this: in an average year, a big city like New York or Paris can expect that only about one hundredth of one percent of babies born will be electromagicians. This year, that number for Paris is almost one percent."

Beside me, I can feel the confusion emanating from Percival. "One percent? That's nothing."

"On the contrary," Kevin says, suddenly very serious. "At a rate one hundred times higher than the norm, Paris's EM population could rival the entire world's population of electromagicians in just a few years. Once all these babies grow up, then what? There would be far too many to remain hidden from regular people forever." He lets that point settle in, and I really have no idea how I feel about it. Let the world know we exist? Would that be so bad? Then again, I have always been a big fan of my own privacy. "What we're seeing in Paris could change the future of humanity as we know it."

There is a long silence until Zee finally whistles, a long low note. "Well, yeah. That *does* seem like something someone should check into."

"Exactly," Kevin says.

"I can't speak for Lyn, but Percival and I can't really afford a flight to France, hotel, meals, all that."

"All taken care of for you, including a per diem. Can I count on you?"

We three look at each other, and in no time, everyone's nodding.

Pers pipes up. "Free trip to Paris, good paying jobs, working with the Order? What's not to like?"

"Great. We can get you on a flight early next week," Kevin says. "Be sure to study that folder. Once you arrive, I'll need you to meet with Genevieve Deschamps — she's High Order. Think of her as Paris's version of me. But read what I've given you beforehand."

"Definitely, will do," Percival says, and we all push up from our chairs to head for the exit. There, as he holds the door for Zee and me, Pers turns back to Kevin, brows furrowed. "Just one more thing. What's a *per diem*?"

———

WE HEAD BACK to my house, which is another one of those uncomfortable changes in the new normal. Used to be, I'd kick and scream *not* to invite people over. Now they come over regularly. "What about this one?" Zee asks me, almost giddily. She swipes through another set of photos on her phone, the third apartment she's shown me in as many minutes. It's just the two of us; Percival disappeared, off to run one last odd job, or maybe tell his former employers to go to hell. Who knows? I'm really happy for them both — and especially happy that Zee has a chance to change her life in a positive way — until I notice she's using her phone without gloves.

"Am I the only EM in the world who can't stop zapping her phone?" I mutter, not really intending for it to become a conversation starter, but of course, she hears me.

"Girl, do you have any idea how many of these things I've fried?" Zee laughs. "After rent, I think my phone budget is my next highest expense. Well, between paying for the service and the replacements. Luckily, I only destroy them when I'm really not paying attention to what I'm doing. I told the phone company it was due to *unexpected electrical fluctuations in my antiquated apartment building.* See? Another reason to move!" She sees my sheepish expression. "What is it?"

"Can you teach me how to not kill my phone?"

"Oh my God, Lyn — is that why you always wear gloves? I just thought you liked the look." I hang my head. A moment later, we're dying laughing at the stupidity of it all. Her phone buzzes, and through tears of laughter she checks her notifications. "Geez. Your brother means business."

"What it is?"

"Check your phone," she says, and I return a glare. "Oh, wait. Never mind. Anyway, Kevin has already sent over two messages — an employment contract. Sheesh, formal much?"

"What's the other email?"

Zee dons a really bad French accent. "A plane ticket to *Pah-ree*, of course, *mon ami*. We leave in four days."

"I don't recommend you talk like that once we get there." Meanwhile, in my head, some dumb little song from childhood or who knows when crops up. *There's a place in France, where the naked ladies dance.* Oh wait, I know where I heard that. From Percival. So mature.

Between the three of us, I firmly expect to be kicked out of the country as an offense to their culture before we ever get near a newborn Parisian electromagician.

7

THE CITY OF LIGHT

I have to admit, the idea of traveling to France has me a little excited. A free vacation with my best friend and my boyfriend? I mean, sure, we'd have to do something about this investigation my brother wants us to do, but that seems almost like playacting. What do I know about running an investigation?

I should have known the potential joy of the whole thing would be tossed out the window in short order. First, Kevin has us fly business class, meaning Zee and Pers are all *OMG this is amazeballs!* the entire trip, until they blessedly fall asleep. I almost never fly anything but coach, but I'm used to far too much plush comfort at home, so the fancy flight has the opposite effect on me. It grates on me. I'm not surprised to find a car waiting for us at the airport. I am, however, stunned by the house.

My home in New York is ridiculous enough. The place Kevin gets for us in Paris — for *three* people — looks like a castle, with a big sort of turret/tower crowning the whole thing. Granted, it's actually more of a city townhouse, given that it's connected to the buildings on both sides, but just the look of it alone, ugh. The moment we step out of the car, Percival asks, "Does the queen live here?" Should I tell him the French hauled their queen out to publicly cut off her head? I think that would just inform everyone of my mood seeing the place, so I opt for silence.

Inside, there are ten rooms, five of which are bedrooms, because of *course* Kevin got five bedrooms for the three of us. I imagine he's in denial about our most likely sleeping arrangements, and that's fine with me. Still, if we accidentally bump into a half dozen of our closest friends around town, we'll be able to put them up. Or maybe we'll rent the extra rooms to partying Parisian college students. Would serve Kevin right.

As we wander the house, taking in the new digs, Pers catches up to me and can't help but notice that I'm significantly less excited than he is. "What's wrong?"

I wave it off. "Nothing. Just... *this*. It's too much, which is so typically, maddeningly *Kevin*."

"I don't mean the house. What's wrong with *you*? You seem like nothing is making you happy these days." I'm silent. He's hitting way too close to home, and we just began a trip to a foreign country. I'm keenly aware that my mouth may end up alienating him and possibly Zee for the whole trip. And possibly beyond. Reaching out, Percival puts his hands on my arms, trying to look me in the eye, though I'm doing a bang-up job of avoiding his gaze. "Lyn, I think I understand. *Everything* is different. Before, you and I just, you know, hung out here and there. Before, the world had this, I don't know, *structure* where Torden was the person in charge. Your brother ruled your home life, and now it's like he rules your *whole* life. Stickmen were mostly rumors. The hardest thing to figure out most days was what to eat for breakfast, and if there would be a storm so we could maybe get a charge. Things have really changed."

"They really, really have," I say.

"And look, if you think this whole boyfriend/girlfriend thing is just adding complication on top of that, then maybe we just decide to enjoy each other's company and go from there. I want to be part of the things you *like* about your life, not that piss you off."

He's right, about so much of it, and how all this change is hard for me to deal with. A girl who has lived in the same bedroom her whole life, a place I both love and hate. But he's wrong about one part. I lean into him and place my cheek against his chest. "It most definitely isn't you. You're the one change I really like." I tilt my head up and he leans down to kiss me.

Just then, Zee passes by in the hallway and audibly sighs. "I can see how this is gonna go down. I think I'll take the bedroom far away, up in the loft. You know, that castle turret thing? It's kinda small for two, anyway, and then you guys can take whatever you want, *down here*. A little distance will do us all some good." She wanders off, shaking her head. Just then both my phone and Percival's buzz at nearly the same moment. We both reach into pockets, but apparently Zee's buzzed, too, and she's faster, calling from the hall. "Looks like we have a meeting today. That was quick. *By decree of the Paris community, and myself, Genevieve Deschamps...*" Zee interrupts reading the email to yawn. I guess she's got a bit of jet lag. Oh, and I'm pretty sure she butchered the French woman's name. "*I hereby request* blah blah blah... Basically, we meet in under an hour. She's hosting us for lunch. I do so hope there will be baguettes and caviar, but maybe this could have waited until tomorrow? I'm exhausted. Thanks for all the notice, lady."

"Do we *report* to her now or something?" Pers asks.

"No idea," I say. "I sort of forgot to read the folder."

"Me, too," says Zee.

"Well, you know *I* didn't read it," Pers replies, grinning his perfect grin. "So I hope they're happy to see us."

———

JUST AS WE'RE contemplating how to get to a meeting in a town we're utterly unfamiliar with, a car pulls up and its driver buzzes at the door — the same driver who had taken us from the airport to the house. His name is Jean and he informs us that he's been assigned to whatever our needs are while we're in Paris, and that he's aware we need to get across town. Clearly seeing that we're confused, he explains that our townhouse is in Paris's 16th arrondissement, which is apparently on the west side. Pointing down the street, he notes how we can see the tip of the Eiffel Tower, just visible, but not too far away. We need to get to the 4th arrondissement, which means less than nothing to me. He says he'll try to give us a little geography lesson as we drive, so we all hop in. Jean is a regular human, so of course we avoid discussions of electromagic in his presence, meaning that if we want to have any last preparations before the meeting, they're going to need to be in some sort of code or in our heads. Luckily, this is not our first rodeo in that respect; EMs have been talking in code around regulars for as long as there have been EMs.

Not surprisingly, Jean has a French accent, but it isn't something as outlandish as what Zee tried out back home. In general, he speaks quite clearly in English. Where I start to lose him is when he uses French names, or at least ones I've never heard before. First, he drives us past the Arc de Triomphe, which is remarkably close to our place. Then he heads down the Champs-Élysées. I know he's taking the scenic route for our benefit, but I'm not complaining. After a lifetime in New York, it's remarkably refreshing to be some place I've heard about for years but never seen with my own eyes. Frankly, I'm dumb-struck by seeing the sights.

Jean says our meeting is at the Place des Vosges, in Le Marais district, something that was built by King Henry IV in the 1600s, as if information like that was completely normal. I search for it on my phone — which thankfully arrived a couple of days before the flight, though I'm still wearing gloves until Zee gives me a lesson — and based on my completely inaccurate spelling, I realize I'm over-whelmed trying to connect the sounds I *hear* to the words I *see*. Whether on my phone's map, or on the cool tile street signs embedded into the sides of buildings, French words definitely do not look the way they sound, at least not to my amateur understanding. Jean continues our tour, but for the most part, my recollection of the drive is *historic-thing, historic-thing, river, historic-thing*.

Finally, we pull up to a rather regal-looking square of buildings — which makes sense given its origins — but not in a castle sort of way. More like very formal apartments surrounding a beautiful, green open space. Jean pulls over and gestures for us to get out and walk under an arch at the north side of the square. "White building, left side, red door, just past the arch. Ask for Genevieve Deschamps."

"Can't you just drive us to it?" Percival asks, peering out the window like some French monster might be waiting for us outside, despite the fact that it's a bright, sunny day and there are about two thousand locals and tourists dotting the square, having a late lunch or just enjoying the weather and surroundings.

Suddenly a small white vehicle that looks like the lovechild of a van and a truck barrels through the archway and blows its tinny horn at us. Trying to drop us off, Jean has blocked the roadway. "That is why. It is a one-way street."

"Ah sorry." Percival opens the door and jumps out, giving the van/truck driver a wave as he holds the door for Zee and me.

Just before I exit, Jean hands me a business card. "Text me when you need another ride." I nod. The van/truck driver has been inching closer to make his point, with the harsh noise of the engine nearly blotting out Jean's voice. Between the rattle and the smell, it brings to mind the diesel delivery trucks that run all over Manhattan. Coupled with the driver's disposition, it makes me wonder if maybe New York and Paris aren't all that different, after all.

I follow Pers and Zee under the archway as Jean departs. Turns out that Percival's concerns about finding our way are overblown — the white building with the red door is easy to find. Not knowing what else to do, we go to the heavy wooden door and knock, but no one answers.

At least, no one answers in a regular sort of way.

"Yes?" a voice says inside my head, the tinge of static making it clear this is electromagic communication, which of course tells us we're in the right place. A door in a populated downtown area that no one will answer without the secret handshake, or in our case, the secret way of saying *let us in*.

Without audible words, Percival replies. "We have come for a, um, lunch meeting. With, uh, Ginnavee Dayshum."

Wow, I think. *That was even worse than Zee's French.* Now I'm terrified to even open my mouth.

Shockingly, the French don't kick us directly out of their country. The door lock clicks, and the red door swings open, revealing a large, dark space that's hard to register in contrast with the bright sunlight outside.

A tall, wiry man with a short mat of brown curls atop his head appears in the doorway, a trick of the light nearly making it look as if he pops out of thin air. He speaks, not the EM way, but the regular way, probably because he's now clearly visible to anyone passing on the street. "*Bonjour*, I am Marcel Brodeur, an assistant to Madame Deschamps." He tries to be subtle as he eyes each of us individually, but his face tells me clearly he'd rather we weren't darkening his door. Oh, and his pronunciation makes it obvious that Pers did a shit job there, too. "Follow me, please."

The man turns as we enter the building. Behind us, the heavy door swings closed on its own, culminating in a low, echoing click of the latch as we are plunged into nearly complete darkness. Blinking to adjust my eyes, I see Brodeur is already halfway down the hall.

Pers leans toward me and whispers. "And I thought your brother was uptight." The sound seems to bounce off the cool stone walls as we hurry to catch up.

8

WINE AND CIGARETTES

"Lyn Hopkins," the woman I assume is Madame Genevieve Deschamps says, with a slight dip of her head in my direction. She studies me a moment, squinting. "I am acquainted with your brother, though I can't say there's a tremendous amount of family resemblance. In any event, welcome to Paris." She's tall and thin, dressed all in black — black blouse, jacket, cropped pants, even her simple but stunning high heels — and her hair looks like she just stepped out of a salon or a magazine shoot. Though I estimate her age at more than double mine, I'm immediately jealous of her classic yet seemingly casual beauty. So, of course, I say nothing. As if she's just now realizing I'm not alone, she finally turns toward my friends. "Mackenzie Patmina, Percival Farimir, welcome to you both, as well. I'm Genevieve Deschamps."

"Howdy," Pers says. He's not really a *howdy* kind of guy, so I know he's using his brand of irreverent humor to try to overcome what seems like meeting the French queen of the electromagicians. Zee just nods and smiles.

My immediate thought is to compare the current situation to what I know already — this woman is basically the equivalent of my brother. She's Paris's leader and a representative from the High Order.

But I've only watched Kevin in that role for a short time, so instead, I think of Torden. That man had a penchant for the weird — I know, understatement of the year, sorry. I remember meeting him in his receiving room, that strange wide room full of candles making odd pools of dark and light. This place, in France, is nothing like that at all. First and foremost, Deschamps stands up to meet us; Torden never did. We're in a wide, posh, well-lit room on the second floor, almost like a hall that runs the building length. There's a bank of endless tall windows on my left with luxurious, patterned draperies framing each one, and oversized doors along the right wall. The floor is wood parquet and the walls have been painted a pale yellow with white accents. The only furnishing are pairs of expensive-looking white chairs arranged below the windows every 20 feet or so, each with a little, ornately carved table between them. The only difference between the place where Deschamps greets us and the other seating areas is the steaming glass-and-gold cup of tea resting on the table beside where she sat. Just then, the trill of a high violin note makes me realize that classical music is being pumped in from somewhere, low and subtle but filling the room with musical ambience. *Oh man, if Kevin sees this place, he's gonna want to upgrade our EM building back home. And what the heck is that? Do I smell lilac?* I look down at the sleeves of my hoodie, feeling remarkably out of place.

Marcel Brodeur walks over to Deschamps and leans in, saying something to her I can't hear. She gives a nod that's so subtle that it looks more like a long blink. "Lunch is ready. Shall we walk to the dining room?"

The three of us look at each other, no one really taking the reins on the situation until Zee speaks. "Sure," she says. "I'm starving. Even in business class, plane food is... well, plane food." Genevieve Deschamps's mouth curls slightly at the edge, like she's so very in tune with Zee's sentiments. Ah, the rich life. I shudder.

———

CALLING the place she takes us a dining room is like calling Mount

Everest a bump in the road. It's a massive space, full of large round tables covered in white linen, most of which are filled with people — EMs, assumedly — eating lunch. The room's decor is similar to the hallway with tall, draped windows and pale walls. From the high ceilings, chandeliers dangle, each looking like they're made from a thousand pieces of leaded crystal. Okay, okay. I know. My recognition of leaded crystal versus glass baubles clearly labels me a wealthy person. I can't help I've been around shit like this my whole life. Still I remain quiet, afraid that if I open my mouth, I'll simultaneously look like a stuck-up brat in front of my friends, and a country bumpkin in front of the elegant lady seated beside us.

Lunch begins with each of us receiving a colorful dish of mixed greens, while some kind of pâté is placed in the middle of the table, along with a sliced baguette. I have far more utensils and glassware options than I would ever know what to do with. Thankfully, one of the waiters rounds our table, artfully pouring white wine into one of our two wine glasses, so I don't have to guess which one to use. The low sounds of classical music still flow from unseen speakers, now mostly masked by the rumble of many conversations, and the clinking of forks on dishes. There are too many smells in the room for me to pick out any one, but the overall scent is mouthwatering. I didn't realize how hungry I was before sitting down and having so many smells waft over me.

Percival is the first to eat, and I wonder if maybe he really is oblivious to all the pomp and circumstance. Zee and I follow, but notably more reserved despite our hunger. In time, our salad plates are removed and we're offered meat, fish, or vegetarian options for our main course. Pers takes the meat, Zee asks for vegetarian, and almost like I feel compelled to do so, I take the fish. *You idiot*, I think. *You don't even like fish all that much.* When the next course arrives, wine comes again. The French like their long lunches, I guess.

As if reading my mind, Zee finally asks a question. "Do you all eat lunch like this *every* day?"

Deschamps gently places her fork beside her plate before reaching for her napkin and dabbing at the side of her mouth, smiing. "Well, yes and no. *Lunch*," she says somewhat awkwardly, "or what we call *le déjeuner*, is the most important meal each day in our country. I understand it is not really this way in the US?" She looks at us for confirmation, and we each nod. "But we have admittedly made this meal more of a welcoming celebration, for our guests such as yourselves."

The food is so good, I don't even mind that mine is fish. I look around the room, at all the other tables filled with people I assume are French EMs, though it's hard to think of many of them as electro-magicians. Different tables are at different stages of the meal, and some are even finished entirely, the adults there puffing on thin white cigarettes. I'm suddenly aware of the smell of smoke, a scent unfamiliar from New York restaurants since it was banned many years ago. "There are other guests?" I ask, the first words I've spoken since we arrived. I look around again, wondering why so many of the people look strange to me.

"Yes, of course," Genevieve Deschamps says. "Not only New York is interested in our rapid population growth. We have guests from Singapore today as well, though I had time to chat with them this morning, so I am spending time with only you now." She gestures to a table across the room where an Asian man and woman are still on their main course. "There are also groups from Rio de Janeiro and Nairobi. More will come soon, I suspect. As each arrives, we like to throw a small welcoming party, like this one."

Percival stops shoveling food into his mouth for a moment, fork still held near his mouth, looking oddly like a raccoon caught in a trash can. "Party? Like The Fuse Box," he says, matter-of-factly.

Deschamps wrinkles up her forehead, like she can't seem to translate the words. "*Fuse Box*? What do you mean?" This begins a five-minute description from Pers about The Fuse Box, both its original, impromptu version, and its current permanent home. Our French hostess looks mildly amused, particularly at the clear distinctions Percival draws between our raucous nights and their reserved French midday meals.

And that's when it hits me — why I am having so much trouble identifying the people around us as EMs. They are *so* much older than the New York crowd. Not all of them, of course, but the population ranges from children (with their parents, I assume) to people much older looking than us or even Deschamps. *This is all a wild goose chase*, I think. *The only difference between Paris's EMs and New York's is that Torden Detonde culled our clan regularly to steal power and extend his own life. This baby boom thing is no big deal.* I mentally make a note to text my brother exactly that when lunch is over.

"So, Madame Deschamps," Zee says, interrupting my train of thought with her unexpectedly decent version of French pronunciation. I guess she's a good mimic. "Given that you've invited us here, and created this celebration, does that mean you welcome us looking into the things happening in your city? The high EM birth rate we've been told about?"

Good question, Zee, I think. Perhaps at least one of us will actually deserve to be sent halfway around the world on Kevin's little mission.

"Of course," Deschamps says after a sip of wine. "I am just as surprised as all of you that there are so many newborn electromagicians here. So, look into it if you like. My people are as well. But I think it is, how would you say... just one of those things?"

I couldn't agree more with her. We're in Paris for nothing. And realizing that makes me further realize I'd better take as much advantage of the chance to be with my boyfriend and friend in such a famous place before my brother calls us home.

"Tomorrow," she continues, "I have made arrangements for you to meet with a member of our community, Charlotte Laffitte. She's a nurse in the maternity ward of *l'hôpital Pitié Salpêtrière* — don't worry, I will provide you with all the necessary information, and I am aware you have a driver to get there. You may ask Madame Laffitte anything you like to satisfy your investigation. Good?" We agree. Deschamps then reaches into the small designer handbag next to her on the table. "Wonderful. So then, if we are all finished with our meal, who would like a cigarette?"

9

THE ORIGIN OF THE SPECIES

Bright and early, we stand at the door, not knowing exactly what to do, when a loud buzzer goes off, followed by a harsh click. For a moment, we don't move, until the dented metal speaker box beside the door blares a tinny male voice. "*Pousse la porte* — oh sorry. Push the door, please."

Pers shrugs and does as asked, with Zee and I following him into the staff entrance of *l'hôpital Pitié Salpêtrière*. I'll just call it the hospital.

The previous day, after a rather long and drawn-out lunch with the Paris EM clan, we were driven back to our castle house by Jean with every intention to use the evening to walk around and explore this city, so new to us. Instead, we spent much of the afternoon in a vegetative state from all the food we ate. When we finally recognized that we might be hungry again, hours later, we took the easy way out and got dinner at a cafe that was only about five blocks away. Frankly, we were all feeling the effects of jet lag and kept catching each other yawning. Dragging our feet, we passed a place called *Le Caneton Rouge*, and I thought it looked too fancy for my liking. But Percival was adamant that we use up our *per diem*; once he learned what those words meant, it was like his daily challenge to make sure he spent it all. "If we don't, we're just giving away money," he said. The argument meant nothing to me, but Zee agreed, so I went along. The one aspect of it I could support was that the cafe wasn't some American chain restaurant, of which we saw many. Why go there? We can do that at home. Nonetheless, by the end of dinner, we were all hurting. Tired and rather bloated from a second big, rich meal — delicious though it was — we made half-hearted promises to each other to see the sights tomorrow and then went home for bed.

Another good reason for the early end to our night was the timing of our meeting at the hospital: 7:30am. What sort of monster schedules a meeting for 7:30am? As Charlotte Laffitte greets us, just inside the staff entrance, I make some offhand comment about the time. Big mistake.

"I'm not even sure what time it is," she says with a sneer. "I only know I've been on shift for five and a half hours, and I have six and a half to go." I try to do the math on that, to figure out when she will finally get to go home, and it hurts my brain. Still, somehow, she looks pretty fresh and ready to go, especially compared to the person I saw in the bathroom mirror this morning. I rub my eyes and make a mental note not to yawn again.

Nurse Laffitte guides us down hallways, making turns seemingly at random. Sure, there are those generally cryptic signs with names and arrows that you see at most hospital hall junctures, but they're even less helpful for us than usual, given that they're in French. Finally, she reaches an elevator bank and presses the Up button. "We will take the lift to the first floor," she says, and immediately I learn two things: an *elevator* is a *lift*, and the floor we're already on — the ground floor — is apparently *not* the first floor. I make a note to search online for common differences between the States and France when we get home, knowing I should have done so before we left the US. But, you know, I wasn't expecting suddenly to have a job, and especially not one that took me across the ocean days after I signed on, so cut me a break.

The elevator — arg, *lift* — dings at the "first" floor, and we get out, dumped right into the middle of the hospital's maternity ward. A wide curving nurses' station is before us, bustling with three people wearing pale green — two men and one woman — either on the phone or working through important-looking folders filled with paperwork. To each side, the hallway curves around the nurses' station, with doors receding in the distance. Laffitte guides us to the left without a word.

Eventually, we reach a closed door that stands beside a long window, and even I know what it is, if only from watching TV and movies: the hospital nursery. As the nurse places her ID card against a reader to open the door, I peer in the window and see a dozen or so little faces, pink and brown and black, barely peeking out from between their little knit caps and a tightly wrapped white blankets with pink and blue stripes. *God, I would be so claustrophobic*, I think. Nurse Laffitte urges us to enter before closing the door behind us.

Inside, I walk among — and smell — the newborns I had seen from the window. Two rows of tiny beds, more like boxes, most with a cute little bug of a human being inside, though several at the end stand empty. What isn't cute is the aroma. Sure, hospitals try to stay clean, and I'm sure they regularly change these kiddos, but the fact of the matter is babies poop themselves, and in a closed room with a bunch of them, it's noticeable. Or maybe my nose is playing tricks on me, since no one else seems to flinch.

It all feels a little illegal, if you ask me. Three foreigners brought into the nursery where a bunch of helpless babies could be abducted, with no one except a somewhat suspect EM nurse stopping us from doing something bad. I shake my head to stop thinking such thoughts, just as Laffitte starts to recite what sounds like a pre-rehearsed spiel.

"What you see here are the babies born in this hospital, either today or within the past couple of days," she says. "It depends upon their health, and that of their mother, to decide when they get discharged. But the ones in here are the healthiest ones, and the number of babies you see here is fairly common. I have worked at this hospital for just over twenty years, and in all that time, I've become very, *very* familiar with the number of electromagicians born here. In a normal year, I might see one. Perhaps none. I think only once have I seen two MEs in a year. But now —" She catches herself. "Sorry, in France, we call our kind MEs, not EMs. It stands for *les Magiciens Électriques*. Do you want to know how many MEs I have seen this year?"

We all nod, wide-eyed, though Zee has a sort of extra bonus expression, like, *Well, why else did you think we were here, honey?* Afraid the nurse will see Zee's face, I pipe up. "Yes, please."

Nurse Charlotte Laffitte walks between rows of newborns, stopping and pointing at the fourth one in the back row, an infant with a ruddy complexion and tiny curl of hair hanging down on his forehead. Other than thin wisps, it was all the hair the kid had. "This child, a boy only one day old, is one of us. The others, they are not. Still, that is very unusual. Because this child is the *ninety-fourth* one I have seen so far this year."

"Whoa," Percival says, grimacing. "That is a big difference."

"Indeed," she says.

"But, um... how do you know for sure whether one of these babies is a regular or an EM? Sorry, *ME*?"

The nurse shrugs, as if we should already know the answer. "I perform the test on each one, of course."

Zee, Percival, and I look at each other sideways. "The test?" Zee finally asks.

Laffitte sighs and slides over next to the newborn with the standalone curl. "It is simple. Like this." Then she reaches into the kid's boxy little bassinet and touches one finger to the flushed skin of the boy's cheek. Suddenly, a tiny arc of blue electricity flows from her finger to the child. The baby boy doesn't even wake up. "But with the others, it is different," she says as she moves to the next bed down the line, once more reaching out her finger. The moment her arc of electricity zaps the second baby's cheek, that child's eyes pop open in shock and its mouth immediately spews forth a frail, mewling cry. Percival, Zee, and I reel back in shock at what she's just done.

"My God!" Zee gasps. "Isn't that *cruel*?"

Nurse Charlotte Laffitte seems nonplussed. "It is only a *little* zap," she says with a smirk. It's the kind of expression that makes me think she could be a serial killer with the right motivation.

Percival leans over and whispers. "So, then it's only a *little* cruel?"

————

ON THE DRIVE HOME, I text my brother:

Met with Paris clan and saw babies. Where do EMs come from, anyway? How did we get made in the first place?

A few moments later, Kevin replies:

Sorry, Lyn. I don't know.

I start to wish we had a scientist or a genetics lab or something a little more professional than a potentially crazy nurse electrocuting newborns. But you know what they say, you gotta play the hand you're dealt. And my hand feels like two jokers and the card that tells you where to send money for the rulebook. Come to think of it, maybe I need to send in my money, because I definitely don't feel like I understand the rules of the game we're playing at all.

10

A STROLL ALONG THE SEINE

I n the evening, jet lag continues to work its magic on us, but of the three, Zee is by far the most affected. Besides, our Parisian lunch — at a restaurant Percival absolutely insisted upon, after only knowing it existed for about eight seconds — was once again quite filling. "Listen, guys, tomorrow. I promise," Zee says. "I'll go see Paris tomorrow. Tonight, I'm gonna crawl my way up to that loft, shut off the light, and *sleep*. Besides, they say that your sleeping mind is better at figuring out problems than when you're awake. And right now, I feel strangely certain that everything is connected. You two go out — have a date. Isn't this supposed to be the most romantic place on earth, anyway?"

Percival and I share a glance, both thinking that a date in Paris doesn't sound like a terrible idea at all. After a few *you sures* and a couple *can we bring you anythings*, we head out, waving to Zee as she locks the door behind us, already wearing her pajamas.

———

WANDERING the streets of Paris at night is a somewhat intoxicating thing to do, even before we think about stopping for a glass of wine.

The sun hasn't even begun to set, and the aftereffects of lunch still linger, so rather than rush to some restaurant, we decide to walk. We're not much more in tune with the layout of the city than we were the day before, so we use the Eiffel Tower as our primary landmark and head in that direction.

Sometimes we hold hands, Percival and I, and sometimes we don't. We tell each other stories, one spurring the memory of another, flowing the ways stories do, but there are also long periods of silence, both of us enjoying the moment without words. We walk underneath the massive Eiffel Tower, amazed by its scale and the rigidly specific form of its structure, then we continue through the gardens beyond, dodging a few locals and scores of tourists as we wind our way along. Afterward, we meander through the city without any true destination, eventually finding ourselves standing at the Seine with the magnificent dual towers of Notre Dame Cathedral staring at us from across the river. I pull out my phone to take a photo and realize we've already been gone two hours. "We should probably find a place to eat," I say, "before it's completely dark."

"Allow me," Pers says, raising his phone like a chivalrous knight might unsheathe a sword. He taps for a few moments and then smiles with his perfect teeth, blond curls hanging into his eyes. "This way, *mademoiselle*." He leads me across the river, sliding between about a thousand other pedestrians.

"Wait!" I call after him. "Where are we going? And how did you pick something so fast?"

He turns around, his grin mischievous. "Maybe only one of us didn't know where we were going..."

I stop and scoff. "What? You —!"

Percival laughs, waving for me to follow, and of course I do. I pepper him with questions along the way, trying to figure out our destination, but he won't budge. Luckily, it's not far. When we reach the entrance to a small, almost nondescript restaurant, he stops. "We're here," he gleams.

Reading the sign tells me nothing, and I'm certain that I butcher the words speaking them aloud. *"La Lune Qui Pleure de Jean-Paul Segal...* I'm sorry to say I've never heard of it."

"Good thing I have, then," he says, pulling open the door and gesturing for me to enter.

"How?"

"You know those jobs I do back home? I mean, *used* to do? Well, some of the people I worked for have a lot of money, and they travel a lot. Let's just say this place was recommended. Oh, *and* they know we're coming."

I pause and punch Pers lightly in the shoulder. "You are *devious.*"

"I know," he says. "But you love it."

I smile, leaning up and kissing him. "Actually, I do."

THROUGHOUT DINNER, I feel like I'm being served the tastiest food by the nicest people I've ever met. Our waiter, Alain, is like the older brother I never had. Oh wait! Crap, I have an older brother. Okay, well, he's like the more jovial, more French, second older brother I never had. Our hostess, Célia, is like a doting aunt. Even the owner and head chef, Jean-Paul Segal himself — okay, I only know him from the sign on the door, but I learn from Pers that he's a renowned chef in the city — comes by and brings with him an assortment of small things to taste, all on the house. Every course has some kind of wine with it, including the chef's little bites, though his accompanying drinks pack a decidedly stronger punch. *So this is what a true family meal might be like?* I think, with a mixture of bliss and melancholy.

"Lyn," Percival says, with an air of seriousness. The restaurant staff are so good at their jobs that they not only know when to come and cater to our every need, they also know when to give us a moment. "I have to say one thing, just to clear things up."

Suddenly the smile that had felt permanently affixed to my face throughout dinner disappeared. "What? Is something wrong?"

"No, no, of course not. Dinner is amazing... *you* are amazing. It's just — well, I have to admit that this is not an everyday kind of thing for me."

"Being in Paris and having the best meal of our lives is not an everyday kind of thing for you," I mock. "Okay, duly noted."

"No, I'm serious. I pulled a lot of strings to make this happen, and of course, paying for it is all through our new jobs with your brother's *per diem*. This isn't the kind of life I can really offer."

Life I can offer... I am simultaneously stunned that Percival is talking about us having a *life* while being completely incensed that he would think he needs to offer me riches to make me happy. I pick up my napkin and dab my mouth a moment, mostly so I don't use that mouth to say something I might regret. No, something I *definitely* will regret. *We're having a great night, Lyn, so keep your damn trap shut. You know sometimes he says things that aren't what he really means.* Rather than make a snide reply, I stay quiet. Maybe he'll pull out of the nosedive.

"I'll just tell you this," Percival says as his eyes gleam in the candle light. "Whatever I have, even if it isn't much, is yours. Whatever I can do for you, whatever I can give you, it's yours."

I raise the napkin a little higher, this time to blot a tear welling in my eye, hoping I'm not too obvious in the gesture. Did he pull out of the nosedive? Why yes, yes he did. "Thank you," I say, as if it's enough, when I know it isn't. "But I don't need anything from you. Just you." Though it's awkward with two plates, utensils, and a burning candle in the way, Pers rises and manages to lean across the table to kiss me. As he sits again, I see our hostess, Célia, looking at us with such a loving smile that she may melt from the joy.

Given the whirlwind of food, company, and emotion, I don't think I've ever had a better meal, and I doubt I ever will. It's the best night of my life.

———

WE WANDER HOME through silent streets. Percival again seems to know where he's going, so I just let him lead the way. Pretty soon, we're strolling along the much busier Champs-Élysées with the Arc de Triomphe standing like a beacon uphill, guiding us homeward. There, we branch to the left, soon making our way to the quiet little side street where our castle townhouse lives.

Though there are streetlights and the sounds of traffic in the distance, our street is so still it's like walking into a postcard. *Greetings from Paris! Wish you were here!*

We reach steps to the front door, and Pers fumbles in his pocket for the key, dropping it loudly on the stone walkway. He giggles as he bends to pick it up, and I follow suit, suddenly aware that multiple courses of dinner with wine seems to have made us both a little giddy.

Percival comes close. "Shall we retire to the boudoir?" he says, wiggling his eyebrows in a way that is both enticingly sexy and remarkably silly at the same time.

"Don't forget. Zee's asleep. We have to be *quiet*," I say, smiling up at him.

My field of vision is mostly Percival's beautiful face, but beyond his dangling blond curls, the tall turret-like part of our home stands high in the sky, dark against the star-filled sky.

I hear glass shattering, followed by a low popping sound from somewhere above, then suddenly the windows of the upper floors of our house burst outward in an explosion of glass and fire. The concussion knocks us backward, Percival falling over me as shards of glass rain down. I scream.

A second explosion rocks the building, seeming to shake the earth itself, and once more huge flames shoot out of the windows. A car alarm starts blaring from the street behind the house, set off by the percussive waves of force.

I push Percival off me, desperately screaming. "Zee! Zee!"

"Oh my God," Percival says, quickly brushing off and racing toward the front door. He fumbles open the lock and runs inside, but immediately starts coughing from the billows of dense black smoke that come streaming out. For a moment, he disappears in the dark interior, but quickly returns. "The stairs are all on fire — I can't get up there that way."

I think about using my electromagic to fly up, try to rescue my friend, but before I do that, instinct kicks in. "Zee!" I shout in our special EM way of communicating, forcing the signal wide and loud. "Answer me! Are you okay?" Percival just stares at me, waiting, but in my head I hear nothing but low static. "She isn't answering." Soon we're both desperately broadcasting, hoping Zee will respond, but there's only silence.

Just then a third explosion sprays debris into the air and tears out a section of the building next to one of the upper windows. Bricks smash down around us and we're forced to retreat to the street.

As we stagger backward, one shard of something hard and sharp flies past my head, nicking me over the ear. "Zee!" I try again in our static connection, but it's pointless.

"It was sudden. Maybe she didn't even feel any—" Percival starts.

"Don't say that!" I shout back. Still, in my mind, it's all I'm thinking. *She was asleep up there. She didn't have a chance. Oh my God Oh my God no* — "Zee!" I scream again, both out loud and through my EM connection.

And finally, I have to come to grips with the idea that my best friend, Mackenzie Patmina, is dead.

As the cold face of the moon looks down on us, I fall to my knees, weeping, with my head in my hands. Percival leans over, wrapping his arms tightly to console me, but he might as well not be there. No one is there. The world no longer exists around me. I am nothing and nowhere and nothing makes any sense anymore. It's the worst night of my life.

"Zee..." I say through wet sobs. *This is my fault. If it weren't for me, we wouldn't have these stupid jobs, we wouldn't be here at all.*

In the distance, sirens begin to wail.

11

STILL I FEEL I'M SINKING

W e don't move. Why should we? How could we? Zee is dead, and our house is destroyed. We have nowhere else to go, anyway. The sirens grow louder, and I realize how strange they are, how unlike American sirens. Rather than the slow up-and-down drawl of ours, French emergency sirens have a more staccato back-and-forth pulse. I'm so focused on it, I don't even truly notice when Percival jumps up, spinning around. There's motion, close by. It must be firefighters or police or something, but somehow it feels wrong. Percival seems upset. Slowly, I look up.

There are men — a lot of men. That's all I can register at first, until I realize the men are clad in black, with what look to be military googles covering most of their faces. And they have guns.

These people, I think. *These must be the people who did it. Who blew up our house and killed Zee.* Instantly, electricity surges in my body. I stand. I ready. I will kill them for what they've done, and I will not feel bad doing it. They deserve it. My friend did nothing wrong.

Guns click and voices shout. "Tell her to cut it out, or we'll have to put you both down."

I clench my fists. Ready.

"Do it! Tell her to release her power or we shoot!" More scuffling, more shouting, more clicks.

Percival appears through the haze that is all around, clouding my vision. His nose is an inch from mine, and he looks desperate. "Please! Lyn! We can't risk it! There's too many of them!"

"What?" I ask, like a child waking from a nap, confused, blinking.

"They'll shoot us, and electricity doesn't stop bullets! Please let go of your power!"

I come fully aware of my surroundings, seeing the men holding their deadly weapons, standing tense, aiming at us. "These people *killed* Mackenzie, Percival!" I flare electricity and it sparks across my body, making zips and zaps and arcs of blue-white. "We can't just let that happen!"

Percival grabs my arms, and I suddenly feel the well of his power, too. If I want, I could raze the land, tear down trees. If I want — and I really, really want — I could kill them all. "Lyn! I can't let you do this now. I can't lose you. Please!"

"Step aside, Pers," I say to him, nothing but confidence. "I got this."

He shakes me. "No, Lyn. No, you don't. They're all around us. You might get one, hell, you might get 20 of them. But if you miss one — just *one* — we're both going to die. And I can't let that happen, Lyn. I love you."

Those words. Even in the moment, when nothing could be further from my mind, they have such weight. *You...?* I falter.

My shoulders sag and Percival must notice the change. "Good, yes. Okay, Lyn, like that. Just let it go. We can live to fight another day."

"But Zee..." I say.

Coming even closer, he looks deep into my eyes. "This isn't going to change that." Then he's so close that he's whispering, just to me. "Let go of your power and I swear that as soon as we have the chance, you and I will rip these people apart. They'll regret ever messing with us, and we'll make Zee proud."

"Okay — okay," I say, and my electromagic falls away. Immediately, we're grabbed and our hands are secured behind our backs by something, maybe zip ties. Something is set between my wrists, some kind of hard object, and immediately my power is gone. Completely gone. I stagger, wondering what on earth just happened.

The emergency sirens are loud now, upon us. A dark sack is slipped over my head and the world goes even darker than it was as I am dragged stumbling away from the house. I can't tell where we're going, but it's not in the direction of the sirens. *They're taking us away from help.* There's a loud clack and we're hoisted up, then pushed to sit. My feet make hollow noises on a metal surface, and below me, I feel an engine rumble to life. *We're in a van*, I think. Another loud clack and even the tiny wisp of light I could see through the dark sack on my head is puffed out. I feel the jolt of movement as the van lurches forward. It forces me sideways, and I feel the barrel of some unseen gun poke into my ribs. Whatever they put between my wrists is still there, and it must be what's sapping my EM power. I never knew such a thing was even possible. "Percival?" I call.

"I'm here," he replies. "We're together."

Okay, okay... think. Someone is taking us away. The same people that blew up our house and killed Zee. But Pers is with me, and as soon as we can, we're going to end this. They have guns on us now, and they've taken our power, but they'll make a mistake. Shit, they already have made a mistake — they left me alive. They have no idea who they're missing with. If I have to go down in a blaze of glory, that's perfectly fine with me.

12

CAPTIVE AUDIENCE

I t's dark, and what little sound there is echoes strangely around me.

At some point, I must have fallen asleep after they put us in the room. Or holding cell, whatever you want to call it. We're in back-to-back chairs, neither one facing the door they brought us in through. Everything is metal — the chairs, the walls, the door, even the floor. They shut out the lights, and after a while, despite our anger and our attempts to wriggle free, there's nothing else to do but sleep.

Yet now I'm awake. I strain my eyes, trying to make out anything, but the darkness is complete. There isn't even a faint glow to pick out shapes. Such a total lack of visibility is disconcerting, it's playing with my head. I need a frame of reference. "Pers?" I whisper, a sound that bounces through the space.

At first, there's nothing, then I hear something behind me shift. I hear Percival grunt softly, waking up. "Lyn?" He pauses a moment. "I can't see — ah, shit. We're still in the metal room? I was hoping that was a nightmare."

"Nope," I say. "Are you okay?"

"Yeah. Fine. Sore from sleeping with my hands tied behind my back, but fine. You?"

"I'm okay—"

"Wait! That thing, whatever it was they had on our wrists. It's gone. I..." Percival goes quiet a moment, then suddenly I realize I can see. Blue-white light shimmers to life, bouncing off the reflective silver walls. It's like opening your eyes to discover you're living inside a kaleidoscope — everything is flicking with electric light. "I can tap into my power again."

I try to do so and suddenly there are two pools of light illuminating the room. I sigh with relief at being able to get my bearings again, even though we're still prisoners. The weird thing, though, is that we're both making arcs of electricity with our hands, which are tied behind our backs, close together. I can see two bright curves in the reflection from the walls, but not see what either of us are doing directly. "What was that thing they touched us with? That has the ability to tap us out like that?" I ask.

"No idea," Percival says. "But I'm not waiting around so they can use it on us again." The light from behind my back grows brighter, then turns into a pair of lightning bolts that strike the floor just to each side of my chair. Everything seems to thrum, like the whole room is vibrating with the energy Pers is pumping into it. After a minute or two, he lets go of his EM power. "Shit."

My mind reels, trying to make sense of what's happened. Where we are. *They killed Zee, but took us captive. Why? They're regulars with guns, not EMs. How do they even know we exist? And how on earth do they have some kind of thing that takes away our powers?* My head starts to ache, thinking about it, and the little arcs of lightning between my fingers pop out, leaving us once more in the dark. "Why'd they do it, Percival? Why'd they kill Zee?"

"I don't know," he says, voice echoing back to me in the utter blackness.

"You said we'd make them pay."

"We will, Lyn."

"*As soon as we can*, you said."

"And I meant it."

I huff, my temples pulsing with pain. "Then we need to do something now, while we still have power and no one's pointing a gun at us."

"Like what?"

"I don't know," I say. "Find a weak spot in this room and burn our way out of here?"

"We're tied to chairs," Percival says, sounding helpless.

It riles me. If it weren't so dark, I think anyone watching might see the throbbing of blood flowing through my veins, flushing my face. "Then let's burn our way out of these chairs. Can you reach me?" I stretch my fingers backward, trying to see if I can connect with Percival's.

I hear him straining. I can feel the faint brush of air as his hand flops near mine, just out of reach. Then I hear his neck and back pop as he drops lower, trying to gain just a tiny bit more distance.

His finger brushes mine. "There!" I shout, breathlessly. "Do that again!"

I can't see him, but I can sense him wriggling in the dark at my back. His finger touches mine again. It's not far enough for us to lock hands, or even curl a single knuckle over each other's. It's just a faint scrape from the tip of his middle finger.

But it's enough.

I blaze with electricity, pulling from my well of power and Percival's, too, suddenly making the room blindingly bright. I will a ball of electromagic to life and it swells to encompass my hands, Percival's hands, and then the bindings holding us. In seconds, our hands are free, and we are no longer tethered to the chairs. I leap out of mine, turning toward the door, power still glowing in both hands. "It's time to get the hell out of here," I say, then I let loose my lightning. The room seems to shake with the force of it, and the door begins to glow. I pour more and more electromagic into it, and the room quickly becomes hot. The door changes from an orange glow to bright blue, and I think I'm close. But...

More power, more.

Still...

Nothing happens. The door doesn't blow off its hinges or melt into a puddle. It's pulsing with blue-white heat, but still stands. Finally, I release my power, and the brightness in the room fades. Now we can only see each other by the glow of the door, though while we watch, even that subsides.

Maybe if we both try...

"What are you doing?" an exasperated male voice with a light but clear French accent says from unseen speakers. "Calm down. That won't do any good, anyway."

I scoff, pulling up my electromagic for a second attempt. "What would you know?"

"A lot. I built the room you're in," the voice says. "Listen, you want to waste your charge firing it into my walls, be my guest. But it won't help you, and you won't get out. This room is specifically designed to hold MEs. Oh yes, sorry. You call yourselves EMs in the States."

"I don't know," Percival says, filling with power. "That door looked pretty much ready to pop. I think if we both go at the same time —"

"Nothing different will happen."

"How can you be so sure?" Pers replies.

"Because we've tested it with ten electromagicians at once. All you're doing is losing your charge and feeding my machines."

"Your *machines*? What kind of place is this?" I ask.

"It is not for me to explain why you're here or what we do here. However, I can tell you that the room you are in was built to with-stand any electromagic you can pump into it, and send that electricity back into the city's power grid. So every moment you waste trying to burn down my door simply adds reserves for the local municipal energy company. If you'd like to try again, I thank you on behalf of the French government."

I spin away from the door. "Damn it," I mutter under my breath.

"Okay," Percival says. "If you can't tell us anything else, who can? And why is it so damn dark in here?"

The room lights slowly come up, revealing silver metal all around us, gleaming on every surface. "The lights were off because you were sleeping. I didn't think this would make you so — how do you like to say it? — pissed off. But you might as well sleep. He won't be here to talk to you for another two hours."

"Who?" I ask.

"Orkan," the voice says, as if that should make sense to me.

"Who the hell is Orkan?"

My only answer is silence.

PART II

FREE WILL

13

WHO DO YOU TRUST?

The door opens and damn if it doesn't wake me up again. I had every intention of staying alert, but two hours in a metal box with nothing to do doesn't help. Neither does Percival, who's slouched in his chair and snoring.

I jump to my feet, hands raised, power rising. Pers must sense something's happening because in a moment, he's beside me, ready.

Before us is an older man, tall and thin, but not gaunt. His complexion is dark but the browns of his skin seem to have faded into brownish-grey, a color that blends easily into the light covering of grey hair atop his head. He smiles, showing white teeth, the skin of his face creasing gently beside his mouth and eyes. He's wearing what looks to be a finely tailored brown suit jacket and slacks, with matching leather shoes that probably cost as much as Percival's monthly rent. He isn't wearing a tie, but his white shirt is immaculately pressed. As if in response to our aggressive postures, the man raises a hand, a simple calming gesture. "Hello," he says in a rich, deep voice that echoes in the closed space. "Please forgive the situation. My people are trained to be cautious." His French accent seems different; he rolls the "r" in "trained" and seems to add extra syllables in places, where most Parisians I've heard tend to drop syllables.

I'm still mulling the differences when Percival jumps in front of me. "You killed our friend, you asshole! And now you messed with the wrong damn people!" Thrusting his hand forward, Pers shoots a deadly bolt of electricity directly into the man's abdomen. It staggers him backward, but that's all it does. In milliseconds, it's clear the guy is just lapping up the power. Percival lets his magic fade away, dropping his hand dejectedly. "Ah, damn it! I thought you were a regular like the others."

"There are many things you do not know," the man says. "May I sit and talk with you?"

"Do we have a choice?" I reply, gesturing toward the metal cage around us.

The man stares at me seriously. His eyes are grey, but not the flat grey of his hair or the brownish-grey of his skin. His eyes are bright, like they're lit from behind with some internal spark. "There are myriad choices for each of us, each day, every moment. Though I share your ability, you two are young. You might choose to physically restrain me and force your way out of here. You might pick up that chair and kill me with it..."

Percival buzzes in my head via our EM communication. "Damn, these are good ideas. We really should have thought of them."

"Shut up," I buzz back. "We're not killing anyone. Not yet, at least. I want answers first."

The man continues, still focusing his eyes on mine. "...Or you might choose to sit and listen to me. You always have a choice, Lyn."

He knows my name, I think. For some reason, that makes me very, very uncomfortable. "Who are you?"

The old man bends in a shallow but graceful bow. "My name is Orkan Zidane. Here, you are in my charge, and as such, I apologize for keeping you in this room." He straightens again to stand tall. "However, I have been out of the city until this morning, and as you no doubt have noticed, many of my colleagues are what you call *regular* humans. For their own personal safety, they are permitted to use restraint — and use force — as necessary with *les Magiciens Électriques*. Restraint is, of course, the preference, over force."

"That still doesn't tell us who you are, or why we're here," Percival says.

Now it's time for my eyes to sear into Orkan's. "Or why you killed my best friend."

Orkan puts both hands up this time, ducking his head in a gesture of innocence. "That, I can assure you, had nothing to do with me. In fact, the reason we brought you two here is for your own safety."

I can tell you this. I'm buying what he says like I'm buying the northernmost province of Canada. Which is to say, I'm buying Nunavut. Oh shut up, I'm in a tense situation. I can't help it if my puns suck.

"Bullshit!" Percival barks. "You imprisoned us *for our safety*? You're lying."

"You are not *imprisoned*," Orkan says. "You may leave whenever you like."

Percival and I blink at each other, confused. Disbelieving, Pers walks to the door and twists the handle. It's unlocked, opening easily, and he swings the door wide to reveal a dark hallway. At the far end is a person with a large gun, but that person does nothing to stop Percival, doesn't even really look in our direction. "Come on, Lyn, let's go," Pers says, one hand holding the outside of the door frame like he's keeping our exit clear by force of will.

"You are welcome to leave," Orkan says, "but before you do, I would like to ask you two simple questions."

My focus bounces from Percival and the door back to the old man standing next to me. A man I don't know, who somehow knows me. After what's happened — with Zee, with our night in this metal cell — I have a feeling deep inside that I'm trying to ignore. It's telling me to listen to him. No, worse. It's telling me to trust him. Rather than let my very understandable apprehension win, or my very unexplainable trust, I stall by talking. "What are your questions?" The uncertainty I'm feeling comes through loud and clear in my voice, and I bite my lip, frustrated with myself for being so transparent.

"Just this," Orkan replies. "First, do you have any idea why someone would want to try to kill you?" I shake my head once, sharply. "And second, if you go, *where* will you go?"

I sigh. One thing I really hate is uncertainty, and now it seems like all I have. Until moments ago, I assumed our captors, whoever the hell they are, were responsible for the explosion at our house that killed Zee. And as for where to go next... my only thought is to run back to Genevieve Deschamps and the Parisian EMs.

As if he's reading my mind, Orkan speaks again. "Who can you trust in Paris? I am quite certain you are not ready to trust me, and I accept that. We didn't exactly roll out the red carpet for you here. However, I know Madame Deschamps has greeted you in style. Perhaps you should return there."

"That's right," Percival says, interjecting forcefully. "We're going back there."

Orkan turns to face Pers. "And as I said, you are free to go. I hope they will keep you safe."

"What's that supposed to mean?" I ask.

"Only this: currently, none of us know who attacked you. I can only assure you it was not me."

"You're insinuating that the Paris EMs blew up our house and killed our friend?"

"I am insinuating nothing, I am merely stating that only one group is definitively not guilty."

"Maybe to you," Percival says. "But we don't know you. You could be lying. You could have done it."

"I understand that it is a matter of perspective," Orkan says. "I can tell you with certainty that we did not, yet you have no reason to fully accept that. Which is why I say that you may leave whenever you wish. If we had wanted to kill all three of you, we most certainly had the opportunity here, wouldn't you agree?" What he said makes sense, and yet none of it makes any sense. It can't be Deschamps and the Paris EMs. Can't be. We were sent to them by my brother, by the High Order. They can't be responsible for murdering one of us. And yet, how can I trust this man Orkan and his people who left us in a dark prison overnight? "Here is my offer," Orkan continues. "Why don't we leave this room, go someplace more civilized, comfortable? There, I will tell you about us, and answer any questions of yours that I am able to answer. Afterward, you may stay with us, or leave, as you decide."

He holds out one hand to me, and I freeze. Does this hand have blood on it, the blood of my friend? Or is this stranger legitimately trying to help? I glance at Percival and see him shake his head slowly. But inside me, that feeling I can't explain rises.

Cautiously, like reaching into a dark hole in the wall that may be filled with spiders or snakes or worse, I extend my gloved hand. When I touch Orkan's, he gently folds his fingers around mine and smiles.

"Come with me," he says.

14

THE WOOL OVER YOUR EYES

Orkan leads us out of the metal prison cell and down the dark hall. We follow blindly, seemingly going deeper and deeper into a dimly lit structure, and my mind begins to imagine scenarios where accepting Orkan's offer was a very bad idea. Scenarios where we are led to a dungeon and chained to wall until we die, or strapped to a rack and stretched until our bodies rip apart, or even stuffed inside an iron maiden full of deadly spikes. Okay, so most of my imagination comes from watching old movies about castles, knights, and evil kings. Mock me, if you like.

Just when I'm certain we're lambs to the slaughter, Orkan opens a doorway and we're blinded by bright lights. After a few moments, I realize it's just sunshine, streaming in through a massive set of windows that stretch floor to ceiling with nothing but the occasional metal vertical to hold things in place. Looking out, I see we're many stories up, overlooking a part of Paris — at least I assume we're still in Paris — that we haven't seen before. Tall glass skyscrapers clustered together, more like our home of New York City than the Paris we've stumbled through. I scan the horizon and I'm relieved to see the Eiffel Tower is there, a distance away but still present. *Okay, good, still in Paris.*

"Please, sit with me so we can discuss things in a more civilized fashion," Orkan says, gesturing to a round table decked out with an embroidered white-and-gold tablecloth and matching linens. The place settings look like real bone china, covered in a golden design of peacocks and birds of paradise, and the utensils sport handles that I'm relatively certain are 24k gold-plated. I may shun the fact that my family is wealthy, but I'm not blind. I've seen stuff like this my whole life, and the fact that Orkan Zidane is asking us to sit down to such luxury means he's trying to impress us. And of course, the fact that he's trying to impress us raises my hackles that what he has to say may not be the complete truth, so he needs to sugarcoat it a bit with golden finery. "Are either of you hungry?" he asks.

I start to shake my head, not wanting to fall into the trap of another handout, but before I can even move, Percival is speaking, enthusiastically. "Very hungry, thanks. What is there to eat?" He plops down in one of the cushioned chairs, ready to go.

I pop my retort into Percival's head via our static EM connection. "Take it easy, now. We're not on Kevin's *per diem* here." Pers throws me a look that probably means *Relax, it's just food*. I sigh and sit next to him, then Orkan takes a third chair opposite us.

"Either you can have the chef handle selections for you," Orkan replies, waving to a man in a white shirt and apron, with a black shirt and tie, "or you may simply tell Victor here what you would like."

The waiter, Victor, awaits Percival's decision, but I can tell immediately that Pers has no idea what to order in such a place, in France. I nudge him in the ribs with an elbow. "You can always just let the chef decide, like he says."

"Yeah, that," Percival responds with a cheesy grin. A curl of his blond hair falls over one eye and he swipes it away absently. It makes me consider his overall appearance — nice enough for a pair of tourists in Paris, I guess, but nothing fancy for such a dining experience as we are no doubt about to have. I look down at my own clothes, realizing it's been more than 24 hours in the same old hoodie and jeans. I really don't fit in anywhere, but right now, I'm just hoping I don't smell. I know Paris is supposed to be the food capitol of the world and all, but does every one of our meetings with prominent EMs need to happen during an opulent dining experience?

Still, we eat, and — prepare yourself not to be shocked — it's amazingly good. We're particularly hungry given that it seems to be past noon and we've been in a prison cell overnight. I'm not even sure what every dish is, and I don't care.

When we finally slow down, Orkan pushes his chair back, swipes an embroidered white napkin across his mouth almost artfully, and crosses one leg over the other. He looks completely at ease. "If you don't mind, as you finish your meals, I would like to talk to you about a few things, things that I find very, very important."

"Well," Percival says with something still half-eaten in his mouth, "I suppose that's the least we could do for the free meal."

This time I jab Pers much harder in the ribs. "Or maybe this guy owes us a meal and a whole lot more for keeping us in a *cell* overnight?"

"Oh, yeah, that," Pers says, grinning with so many gleaming white teeth showing. I'm vaguely glad I don't see food between any of those teeth. Though part of me wants to punch out a few.

Orkan pretends to ignore our bickering, clearing his throat to regain our attention. "You are familiar of course with the High Order?"

I imagine it's not a real question, but I answer it anyway. "Yes, and haven't you violated basically every law of theirs? What do they call it, the Oath of the High Order? You have regular people working for you, you put us in some kind of EM-proof jail cell —"

"All of that would matter," he says, "if I were a member of the High Order. I am not."

"What are you then?" Percival asks.

Orkan smiles, his grayish-brown skin creasing yet defying us to guess his true age. "Many years ago, there was a rift in the High Order. It began with one issue, but soon swelled into a host of differences, to the degree that reconciliation became impossible."

What he's saying tickles at my memory. "Kevin told me that my parents were involved in a split with the High Order. It started because of Torden Detonde."

"The very same rift I am describing."

"Did you... *know* my parents?"

"Yes, Lyn, I did," Orkan says.

"Then do you...?" I can't bear to say the words.

"If you are asking me what happened to them, I could not say. Personally, I have not seen them for many years."

"They're dead," I say. Not because I want to or because I want it to be true, but because it's the only thing that won't rip me apart. As horrible as the truth is, at least when you know the truth, you know the whole story. No one can surprise you, not any more. That's why I hold on to it.

"Perhaps. In any event, I want you to hear about the outcome of the rift, because I think it is important that you understand your options. With a number of others, I founded a new sect called the Prime Order."

"Not the most original name," Percival mutters, still shoveling food in his mouth. I kick him under the table.

"As you say, but our intent was not to fight with the High Order. Our intention was to convince every electromagician on the planet that our ways are better. And once we do that, there will be no more High Order."

"No more High Order?" I gape. "So you are trying to kill us."

Orkan waves his hands and chuckles. "No, no, of course not. We don't want to *kill* the High Order, we want them to *join* us."

"Okay," Pers says, looking as confused as I feel. "What's the difference? High Order, Prime Order? Do you have, like, a better logo or something?"

"We have a better life."

Half of me knows this is a sales pitch, but I want to hear it. "Explain," I say.

"Put simply, the Prime Order is about electromagicians taking their rightful place in the world. We exist, and we are strong. There is no need for us to hide in the shadows any longer; regular humans need to know about us, and we need to have proper representation and protection in the laws of this world. For this reason, the Prime Order does not adhere to some holy set of rules, as the High Order does. Instead, anyone who declares themselves Prime Order is free to live as they see fit."

"No rules?" Pers asks.

"Well, that's not entirely true," Orkan says. "We have rules — equality, justice, freedom — but the difference is that every one of us votes on these rules. They are not handed down from some elders like they are religious artifacts. And any member of the Prime Order is welcome to suggest a new rule, or even the modification or removal of an old one."

"Whoa," Percival says, voicing my thoughts as well. "I'd have a say in things?"

"You would," Orkan says, smiling.

I shake my head. "Wait a minute. If you are cool with revealing EMs to regulars, why are you living in secret, too?"

Orkan looks at me seriously. "Out of respect. Respect for our High Order brothers and sisters. That's why we want the High Order to join us. Once we are united, and the rift is gone, we can announce ourselves to the world as one."

I grimace, suspicious of Orkan and the Prime Order's motives. "That's magnanimous of you."

"Actually, it's really about sensibility. If we were to come forward — just those of us in the Prime Order — we would be few. Our numbers and our spread around the world, so far, do not compare with the High Order. Regular humans might easily decide we are at best a novelty, something to investigate. At worst, we would be freaks. Something to shun, abuse, experiment upon, possibly even destroy. Therefore, we need *all* of us to have the sort of widespread impact that the regular human world cannot ignore and cannot manipulate."

"And then what?" I ask.

Orkan shrugs. "Then we live, like normal people. We engage in society. We are recognized as members who can live, work, prosper, pursue happiness, whatever we want."

"Come out of the shadows," Percival says, almost wistfully.

"Exactly."

"And you want us to join you?" I ask.

"Yes, of course," Orkan says.

"Right now?"

"Yes, if you like."

Suddenly, the importance of the moment must hit Percival. "What about jobs? The High Order gave us these jobs, and they pay really well, and, you know, they did send us on a free trip to Paris and all."

"I'm afraid the Prime Order is not in the business of employing every electromagician."

"Hm," Pers says. I stay quiet. Obviously my concerns about work and income are much different from his. "So then it's not quite paradise, is it? I mean, we might be recognized as part of regular society, but it's still up to us to make ends meet. No special privileges, we're just like everyone else?"

"Yes, but isn't that the way it should be?" Orkan says earnestly. I can tell he's already lost Percival.

Confirming my suspicions, Pers shakes his head, sending blond curls dancing across his cheeks. "Nah. I don't think so. I've lived that life, scraping, clawing, odd jobs for anyone who will pay. I *like* my current situation with the High Order."

"But I'm offering you freedom, true freedom," Orkan says, leaning forward.

Percival leans in as well, putting on a face I've rarely seen. The face I suspect he uses doing some of those odd jobs he never wants to tell me about. His tone of voice is serious, and maybe even a little scary. "If you're offering us freedom, then I guess we're free to go." It isn't a question.

I watch them sit there angled toward one another for a long moment until finally Orkan eases back into his chair. "Of course." He gestures, and a man in a dark suit walks up behind him. "Is the car ready?"

"Yes, sir," the man says.

Orkan stands, primly dusting his lap as he does so. Once satisfied, he nods toward us. "Please. Follow me."

———————

WE WALK into an underground garage where a nondescript white van is waiting, the engine already running. Orkan waves Percival and me toward the rear doors, which are already open. Inside, there are seats along both walls, benches like you might see in some Hollywood heist movie, but no windows. There's even a solid partition between the back of the van and the driver's area, so once the doors are closed behind us, we're in darkness.

The van slowly rolls out, and we bump along unseen streets. Orkan is notably silent.

"Pers," I say to him alone via our EM connection. Our special way of talking can either be one-on-one or a widespread broadcast, making me I'm thankful that I have the option to talk to Percival without Orkan or anyone else hearing me. "This doesn't seem good. I think we pissed him off."

Beside me on the bench seat, Percival is motionless, but inside my head, he responds. "Whatever. If this Orkan guy tries something, you run. I'll take care of him."

I scoff mentally, so that he can hear it. "That's very brave and all, but what if the driver has a gun? What if he drops us somewhere and they shoot us?"

"Now I think you're just being dramatic."

"They brought us in with a bunch of guys with guns."

Percival doesn't reply, which means that he's considering the possibilities in what I'm saying. I glance over and notice his brow is now furrowed, and his eyes are locked on Orkan, mistrusting the older man.

Suddenly the van stops and we hear the driver get out. The rear doors open, revealing nothing more than a sidewalk and some trees. We could be anywhere, though there's traffic noise. A lot of noise. Enough to mask other sounds, you know, like gunfire? Percival and I are tense. Orkan reaches into his suit jacket, and immediately I realize that guns don't have to be handled by regular humans only. When Orkan's hand reappears, I'm visibly relieved to see it's only holding a business card.

"Call me if you change your mind," Orkan says.

I take the card as I exit the van, nodding but remaining silent. Unlike Percival, I'm not against what the Prime Order has to offer. Then again, I'm not against what the High Order has to offer. Both have pros and cons, and like pretty much everything else in my life, I'm not entirely sure I belong with either. The cons of both seem to outweigh the pros.

Pers gets out of the van behind me, and the driver closes the rear doors before hopping back behind the wheel and driving off. Just past where the van had been idling, the massive form of the Arc de Triomphe stands, one of the very few places I actually know in Paris, amid what looks like an island float within a traffic circle.

"We're close to home," Percival says.

"Home isn't home anymore," I reply, thinking of Zee.

Percival and I stare at each other with no idea where to go or what to do next, as a seemingly endless stream of cars circles around us.

15

A NICE AFTERNOON DRIVE

"You're coming home," Kevin says over the phone, like it's a command. I guess he's technically my boss, but I've never jumped at his beck and call before, so I sure as hell ain't starting now.

"No," I reply, flatly.

"You're in *danger* there, Lyn. You have to come back."

"If I leave Paris now, whoever killed Zee gets away with it. And then her death means nothing. No way."

"Lyn, that's an order. You're coming home. I'll send a car to take you to the airport."

"An *order*...?" I say. "If that's an *order*, Kev, then you can take your little job and shove it up your ass. The only things working for you and the High Order has gotten me so far is a dead best friend, a blown-up house, a night in a jail cell, and more questions *by far* than answers. So, *no*. Keep your car, keep your plane tickets, keep your job, and your money. I'm staying here and there isn't a damn thing you can do or say to change my mind."

Kevin is silent. He's not used to people other than himself getting their way. "Fine. Stay. But let me help you."

"Better," I say. He's my brother, and other than Percival, I'm not sure there's anyone else I can trust. *Please tell me I can trust you, Kevin.*

I hear clicking as my brother taps out something on a keyboard. "I can give you the name of an EM who—"

"No good," I say. "There are already enough EMs in Paris who know we're here. If you help us, I want it to be strictly business. Don't use our names and don't make it an EM thing."

"Got it. Okay, yeah. That makes sense." More clicking. "I can get you another house in two hours. What names do you want to use?"

I put my hand over the phone and lean toward Percival. "We need fake names."

He nods with a furrowed, thoughtful expression. Like needing fake names is a normal request. Maybe it is, for him and his odd jobs; I don't want to know. "Okay. We're American newlyweds on our honeymoon. Our names are Paul and Stephanie Kramer."

I grimace at him, brows furrowed. "You came up with that *way* too fast." Nonetheless, I relay the info to Kevin.

"Tell me where you are. You'll have new passports in an hour," my brother says.

I gasp dramatically, full of sarcasm. "Kevin Hopkins! Are you going to do something *illegal*?"

I can feel him rolling his eyes through the phone. "Lyn, I run a secret organization of powerful people that the world at large doesn't know exist. Sometimes you have to bend the rules to make things happen."

"Fair enough," I chuckle. "Thanks, bro."

"You're welcome, Lyn. And don't call me *bro*." There's a long pause and for a moment I think Kevin hung up. "And Lyn... I'm really sorry about Mackenzie." He cuts the line before I can reply and without even saying goodbye. All things considered, I hope that's not a bad omen.

———

PERS and I chill on a nearby bench for less than 45 minutes when a guy on a noisy diesel moped pulls over next to us. He's wearing jeans and a jacket that has an embroidered logo on the pocket, but the words are in French, so I have no idea what they say. Still, I understand enough, because above the words there is the image of a stick figure running with a box. Delivery company. Confirming that, the guy gets off the moped, hops it onto its kickstand, and goes around to the back where there is an oversized box mounted above the rear wheel. He opens the box, rummages around briefly, and comes up with a cardboard envelope. Then he says two words in an extremely thick French accent, made even more difficult to understand given that traffic still circles nearby, his diesel engine continues thrumming and popping, and the guy never takes off his helmet or even opens the visor. So it's like trying to comprehend a foreign language being spoken through a thick, wet sock during an auto race. I tilt my head, completely confused.

Percival, on the other hand, stuns me by jumping up. "That's me — Paul Kramer!" Oh yeah. The fake names. Pers takes the envelope from the guy, and immediately our courier hops on his moped and filters back into the ever-present flow of traffic.

Tearing open the package, Percival pulls out two US passports. He flips open each before handing one to me, and I open the little book to see a mugshot of myself next to the name Stephanie Kramer. *Guess I better get used to that.*

"Steph?" Percival says.

I sigh. "Yes, Paul?"

He gives me a cheesy grin. "You know what I could really use right about now?"

"A nap? A stiff drink? Oh wait, no this is you we're talking about, Per — I mean, Paul. You want to eat."

"Nope. None of that." Percival has the envelope and new passport in one hand and his phone in the other, which he turns around so I can see the screen. My reaction is visceral, and almost lustful. It's a map with blobs of darkening green, but the real eye catcher is the line of yellows, oranges, and deep reds on the upper left side of the screen. Even though the lines on the map aren't familiar, I know the colorful approach of bad weather when I see it. "I need a charge. And so do you."

I squint at the map on his phone. "Where is it? How far?"

"Northwest of Paris, twenty-five, maybe thirty miles." He reaches into the envelope to produce something else my brother sent us — a pair credit cards, one embossed with the name PAUL KRAMER, the other STEPHANIE KRAMER. "I say we rent a car."

Given the shit we've been through, the utterly normal act of charge hunting seems like a beacon of sanity, so I immediately agree. I pull out my phone and do a quick search. Triangulating, I turn and point toward a building just off the circle. "I love big cities. There's a rental agency right there."

"Then it's fate," Percival says, offering me his hand for the walk. PDAs still make me uncomfortable, but I take it anyway. *We're supposed to be newlyweds*, I tell myself. Not that Pers made any mention of public hand-holding being part of an act.

———

DRIVING out of the city is initially nerve-wracking, pretty much like driving in New York must be. Not that I've ever actually done that myself, and not that I am driving now; Percival is behind the wheel, and I'm just taking in the sights as we leave town. It's amazing to me how quickly we go from one of the most important cities in the world to what appears to be farmland. Above us, the clouds look increasingly angry, and despite it being only mid-afternoon, the world around us is getting darker. All of that is, of course, great news for us. Flickers of light illuminate the roiling clouds ahead and we know we're going in the right direction.

Percival asks me to find the best place to stop, so I flip back and forth between my weather app and a topographic map, the standard apps any EM needs. Normally, elevation is our friend, but the storm isn't cooperating. "Turn left here," I shout, pointing toward a tiny road the heads up a gentle rise.

"It's a dead end," Percival complains, and he's right. I can see on the map the little road stops at a long building. To one side of the road, there's a wide swath of smoothly manicured lawn, with another similar stretch perpendicular to the first. "What is this place?"

"Airport, sort of," I say, and as if to prove my point a sleek white glider streams by on our left, thumping softly on the grass runway and rolling up the hill until its momentum fades and one wing tilts to the ground. As someone not completely in love with flying in planes, the crunchy, sandpaper sound of the wing dragging on the ground does not fill me with confidence in the plane's structural integrity for any future flight. Quickly, its occupants — a man and a woman — jump out and each grab a wingtip, pulling the glider up the hill toward the hangar. "Must be thrill seekers to be up in those clouds," I say, eyeing the unrest above us.

As Percival parks in a rocky patch of open space across the road from the runway, large drops of rain begin to pelt the windshield. By the time we get out of the car, the couple is already guiding their glider into the hangar, pulling the wide doors closed behind them. We look around, but there seems to be no one else, so Percival leads me toward the second runway, just far enough from the hangar that the slope of the hill obscures us from direct view. In the distance, we see lightning strike, and like every child ever, we start counting in our heads. *One, one-thousand, two* — The harsh slap of thunder breaks the relative silence and Pers gives me an approving nod. "Nice work on the location," he says.

"Not my first rodeo," I reply with just the right tone of manufactured arrogance.

Percival studies the clouds earnestly. "You know, Lyn, there is just one thing I read up on before this trip — the weather. They don't get nearly as many tornadoes as we do, but they do get something we almost never get in the states, especially this time of year."

"What's that?"

"*Superbolts*," he says.

I'm intrigued. "Explain."

"Superbolts are incredibly powerful lightning bolts — about a thousand times more powerful than a normal bolt. They typically happen over water, but because France is right on the edge of the Atlantic, they can happen here over land. If we're lucky, this storm's packing some superbolts."

"That would explain the purple blotches on the weather map. We'd better split up," I say, starting to move away from him.

He grabs my hand. "Hold on. Let's get the charge together. You know, like back in Jersey, on the tower in the park?"

It's a stupid idea, given that each of us would only get half of any bolt's charge when we do it together, but a superbolt? The charge of a thousand lightning bolts all at once? I could deal with *only* getting five hundred bolts worth of charge, so I nod. Percival pulls me close as the storm whips at my hair, swirling and pummeling us with rain. Electromagicians tend to act as their own lightning rods, so with the two of us together, it's pretty much guaranteed that we're going to draw it to us. It isn't long before a bolt strikes us.

We tense as the power flows in, still holding each other's hands. Anyone watching would surely think we've been killed. Or at the very least, we're having a religious experience. But I can tell from familiarity that the bolt to hit us is just regular lightning. I get a charge, but it isn't excessive, especially since I split it with Pers.

That all changes in moments when we are struck by the biggest, most powerful jolt of energy I've ever felt. I've been in tornadoes that zapped me probably two hundred times. This was more, and all in one instant. The energy threatens to blast us away from each other, but Percival wraps his arms around me and holds tight. The feeling — both of him and the superbolt — is euphoric. I can't properly explain how incredible it is, but I know we're floating, our feet leaving the ground from the intensity of the experience. For a moment, I forget about Paris, EM babies, and even forget about my best friend, Zee. I'm filled with power like never before, and it takes over all thought and reason.

Finally, the moment is over. We stand there, getting drenched for another ten minutes, maybe fifteen, not talking, just holding each other. I think another bolt or two hits us, but honestly, it's like having a gnat land on you just after being run over by a truck. It means nothing.

When the storm seems to be moving off, we head back to the car. We're in such a state that it doesn't even dawn on us that there are far more cars parked along the road than when we left. In fact, there are a lot of people standing around, too. I wonder if any of them saw what just happened to us, but most of me doesn't care. The feeling is that good.

We're almost to our car when I realize that I know some of the people crowded nearby. Two in particular. The recognition is a fairly effective buzzkill, to say the least. Immediately my hackles go up, and I'm pissed that my happy state is being trampled on by these outsiders. "Marcel Brodeur? Madame Deschamps? What are you doing here?"

Deschamps purses her lips as she looks us over, and it's clear we've done something wrong. "Lyn. Percival. I want you to meet someone." The older EM clan chief waves to the group standing behind her, every one of them electromagicians, and a young woman filters through to stand before us. She has short dark hair and sports notably more piercings in her right ear than her left. That combined with a trendy jacket and boots makes her look infinitely cooler than I've ever been in my life. "This is Michelle Brisbois. She is our lottery winner."

"Lottery?" Percival asks, echoing my thoughts.

"Yes, *lottery*. Something you clearly know nothing about. Our community believes in fairness and equality, and so each of us enters a lottery. We have become quite adept at predicting the possibility for superbolt lightning, and when our team says such a phenomenon is imminent, a name is pulled. Today, Michelle's name was pulled. *She* was supposed to get the superbolt today, but of course the two of *you* beat us to it."

"Oh," I say, because what else is there really to say? The effects of the superbolt are still lingering, and besides, it isn't like we took it from this lottery winner, Michelle, on purpose, right? Still, manners get the best of me and I find myself apologizing, anyway. "Sorry?" Yes, it comes out sounding like a question. So maybe my manners are a little rusty.

Genevieve Deschamps simply turns around and walks back to a waiting van, climbing in without another word. The rest follow suit, some in the van, and others to various vehicles of all sizes parked near our rental. The last of the bunch is Marcel Brodeur, Deschamps's assistant. He looks at us like you might look at the bottom of your shoe after stepping in something. "I advise that you check with us before you make any other major moves while visiting France." I don't like his tone one bit, and his words even less. Brodeur turns and hops in the van, sliding the door closed with a loud *clunk* before the EM vehicles head off in a sort of grumpy funeral procession.

Standing there, dripping wet and dumbstruck by the unexpected scolding, Percival looks me up and down. "Well, Lyn Hopkins. In one day, you've managed to shun one faction of Parisian electromagicians and piss off the other. I don't think we'll be receiving a lot of applications for your fan club postmarked from France." He smiles, trying to get me to do the same, and I know he's just kidding around. Too bad it feels an awful lot like the truth.

16

THE SOUNDS OF SILENCE

J ust as we're returning the rental car — and yes, the clerk there is the same one we rented from not three hours prior, so of course he goes overboard giving us weird looks — Kevin texts me.

Got you a place. Montmartre, under the name Mr. and Mrs. Kramer.

It's followed by an address, which I promptly open in my map app. Walking is a possibility, but cool fall breezes and the lingering storm means it would be a chilly and wet proposition at best. Instead, we head back to the circle around the Arc de Triomphe and grab the first available cab. Not surprisingly, the driver doesn't speak English, and there's no way I'm giving directions in French, so I just hold out my phone with the map and address pulled up. The guy studies it for a moment, probably calculating a route in his head — hopefully a relatively direct one, and not the one that makes him the most money. He hands back the phone and pulls out into the always bustling traffic. It's a dance, and I'm almost certain one that's going to end in a car accident, but somehow we make it through and he exits the circle to follow a long, straight road toward the east.

Once we arrive at our new place, a kindly older woman named Madame Martin shows us to our flat. It's on the fifth floor, and she asks if we have bags to carry up. We shrug, and I realize how completely implausible that is, given our honeymoon story. How could two Americas on an extended vacation in Europe have absolutely nothing with them? "We were robbed," I blurt out. "We need to shop for new clothes. And bags."

"Oh, my heavens!" Madame Martin says passionately with such a lovely French accent. She purses her lips, wrinkling up her already wrinkled face. "I am so sorry you have come to my country to have such a terrible experience!" I have to stop myself from wanting to give the sweet old woman a hug.

Beside me, Percival is half-grinning when he suddenly realizes he should look upset at having been supposedly robbed. He quickly frowns, putting one arm around me. "Yes, it was awful. But, we hope that, staying here, we can have a much better experience. Is it safe here?" I elbow him in the ribs for such a dumb question.

"Yes, yes, of course, of course!" says Madame Martin, trying to sound reassuring as she holds out a pair of keys on a ring. "This key is for your room, and this one is for the front door to the building. But there is also a code needed to enter, so really you are secured three ways. Very safe."

Moments later, Madame Martin leaves us alone in our flat, which is small but cozy. It's basically a decent-sized bedroom, with a bathroom off to one side, and a small sitting area. We're on the top floor of the building, which apparently means that our windows are tiny little things that barely open, just enough to let in some fresh air or get a sliver's view of the Paris skyline. I wonder for a minute about the comparative smallness, especially considering the massive house Kevin had previously rented for us, until I remember our story. We're newlyweds who got robbed. The little room is totally appropriate for a honeymooning couple on a budget. In fact, it's almost cozy-overload, the kind of place someone might call a Love Nest. The only problem is that I don't feel like romance at the moment. "Hey, Pers. I need a little alone time. I'm gonna take a walk."

He looks at me with concern. "Okay, but keep your eyes peeled.

It'll be dark soon. Anything strange and I want you to contact me immediately. Promise?"

"Sure. Promise."

———

"Hi, Zee. It's me," I say in my head, sending my EM voice to Mackenzie alone. But the craziness of the world has me doubting myself, so I double-check to see if I'm really focused on talking to just her, like I've done so many other times, or if I'm broadcasting wide now that she's gone. No one responds, and I'm close enough to Percival that he'd definitely hear it if I was broadcasting, so I figure I'm safe. I walk uphill with no particular destination, continuing to send out my internal voice to my best friend using my magic. "I wish you were here. I really do. I'm so sorry, Zee. I —" A tear begins to roll down my cheek, and there are enough people around that it's going to look strange for me to be bawling as I walk along, so I decide to just talk to Zee like normal instead. Talk like nothing bad ever happened.

Night falls in the city while I walk along trying to compose myself, as the oranges and purples of the evening sky give way to blues and blacks. "So, listen. There's a lot of weird shit going on around here. You remember that Madame Deschamps and the Paris EMs? Or I guess they call themselves MEs, which is a perfect reflection of how backward everything feels here. Well, there's also this other group, not part of the High Order. They're called the Prime Order, and yeah, that basically makes it sound like they're two sides of the same thing. Anyway, their leader, a guy named Orkan Zidane, says he wants *all* EMs to join the Prime Order, and then he basically wants to take us public. What do you think?"

I wait, listening to silence pocked with static. Sometimes the best person to talk to is someone who just listens.

"I mean, I'm not against coming out of the shadows. It's generally a pain in the ass to be an electromagician *and* keep it quiet. You remember my screw up at that campsite in the mountains?" I chuckle. Only nothingness responds to me, but somehow static has a warmth that I cling to, that I want to believe in. "Joining some other group to avoid the issues with being part of a first group doesn't seem like a real solution. It just seems like denial, or fooling yourself. Oh, and the Prime Order people have regulars with guns and an EM jail. So I guess that part is different."

I slow my walk, thinking. Ahead, there's a large, white domed church. Probably a very famous place, given the huge crowd gathered in the open space before it, but I'm clueless. No idea what the church is called, or why tourists would flock to it.

I reach the edge of the open space and suddenly get it. Well, I still don't know what might be special *inside* the church, but outside? It sits on a hill overlooking the entire city of Paris, and the sight is amazing. Domes and spires dot the otherwise almost uniformly flat landscape below, but one thing stands out clearly: the Eiffel Tower. It seems so far away, almost small. More like those cheap tourist replicas for sale at every little shop than the massive structure Percival and I walked beneath just recently. Atop the tower, bright spotlights beam out in four directions, rotating like a lighthouse, almost mesmerizing in their slow revolutions. Suddenly, the tower starts to flicker all over with a thousand tiny, winking lights, making it look even more surreal against the night sky. For a while, I stare at it, transfixed.

I shake out of my surprise, turning my attention back to channeling thoughts with my EM power. "Sorry, Zee. Didn't mean to leave you hanging there. I just came across this ridiculous view of the city. You should see it —" I realize that somewhere below me, in some part of the city I'm looking down upon, there is a castle-like house half blown apart from the explosion that took the life of my best friend. I can't help it, but the tears return.

I pull out my phone and start scrolling through photos. The first is a picture of Percival and me having dinner at that amazing restaurant. The second, the two of us along the river Seine with Notre Dame behind. I swipe once more, though I know what's coming. The third photo is Zee, standing outside that house, the day before it happened. Her arms are outstretched, with her head tilted and mouth agape, making some silly expression to mug for the camera.

I stand there, staring at the image, as the crowd shuffles around me, people taking selfies, shots of the city, or pictures of the huge church standing above us on the hill.

Something feels strange.

I look up, but the bright glow of the screen leaves me partially blind in the surrounding darkness. There are a couple of trees nearby, just beyond a little metal fence that is probably meant to guard hapless tourists from falling down the hill backwards while they're more concerned about getting a great shot than watching where they're going.

Someone is standing under the trees. I think that person is looking at me.

I blink. A light breeze ruffles the leaves of the trees, dappling the space below with bits of moonlight. Tiny pools splash over the person standing there. I see tendrils of wild grey hair.

No.

Moonlight falls briefly across the person's face, a face I know all too well.

Torden Detonde.

Suddenly, I realize the problem with my phone shining up into my eyes. Not only is it continuing to partially blind me, it's acting like a spotlight pointed directly toward me. Shit.

I quickly fumble to punch the off button on my phone, but when I look back up, the space under the tree is empty. There are people moving everywhere around me, countless dark forms. Am I confused, or possibly seeing clearly at last? *Torden isn't here. You're just a nervous mess*, I tell myself.

In my head, I hear a static pop and a whooshing, rhythmic sound, like wind... or breathing. *Zee?* No, that's impossible. *What the hell is wrong with me?* I think. I need to get back to Percival, and fast. I don't feel safe alone anymore, but of course, I don't know exactly how to get home. *Every time. You do this every time. Idiot.* Quickly, I text him.

Send me your location, pls.

Almost immediately, he replies.

Lost again?

I'm about to send back something snide, but thankfully, before I can, Pers has the sense to do as requested. A map with a red pin pops up on my phone, and I tap things until I have walking directions.

The whole way home I'm looking over my shoulder, knowing that our honeymooner aliases are useless if I've already been discovered.

I need to make a call, but the last place I want to be is out on the street while I do it. Partly because what I have to say is private. And partly because I plan to use a lot of four-letter words.

17

PLUS ÇA CHANGE, PLUS C'EST LA MÊME CHOSE

"**I**s Torden Detonde in Paris?" I ask, not even attempting to hide my anger.

The deep, richly accented voice of Orkan Zidane replies. "Sometimes."

"Sometimes? What the hell does *sometimes* mean?"

"Exactly what you think. Sometimes Torden is in the general area of Paris, and sometimes he is not."

I huff loudly. "For a guy who's trying to recruit us to your team, you're doing a wonderful job of pissing me off. And a pissed off Lyn Hopkins is not signing up for the Prime Order anytime soon." Percival stands next to me, leaning in to eavesdrop, which I fully permit. He nods enthusiastically, egging me on.

"Lyn, apologies," he says. "My intention is not to anger you; I am merely telling you the truth. I am aware of Torden's expulsion from the High Order and from New York City. He has, on occasion, appeared here in Paris. But my understanding is that Paris is not his only current home, so when I tell you he is here sometimes, I mean that only in the most truthful of ways."

I pause, considering. "Hold on. If you know all that, you know that the High Order wants Torden for crimes he's committed. Why haven't you turned him in to Genevieve Deschamps, then?"

"That answer is both complex and simple. Hopefully you recall some of what I told you about the Prime Order, yes?"

"Yes, I think so."

"Good. Then you may recall that we seek to operate in a democratic way, where each of our community has a say in the management of the community and its rules."

"Great, very open minded of you," I say, my voice dripping with sarcasm. "Still not seeing how it's relevant, though."

"Lyn, it is the policy of the Prime Order *not* to interfere in issues related to the High Order. It would be an affront to the independence and autonomy of the High Order for us to impose our will or judgment."

"You've got to be kidding me!" I shout into the phone. "Torden *killed* EMs. He *made* the Stickmen. And worse, he created his own monstrosity out of a bunch of Stickmen." I don't bother to tell Orkan that we call said monstrosity a Mega Golem, because suddenly saying that name out loud seems kind of ridiculous.

I can sense Orkan's frustration. "Stickmen have existed for many, many generations, all over the world. Torden may have figured out how to manipulate them, but he didn't invent them. Besides, Lyn, my community is not a part of the High Order. No matter what that man has done, I cannot act as judge and jury for him. The Prime Order doesn't work that way."

"So, what? You need to vote on it or something?"

"We would need a majority, yes, and then a sentencing committee would be created to decide—"

I laugh. "A *committee*? Holy shit, you all are worse that the stuffy High Order. How do you get anything done?"

"We are a committed and tight-knit organization. I can assure you that when there is a need, we can move remarkably quickly." He sounds mildly defensive. Maybe he's telling the truth.

"Look, up until now, I've basically seen you and a bunch of regulars with guns. How many are in the Prime Order, anyway? EMs, I mean. Not armed guards."

"Just over one thousand," Orkan says calmly.

I'm stunned, comparing that number to the entire New York clan. Or the Paris High Order I've been exposed to, for that matter. "A thousand? All here? I thought you said you didn't have enough people..."

"No, the entire population is not located in Paris. But unlike the High Order, we don't have a lot of communities in other cities," Orkan says. "For now, Paris is one of only a few cities of the Prime Order... *le Premier Ordre*, and we have one of the largest groups. But, of course, we have recruited members from all around the world."

"And when did the Prime Order start?"

"Hm," Orkan says, a sound that is part thought and part annoyance. "Twenty years. About twenty years now."

"And in twenty years, you've recruited a thousand EMs, total?"

"Yes."

"Hold on a minute." I feel like things are coming together, and I don't like it one bit. Paris is my first glimpse of another city's community of EMs, but combining that with the group in New York, I'm starting to wonder. Given all the other cities I've heard talked about in our High Order community circles, there are thousands of us around the world. Ten thousand? Maybe more. Maybe a lot more. "If you want more and more electromagicians to join the Prime Order, and it's taken you this long to get a thousand, maybe you've stopped trying."

"I can assure you we have not," Orkan says with a mix of annoyance and amusement. "Didn't I just try to recruit *you*?"

"You did, but even adding Percival and me to your ranks isn't going to change much, is it?"

"It might. Some like you... you could have a profound influence on others from New York, possibly even your brother. And perhaps others from afar."

Fine, that does make a little bit of sense, but something else is still bugging me. I decide to spill the beans. "Wouldn't be easier if you just *made* new electromagicians whenever you wanted to? You know, created your own ready and willing population?"

"Lyn—"

"No really, doesn't that seem a whole lot easier? That nurse — Laffitte — she told us there have been ninety-four EMs born just this year. That would be a big boost to your organization, wouldn't it?"

"Lyn—"

I press on, feeling like a lawyer, just about to get a witness to tell it all, right there in front of the jury. "A ten percent jump in a year? That would help, wouldn't it?"

"Lyn, many of our ways may seem cryptic to you, and so might our actions."

"So, you admit it? How are you doing it? How do you *make* an electromagician?" Percival and I are practically falling into the phone, so eager to hear how it's done... and where we ourselves might have come from.

Orkan sighs deeply. "As far as I know, our abilities are the product of many generations of genetic mutation. Is there a way to manipulate such a thing? Perhaps. But in the Prime Order, as I have said, we each get a vote, and we each get a say in our rules. One of our primary rules is that we will *never* forcibly make any electromagician come to our cause."

"That seems to leave an awful lot of room for interpretation."

"Not to me, it doesn't. Lyn, we subscribe to the belief that each of us has autonomy and freewill, each has our own ideas. You now have made decisions about us, and whether I tell you they're untrue or not seems to be immaterial. You will believe what you believe."

"Bullshit. You're lying to me."

"You will believe what you believe. And I hope we can discuss this more soon, when you have had time to reflect on what I've said." Orkan cuts off the call, leaving me in silence.

"That's it," Percival says, smiling broadly. "You figured it out — so we need to report back to your brother."

"Sure, soon," I say, not hiding how ticked off I am. I might have figured out one thing, but there are so many unanswered questions.

How? And what about Zee? For that matter, was it just my imagination, or is Torden Detonde stalking me?

"Soon? Nah, come on. Let's call Kevin now, then we can wrap this up and go home." Percival is still smiling, those gleaming whites showing.

My next words turn his expression upside-down. "Every time we discover something, something else makes no sense. I'm not leaving here until I fully understand. Everything. First and foremost, who killed Zee, because I can forgive this guy Orkan trying to bulk up his numbers, but I cannot forgive what happened to her. And I have a strong feeling that understanding how EMs can be *made* is the lynchpin to figuring out who blew up our house."

There's a sharp knock at the door and I jump, suddenly filled with electric power. I'm glowing light blue and emitting arcs of energy in our fifth floor flat.

Percival sees me and goes wide-eyed, stepping between me and the door with his hands raised. "Whoa, Lyn, chill! I didn't want to leave the apartment while you were out, so I ordered food for us. Don't kill the delivery guy!"

I roll my head back, looking at the ceiling, and letting my power subside. A few moments later, Pers is at our small dining table, opening a bag of something putting off such an aroma that my stomach suddenly realizes how hungry it is and goes into full-growl mode.

And that is how we end up eating Chinese food out of plastic containers in the gourmet food capital of the world.

18

PRIME MOVER

My head is buzzing all night, and I barely sleep. One thing is certain: EMs and their stupid little clans are a major pain in the ass, and I wish — not for the first or last time — that I was just someone *normal*. All the hiding, all the secrets. The only thing electromagic power gives us is hunger. A need for more.

Percival is lightly snoring beside me, and I look over at him in the near dark. I can't tell if the glow from the windows is just city lights or the barest hint of morning. Either way, it's enough to illuminate a wave of blond curls falling over his face. *How do you do it, Pers? How do you just accept all this and let it be? You're so damned comfortable in your skin, and I always feel like I want to jump out of mine.*

Something thumps in the stairwell outside our door, and this time, I'm pretty sure it's not Chinese delivery. A second noise confirms my fears: it's getting closer. *Shit, was this what it was like for Zee? A thump in the night and then boom! Game over?* I hop out of bed as quietly as possible, straining to hear any sound. One of the steps near the top creaks and that's it. We're done for. I give Percival a quick, rough shove. "Get up!" I say in a harsh whisper. "They're here!"

Percival blinks, sucking in a sharp breath. "Wha— who's here?" He notices me glowing with power. "Lyn, what are you doing?"

"The people who killed Zee. I know it. They've come to do the same to us."

There's another thump, this time seemingly just inches outside our door, and Percival, only half awake, jumps up. Now he's glowing with power, too, and the room is awash in pale blue light. "We can't stop a bomb, Lyn. We need to get out." He turns toward the window — the tiny little top-floor sliver of a window. I think it before he says it. "But that's no way out."

"Hold my hand," I say. At first, Pers is confused why I want to play girlfriend in such a situation, but seeing my face, the power flowing through me, he gets it. Whatever's about to happen is going to meet the fury of our combined EM power, not two soloists. And maybe, just maybe, if they try to blow us up, our power can protect us for a couple of seconds until we fly away through some new hole blasted in the roof. The idea doesn't fill me with confidence, because of course it isn't exactly the kind of thing I or anyone else has practical experience with. It's mostly a prayer. "Be ready. Anything can happen."

A new sound comes from beyond the door, a scuffling sound, like someone is down on their hands and knees. *Planting a bomb? But wait,* I think. *If they're planting a bomb, won't they want to get out of the building before it blows up? So maybe there's a timer or something.* It gives me an idea.

"Pers," I say quietly. "If it's a bomb with a timer, maybe we can defuse it."

Percival turns, still holding my hand, but looking at me like I've grown a second head. "Is that a skillset you possess, because I'm afraid I don't know how." Sarcasm. Even in the face of death.

"We could at least *try!*"

Just then, something is shoved under our door and slides a foot or so across the wooden floor. A folded piece of paper. *What the—?*

Percival releases my hand and walks over to pick it up. As he turns it over in his hands, I can see words written in red ink on the top, even in the low light. *The Kramers.* The handwriting doesn't look familiar.

Pers unfolds the paper, reads it, then holds it out for me to see. Inside are just four words: *Watch over the children.*

"Huh?" Percival says, and I have to admit my reaction is about the same. In fact, we're so stumped, we both release our EM power. There's renewed shuffling outside the door, and curiosity gets the best of Pers, so he quickly unlocks the door and swings it open into the room.

On the small landing outside our door is the dark form of a person, slowly standing up. I almost reach for my power again until I recognize the wrinkled woman's face. She gasps and staggers backward, releasing a torrent of startled French words. Then Madame Martin catches herself and speaks. "I am so sorry, I thought you two would be sleeping. It is still very early. I did not mean to wake you." She looks at Percival wide-eyed and I realize he's in a pair of boxers and no shirt. Thankfully, I slept in my clothes, so I'm half-naked, too, but it reminds we need to do some shopping. Replacement clothes, toothbrushes. Vaguely I realize my breath still smells of lo mein. Yuck.

"It's no problem, Madame Martin," Percival says, not the least bit self-conscious at having a conversation in his underwear. "We're awake, but... I have to ask. Where did you get this note? Who gave it to you?"

The old woman shrugs. "It was inside the front door when I began my day. Slipped through the mail slot. I do not know who it's from, but don't you? Did they not write their name?" Percival shakes his head. "Hm, that is strange. I hope it isn't bad news."

"No," he says. "Nothing like that."

"Oh well," she sighs, brushing her hands down the sides of her skirt, probably a nervous habit. "If you don't mind, I need to make coffee for the guests. You are both welcome to come down for it, any time." She smiles, the practiced but endearing smile of a gracious host.

"Thank you," I say, putting a hand on Percival's bare shoulder. "We'll come down... once we get dressed."

Madame Martin's eyes sweep across Percival's bare chest once more, blinking rapidly, then she turns and trudges down the stairs.

Closing the door, Pers waves the note. "Any idea what this is supposed to mean?"

I twist my face into a confounded grimace. "No, but it looks like we have a problem. Someone knows we're here."

Pers raises a hand, finger up. "Ah — they know the *Kramers* are here."

He hasn't put two and two together yet, clearly, so I decide to mess with him. I reach up and put my arms around his neck, gazing deeply into his eyes. Percival smiles like he thinks something very nice is about to happen. Then I ask him a question. "Given the Kramers were invented yesterday, don't you think it's strange someone knows we exist?"

He looks crestfallen. "Oh. Yeah."

"And the note itself? *Watch over the children.* That sounds like it might have something to do with why we came to Paris in the first place, doesn't it?"

Pers nods. "It does, sure. Do you think your brother sent it?"

"I seriously doubt it. Kevin would just text me. Why bother sending a cryptic note on paper, forcing the old woman who runs the building to climb the stairs to deliver it? Plus, Madame Martin said the note was left at the door. The chances that my brother left an unsigned note at the door, hoping it would be delivered to us, are about zero. It has to be someone else, and that can only mean one thing." Percival still looks stumped, falling into the trap of beauty not brains as he sometimes does, so I elaborate. "If someone knows that Paul and Stephanie Kramer are here, *and* they know something about what Percival Farimir and Lyn Hopkins are supposed to be doing in Paris, what does that sound like to you?"

"Like our cover is busted. Already."

I smile, happy to see brains giving beauty a run for its money. "Exactly," I say. So that he doesn't think I'm being too harsh, I give him a quick peck on the lips, then turn for the bathroom. "So then I guess we know what we need to do today."

"Buy new clothes and stuff?" He grins.

"Yeah, that. But afterward, the Kramers have some children to watch over..."

Percival raises an eyebrow. "The hospital? Nurse Laffitte?"

"Bingo," I say, pulling out my phone. I scan the map app not for a route to the hospital, but for convenience stores. Because I'm pretty sure the one thing worse than day-old lo mein breath is day-old lo mein breath with coffee on top.

19

INSIDE JOB

"No one told me you were coming a second time," Nurse Laffitte says, eyeing us in a way that immediately arouses my suspicions. Though she greets us inside the staff entrance just as she did before, her body language is notably different. It's like she's placing herself in our way on purpose, rather than guiding us in.

Maybe everyone in this city is up to no good, I think. Percival and I put a healthy dent in the Kramers' new credit cards, spending hours shopping for everything we could think of, including luggage to carry it all. In the end, I think the best proof that we went overboard was us struggling to drag our new stuff to Madame Martin's fifth floor flat. It took me ten minutes to catch my breath before I even considered heading across town, and now, standing unwanted in the hospital entryway, I almost obsessively itch at the tag of my new hoodie as I try on an innocent tone. "We just had some follow-up questions and figured it would be best to come here to talk in person, rather than have Madame Deschamps act as an intermediary. Do you have an office or someplace where we can talk in private?"

The woman scoffs. "Office? Definitely not. The best I can offer is the nursery again."

The thought of going back in the nursery where this weirdo nurse zaps infants with EM power doesn't thrill me, but Pers jumps in. "That'll do just fine," he says, gesturing for her to lead the way. Reluctantly, she does.

Once the door to the nursery closes behind us, she turns to look at us with a dry expression. She doesn't speak, but her message is clear: ask your questions and be gone.

"Okay, first off, has anything changed?" I ask. "Have there been any more EMs— I mean MEs born?"

"No."

"And the boy — the one you showed us last time?"

"Home now, with his family."

Inside my head, I am completely flailing. I want to watch over the children, but how? What do I know about babies and nursery wards? And for that matter, what do I know about interrogating someone? I have no idea what to ask the nurse, and based on her expression and mood, I suspect she's minutes away from shuffling us out, telling us she has work to do. "Anything unusual about the family of the boy?"

"Nothing," she says. "Look, is there anything else specific you need to know? I'm on duty —"

"Yes," Percival interjects. "And we are thankful for your time, really. Just a couple more questions. Is there anything you can tell us about how these electromagician babies are made?"

Nurse Laffitte looks down her nose at him, blinking her eyes with sarcastic surprise. "Are you telling me that you do not know where babies come from?"

Immediately, Pers turns red. And, frankly, so do I. We've become what you would call quite familiar with the general process. He sputters a reply. "No, not that, of course. I mean, do you know what makes a baby become one of us rather than becoming just a regular person?"

The nurse shakes her head. "Human genetics are — what is your English phrase? Above my pay grade?"

Percival scratches at his chin, clearly trying as hard as I am to come up with something reasonable to ask. "Would you be able to provide us the names and addresses of the ninety-four EMs born in this hospital this year?"

"If I did so and anyone found out, I would most certainly be fired. I would also probably be arrested."

Pers, to his credit, doesn't let go. "But you know that we are here on official High Order business, and that Madame Deschamps herself has sent us to see you."

Laffitte rolls her head around on her neck, making an exasperated sigh. "Fine. But I will need a day or two."

"Thank you," Percival says. And then he goes too far. "The High Order thanks you."

The nurse squints at him like she's having second thoughts about agreeing, so I desperately try to think of a distraction. I say the first question that comes to my mind. "Are you the only EM, only ME, that works in the hospital?"

"No," she says flatly, turning away from Percival and checking her watch. "There is another."

I hope that I've kept her from backing out on her promise, but I know she's ready for us to be gone. *Perhaps we can get more out of the other one.* "Can we meet this person, talk to them?"

"Possibly, but..." Nurse Laffitte looks at us, then away, unsure she should tell us more.

"But what? We won't take up much of their time. Would this other EM have access to the babies, too?"

"Yes, he is an administrator, and able to access everywhere in the hospital, I should think."

"Are you concerned that he wouldn't speak to us because of his position here?" I ask.

Laffitte sighs. "No, not that. Not that at all. Look, I was trying to avoid this, but I need to get back to work, so I will be blunt. Are you aware that not all of *us* are part of the High Order?"

Pers and I are both taken aback. "Actually, yes," Percival says. "We know about the Prime Order. Is the other electromagician who works here one of them?" He looks at me sideways with clear excitement. Over a direct EM connection from his head to mine, he practically shouts. "If Orkan Zidane has one of his Prime Order minions working here, I bet you're right that he's behind all this!"

I try not to look at Pers, because Nurse Laffitte will most certainly guess we're communicating privately, I just send back a single word. "Maybe."

"Well, good. I don't know what Madame Deschamps has or has not told you." Neither of us bother to mention that Deschamps is absolutely not the source of our knowledge. "The man I am talking about is named Anton Bisset. He is the Director of Patient Care Services. I cannot tell you for certain that he's in the Prime Order — it isn't like he's handing out business cards saying so. But I can take you to his office and you can ask him whatever you like, if he'll answer. I wouldn't know because he and I rarely speak. Not only are our jobs quite different, but since he is not part of my ME community, we typically avoid each other."

"That's fine," I say. Strangely, butterflies begin to flutter in my stomach. Could we actually be making some progress? "If you can just take us to see him, we can go from there."

"Then come with me."

———

AFTER THE NURSE tells her colleagues she needs five minutes away from her post, we follow her down long halls, into a completely new wing of the hospital. Here, the smell of disinfectant fades away, and the surroundings look more like an average office building rather than a place that handles sick people. A few passersby nod or say *bonjour* to Nurse Laffitte, though none give us a second glance. I get the distinct feeling that a hospital like this is just too big for anyone to really know the comings and goings of another, or at least that the occasional visit to administration isn't too unusual.

Finally, Laffitte stops at a dark-haired woman's desk just outside a pale wooden door. To one side of the door is a plaque that reads *Anton Bisset* and what I assume is the French version of his job title, a reminder of how little I comprehend once it's not in my native language. Compounding that, Nurse Laffitte asks the desk woman — assumedly Bisset's assistant — something, gesturing toward the door. I guess it's along the lines of *Can we talk to him?* or *Is he in his office?* but of course, I'm not sure. However, when the woman replies with *oui*, that's at least one thing I understand. Stepping around the assistant's desk, Laffitte walks up to the door and knocks twice, lightly.

There's no answer.

She knocks again, but still no one replies. After another moment, she turns back to the assistant with a quizzical look. They exchange words in French, then Nurse Laffitte updates us in a hushed voice. "Mr. Bisset's assistant says that he was in his office before she went to lunch. She has not seen him since, but believes he is inside. Perhaps he is on the phone and did not hear me knock, so I have asked his assistant to enter first. I don't wish to barge in on a hospital administrator. Especially this one."

Percival nods. "Okay, thanks."

We watch as the assistant eases the door open and peeks her head inside. A second later, she looks back, her expression showing only mild surprise. "*Il est parti*," the woman says.

Laffitte furrows her brow. "She says he is gone."

"What, like gone for the day?" I ask, checking my watch. "It's not even two in the afternoon. Is that normal?"

The nurse translates my question, but in response, Bisset's assistant merely shrugs.

Rather than speak aloud, I buzz my static voice into Percival's head. "If this guy suddenly left because of *us*, that means we're on to something."

"Damn straight," he buzzes back, smiling.

Nurse Laffitte, probably aware we're speaking silently, clears her throat. "Given that the director is not here, shall I show you two out?" She looks like nothing in the world would make her happier.

"Um, is there a picture of him somewhere?" I ask, grasping at straws. Once more, Laffitte translates. Bisset's assistant nods and goes into the man's office, coming out a moment later with a small, framed photograph. It shows two older, grey-haired men in suits shaking hands. "Which one is him?"

This time, there's no need for Nurse Laffitte to pass along the question. "That one." She points to the taller of the two men, a wiry, sharp-featured guy whose face reminds me of a rat. I look closer and nod. It's his skin. That old-yet-not-old look it has. I know that look. It reminds me of another ancient electromagician.

20

STAKEOUT

We spend the remainder of the day running in circles. Hospital director Anton Bisset, for all we can tell, appears exactly twice online: once on the hospital's own website, and once on a site for networking professionals. His profile on the networking site is about as bare-bones as you can get. Even though we can't read French, a quick auto-translate of his page reveals nothing more than his name, title, and employer. He doesn't list a single previous job, social media account, or even any contact information.

Meanwhile, I can't help but feel we're missing the point. Sure, Bisset's sudden disappearance seems extraordinarily suspicious, but the question no longer seems to be *if* he's involved in the wave of new EM babies, but *why*. I sit at the little round table in our rental flat, tapping a pen violently against its wooden surface.

Percival paces the floor behind me, thinking. "Lyn. Hon. Please stop."

Not understanding, I freeze. Which of course means that the pen tapping goes silent. "Stop what? And did you just call me *hon*?"

He opens his mouth to answer, though I don't know which question, when a timid knock comes at the door, surprising both of us. "Who is it?" I ask.

The muffled voice of Madame Martin replies. "*Excusez-moi*, but after the, um... last time, I did not want to startle you."

Percival swings the door open. "It's no trouble. And you don't have to worry about startling us." The flicker of Madame Martin's eyes over Pers's formfitting new tee make me think she's a little disappointed not to find him partially undressed once more, so I cover my mouth with one hand to hide my smile. "Is something wrong?" he asks.

"No, no, nothing like that," she says. "But there is another note for you." She holds out a large yellow envelope.

"From the same person?" Percival asks.

She shakes her head. "I do not know who left the first note, but this came via courier. From the hospital, I was told."

Percival and I share a glance with eyebrows raised. "Oh, I see," he says. "Well, thank you so much for bringing this to us. Next time, you don't need to climb all the stairs." He's trying to be polite, but Madame Martin seems to take offense, though she quickly hides it.

"I have walked up and down these stairs many times a day, every day, for many years. It is no bother," she says, eyes once more flickering Percival's way.

She has a little crush on him, I think. *How adorable!* "Thank you, Madame Martin," I say, smiling warming at her. Adorable is a perfect description of her.

"*De rien*," she says, returning my smile before heading back down the stairs.

———

"THIS DEFINITELY FEELS ILLEGAL," Percival says.

I give him a smug grin. "Well, you would know, right?"

"Unkind, Lyn."

"Sorry, too easy," I say. "Anyway, let's assess what we have. Nurse

Laffitte sent us every name and address of the ninety-four EM babies born this year, with a photo, and even their blood type."

"Which we have determined is useless information," Pers notes.

I nod. "Correct. The distribution of EMs across blood types seems to be pretty much exactly the same as the general population. So we can most likely ignore that as any sort of important data."

"Then this entire list means nothing to us. Doesn't help us at all, right?"

"I don't know," I say, twisting my expression as I think, recalling the note slid under our door. "But if we are really going to watch over the children, we at least need to know who the children are, right?"

"Yeah, of course."

An idea strikes me. "And what would be the best way to do that?" I smile as Percival looks at me sideways, trying to guess my meaning.

"We... uh. Nope. No idea. How do we do that?"

I point to the final name on the list. "That boy we saw at the hospital. He went home. Let's go watch his house and see if anything weird is happening." I'm thrilled with myself for such an awesome idea.

Percival crushes my joy. "You want to go full-on perv and spy on an infant in his crib?"

"Well, you don't need to say it like *that*."

"Is it really any different if I say it another way?"

I mutter an angry growl before responding. "No."

"Okay, so we go to his house. Then what are we going to do?" Percival looks at me, confused.

I stammer my reply. "We're going to, uh, spy on an infant in his crib."

Pers shakes his head. "So glad I took this job. Well, let's do it."

———

It's full dark as we take up residence in a small grove of bushes across the street from the newest EM's family home. The kid's name is Luc Porcher, and he's all of five days old. Luckily for us, his bedroom is on the front of the house, so we can clearly see his parents — Olivier and Lea — as they tuck in their little one for the night. Not an hour and a half later, they repeat this process a second time. At his age, I suspect young Luc is being put to bed four or five times a night.

As the light once more goes off in Luc's room, we sit silently on the grass, watching. It's about as exciting as it sounds. Nothing happens.

The autumn night air leaves cool behind and heads straight for flat-out cold, while our body heat seeps from of us quickly, especially on the chilly ground. Percival puts an arm around me for warmth, though I admit I don't melt into him.

"What is it?" Pers asks. "Just too much going on? I mean, I get it. Things have been absolutely insane since we got here, and there's no getting over Zee."

I shiver at her name. "No. There isn't." The house in front of us remains dark and still.

"But are *we* okay?" he asks.

I pause. *Are we? How do I carry on like nothing's happened when my best friend is dead?* I don't reply, which I know means that Percival thinks things are definitely *not* okay. He pulls his arm back, and immediately I realize two things: I am noticeably colder, and I really don't want him to pull away from me. "I'm sorry," I say. "Just give me some time to figure things out."

"Of course," Percival says. "Absolutely." It sounds like a pat response, almost rehearsed.

I begin to wonder. If Pers is rehearsing lines for me, what does that say about *us*? I don't know for sure, but it probably isn't good.

With a gloved hand, I pull out my phone, tapping, scrolling. It's just a distraction. Just a means to avoid the here and now. Percival's hand closes on mine. "Let me show you something," he says. Slowly, gently, he takes my phone and sets it aside on his thigh, then pulls off my glove. "You know how you can willfully bring up your power?" I nod. "Well, I want you to try the opposite. Try to push it down, instead. Hard."

"You know I've tried this before. But, okay," I stammer. I give it a go, face tensing with the effort as I imagine my power stuffed inside a box, and me slamming the lid tight.

"Okay, I'm going to put your phone back in your hand now. Keep pushing your power down." As if he's disarming a bomb, Pers retrieves the device and moves it closer and closer to my flesh, until it finally touches.

Nothing happens.

The screen of the phone is normal. It's working. Unbelievably, the cursed touch of *me* hasn't destroyed the thing with electricity. I smile, looking from my phone to his face and back. "It — it works!" There's a quick pop and a flash of energy arcing from my finger to the device in my hand, and quickly I let it drop.

Percival scoops the phone from the ground, where it fell face-first into a clump of grass, then dusts it off. "No harm done! It's fine."

I shake my head. "Yeah, but that was too close."

"You'll get the hang of it, Lyn. Eventually, it'll be second nature." All I can say is that I don't share Percival's confidence.

We hear a car approaching and grow tense, both of us ducking even further out of sight. I quickly collect my phone and thumb the off button, only registering a moment later that I did it without gloves. *Maybe there is something to this...* I drop it into my pocket quickly before my luck runs out. The last thing I need in a foreign city is a dead phone. *But you already got a dead friend*, I think, immediately throwing myself back into a dejected funk. Ahead, the house is still and dark, and the car rolls by like there's nothing in the world to worry about. I begin to think that's the real truth on display.

"Maybe we should go home. Maybe we're barking up the wrong tree," I say. I have no idea what else we can do, no idea how to *watch over the children*, and no idea who told us to do so, anyway. Feeling small and useless, I extend my hand to Percival.

He interlaces his fingers with mine and says something that is so simple yet makes so much sense. "We should look into all the names on the list — the EM babies that Nurse Laffitte sent us. Maybe there's nothing, but maybe whoever is responsible for making so many of them isn't interested in them until later. You know, maybe a newborn EM is a little too raw."

At this moment, a lot of things feel a little too raw to me, so I nod. We've been through so much in so little time, but at this moment the loss of Mackenzie is like a knife in my lungs, making it hard to breathe. Nonetheless, I squeeze Pers's hand so he knows I'm still there, still on his side. We're still on each other's side. It's the only thing that seems constant. That seems reliable in our screwed-up world.

We stand up from the bushes and walk out to the street as if that's a normal thing to do, then head toward the nearest busy intersection in search of a taxi.

"Lyn?" Percival says, holding my hand tight.

"Yeah, Pers?" I ask.

"We're going to figure this all out, and we're going to make somebody pay for what we've lost." He doesn't look at me as we walk, but I think I see the glisten of tears on his cheeks, reflected from the streetlights we pass underneath.

"Yeah, Pers," I say. Because there's nothing more true than that.

21

IMPRESSIONS

"Any news?" Kevin asks. It's midmorning in Paris, and absently I calculate the time in New York, subtracting hours. Early. Really early.

What do I say? I think. *Uh, Percival and I have all new wardrobes, so it's like looking at a stranger whenever I look over and see what he's wearing. Or when I see myself in a mirror, even.* Instead, I tell him about the missing man from the hospital, and our pointless stakeout. "Honestly, maybe if we were real cops instead of just pretend, we might get somewhere."

"I can help there, at least somewhat," Kevin says. "I mean, I can't give you a badge and a gun, but if it's data you need, that's pretty much my specialty."

"You can hack police computers? In French?"

My brother laughs. "Nine times out of ten, the only things that aren't in English are comments in the code, and the data itself. But if you're looking for a person, well, a name is a name. As long as you know how to spell it."

"Okay fine, but this is definitely illegal." I realize there's probably a lot more to my brother than I know. And given that I didn't realize he was an EM for years, that's saying something. About me.

"Don't worry about it, Lyn. I'm not stupid enough to make anything traceable back to me."

"How?"

"You've already said the words *hack police computers* during this call. I think describing *how* might be pushing our luck. Thankfully, I had the sense to set up your phone with full communications encryption running silently, so unless you've suddenly made some pretty significant changes to the default settings, we should be good there."

"I have no idea what you're talking about." I pull the device away from my ear and look at it quizzically. "My phone is just a phone."

"Good, keep thinking that. It means you didn't mess with what I did, and that's for the best."

"Are you... *spying* on me?"

Kevin laughs. "No, silly. The encryption I set up is what *keeps* people from spying on you."

"Oh. Well. I guess that's good."

"Okay, so give me some names," Kevin says.

"Sure. Anton Bisset is the director from the hospital who disappeared."

I spell it and hear tapping from Kevin's end of the line before he responds. "Hm. There are police records for someone with that name, but they're from 42 years ago, so I'm not sure how relevant —"

"Torden Detonde is two hundred years old, and from the photo we saw, Bisset has the same sort of look." Just the mention of the name makes me realize a tiny little detail I've failed to mention previously. "Oh, and I think I saw Torden. Here in Paris, the other night."

"What?" Kevin says over the phone.

"What?" Percival says standing next to me.

"Sorry," I reply to both of them, offering Pers a sheepish shrug. "We've had a lot going on."

"Well, hold on," Kevin says. "You said you *think* you saw him? Did you or didn't you?"

"It was dark. And my phone was half-blinding me. It was just for a second, and when I looked again, he was gone."

"Hm," Kevin says. And that's all he says, upon discovering that the man who tried to kill me may be close by now. His lack of a response is... well, pissing me off.

So I drop another truth bomb on him. "Also, we had a note sent to us here at the flat, addressed to the Kramers. It said *watch over the children*."

Kevin lets loose with an exasperated sigh that sounds like the uncorking of a bottle. It's an appropriate comparison, since the sound also appears to uncork a torrent of curse words. Honestly, I almost prefer the familiar sound of Kevin cursing over his silence about Torden. Finally, he settles down. "Lyn, you've got to keep me informed if I'm going to be able to help you."

I don't usually talk back to my brother, but everything about this trip is driving me to the edge. Okay, that was a total lie and I often talk back to my brother. However, I feel he at least deserves it this time. And most other times. "Look, Kev. You sent me here to do a job, a job that ended up getting Zee killed. Things are happening. We're pursuing angles. I'm not going to spend all of my day relaying every last thing to you. You're getting your update now. Deal with it." I consider hanging up on him, but don't.

"Okay, sorry, Lyn. You're right. I'm just worried about you. And Percival." Kevin pauses, and I hear genuine emotion in his next words. "And I feel completely responsible for what happened to Mackenzie. *I* sent you all there. I sent *her* there."

My emotions begin to well up, but I replace them with anger. "It's time we did something about that. Give me an address for this Anton Bisset guy. And a picture of him, if there is one." I realize I should have leaned on Nurse Laffitte for at least the address, but getting the info from Kevin's hacking works just the same.

"Sure, one second," Kevin says, tapping again. He stammers through an address and I'm pretty sure his version of pronouncing French is no better than mine, so the likelihood that I am properly understanding what he's saying is very low. "I'll text you the address. And mugshot, though it's an old one."

"Great," I say. "We'll head there today. Oh, and the photo — when you send it, is it encrypted, too? Because I have some of my own to send you."

"Yes, definitely," he says. "Photos of what?"

I reach for the large yellow folder sitting on our round table. "A list of names. Kids' names. The ninety-four new EMs born this year in Paris."

"You need their addresses, too?"

"No, we have those on the list. But I don't think we're going to get anywhere fast by sitting outside kids' houses every night."

"Then what you do want me to do?"

"There's something about these kids — something unique, and I don't just mean that they're electromagicians. Look for anything out of the ordinary. A way to tie them all together, something."

"On it," Kevin replies eagerly. "Send me the photos." He ends the call and I set to work photographing each page from the envelope.

———

THE ADDRESS for Anton Bisset is one of those long French names that sounds much different than it looks. I know because I try about eight different pronunciations with our taxi driver before giving up and just pointing to the text message from Kevin on my phone. *Too bad the Kramers can't use a private car. Wouldn't fit with our story.* The driver squints at the screen for a moment, then nods, and I guess we're on the way. It's a small street, barely ten houses long, tucked across from a diamond-shaped swath of green called *Parc Montsouris*, so I'm not surprised the taxi driver doesn't know the route by heart. As he travels through the city, I watch the blue dot that is us on my map slowly move south toward the red pin that is our destination.

"When we get there, are we just going to knock on the front door?" Percival asks.

"I don't have a better idea. Of course, if he left his office to avoid us, he may do the same at his home."

When we finally reach the right place, half of the narrow entryway to the side street is blocked with temporary construction barricades, so the driver simply pulls over nearby. "*Ici, bien?*" Having grown up in New York, I know a cabbie who has gone as far as he wants to go, so no translation is required. I nod, pay with my fancy new Stephanie Kramer credit card, and hop out. Past the barricades, the street is no bigger than an alley, so even if the driver had pulled in, he would have had to back out.

I double-check the map on my phone to find that the house we want is the first one, just past the barricades decorated with a large orange logo made of three letters: *MdE*. Percival glances over the top of the temporary walls and shrugs. Being notably shorter than him, I don't even bother trying. Instead, I walk up a short set of stairs to stand at the front door of Anton Bisset's house. I really have no idea what to expect — anything from no response to an attack — so while I don't immediately fill myself with EM power, I do prepare myself in the event it's needed.

I knock.

Nothing.

I knock again.

Muted from inside, I hear footsteps, then latches are unlocked and the door slowly creaks open. Looking at us with a puzzled expression is an older woman, her hair sitting in short grey curls atop her head. "*Bonjour, je peux vous aider?*"

"Oh, um, hi. I'm very sorry, but I don't speak French. Do you happen to speak any English? We're looking for someone." As soon as all of those words come out of my mouth, I figure I'm screwed. *Do you speak English?* would have been much simpler. Though I suppose neither version matters if the answer is *no*.

"Yes, a little," the woman says. "May I help you?"

I don't even hide my relief. The relief universal to the stranger in a strange land who suddenly discovers she can be understood. "Thank you, yes." I hold up my phone, showing the decades-old mugshot of Anton Bisset. "I apologize for the old photo, but we are looking for this man. Do you know him?"

The woman strains her eyes, peering at my phone. "Yes, very well. He is my husband. And that photo is not from one of his better days."

She gives us a wry smile, and I find myself liking this person. Which is a conflicted feeling, since she is connected to Bisset, and Bisset seems connected to everything bad going on in Paris. "I hope you are not with the police, after all these years. It was really just a misunderstanding."

Percival steps forward, tapping into his natural charisma. "No, nothing like that at all, ma'am. We might have old friends who are mutual acquaintances, and since we were in Paris, we thought this was sort of a once in a lifetime opportunity to say hello."

Madame Bisset smiles, and I can tell Percival's charms are working again. *Is every older French woman instantly in love with him?* In a strange way, I feel jealous. Has anyone ever fallen instantly in love with me in my entire life? Don't answer that. "Please, come in," she says. "Anton is in the garden. I can take you to see him." She leads us through a house that is dark and crammed with furniture and various objects, as if they can take the place of memories. Nothing, of course, means anything to us, but to the Bissets? I bet every trinket has a history. Or worse. Perhaps these items held stories in their day, but maybe they're now forgotten. "Anton, there are people here to see you," she says. "They only speak English."

A man — the same wiry, rat-faced man I saw in the picture at the hospital — rises from his cushioned metal chair to stand on the small stone patio bordered by a strip of grass these two consider a garden. Still, in the city, any big city, I know that space equals luxury. The tall old man extends his hand, though I'm reluctant to shake it. *"Bonjour,"* he says. "I am Anton Bisset. Do I know you?" How can I shake the hand of a man who might have been a part of Zee's death? But I don't know it to be true. What else don't I know? Who sent the note, *Watch over the children*? Could this man be on our side? No, surely not. Why would he have left the hospital when we came to see him? I make no effort to shake hands, and to Percival's great credit, neither does he. After a moment, Bisset lowers his wrinkled hand, giving us a curious look. "You seem like you have something you wish to say. Please sit." Not waiting for a reply, he takes the chair opposite us.

Tentatively, we join him at the table, but the woman, Madame

Bisset, merely smiles and wanders off, back into the house. I don't know where on earth to begin, but Percival breaks the icy silence, glaring at the old man seated before us. "Took off when you knew we were coming, huh?"

The old man returns the stare, but not in anger. Calm, confident, assured. "Let me inform you of two things," Anton Bisset says. "My wife is not nearly as innocent as she seems, and, if you press us, she will kill you." The threat is so sudden and severe that I find myself blindsided.

Subconsciously, I had assumed that both of the Bissets were EMs, since that tends to be our way, but we all know that an EM firing electricity into another EM is useless. Still, we turn, and sure enough, it's worse than I had hoped. Innocent grey-haired Madame Bisset is now holding a sleek black handgun, alternating between pointing it at Pers and me. We can save ourselves, here in the garden, by flying upward to the sky, but we can't learn the truth without playing by the Bissets' rules, or starting a fight. So we remain seated. "Why? What's the goal? What are you trying to do?"

Anton Bisset smirks at us, and just as I previously felt a strange liking of his wife, I'm now certain this man is bad. "There is really nothing. You Americans are so brash. There's nothing here to worry about. Go home. Tell your brother to worry about his own affairs, not ours."

"Then why did you run?" Percival says. "Why did you leave the hospital when we came to see you?"

Anton looks toward his wife with an attempt at compassion, but on his rat face it feels hopelessly false. "Agnès was ill. She needed someone here with her, so I came home. You're so quick to assume, quick to judge."

I decide to change the subject. "You're not a part of the Order, of Genevieve Deschamps's community in the city. Why?"

"Yes, of course, the *High* Order," he says, almost as if the muscles in his face feel compelled to revert to a sneer. "So pretentious."

"As if your *Prime* Order was anything less," Pers snaps.

Anton Bisset laughs. "I'm neither High Order nor Prime Order," he says.

Half of me is taken aback. *Neither?* Yet, the other half of me strangely thinks it feels right. *Of course neither. Both orders are pretentious. Why can't we just be ourselves?* Then my mind starts wandering in strange directions. "Is there... a third Order?"

Again, Bisset laughs, and I feel so happy that Pers and I could give him such a joyous afternoon. "Not that I am aware of," he says.

"So, you're independent?" Percival asks.

"Is that a bad thing?"

I shake my head, angry at myself for being distracted by nonsense like who's in who's club. "Doesn't matter. The babies. What are you doing to them?"

"Me?" Bisset says, grinning with false innocence. He's smug, dismissive, and insulting. Reminds me a lot of someone else. Apparently, it also annoys the shit out of Pers.

"Yes, you, asshole," Percival shouts, jumping up from his chair. "Why are you making so many new electromagicians? How?"

Anton Bisset's smile droops and he looks over my shoulder to where his wife is standing. "If they don't leave in the next 30 seconds, shoot them both."

Twenty-four seconds later, Percival and I find ourselves back on the street corner, next to the construction barricades. The Bissets stare at us from their front window until we're forced to walk away in failure.

So that went well.

22

BLIP OF THE RADAR

"Got something," Kevin says, as I settle into the singular chair in our flat. Pers flops on the bed, a thin golden line of the setting sun tracing rays down his body.

"What?" I ask, notably ticked off.

"Missing persons. Two cases," he says. "Even more interestingly, it was the first two EMs born in Paris this year."

"Hold up," I say. "First you need to hear what happened to us today." I give my brother the short version of our time with the Bissets and their convenient handgun.

"Jesus," Kevin says. "Well, that certainly makes them seem guilty. Now listen to this." My brother recites a litany of useless information on ninety-two kids and I sit there, totally and completely bored by his words. "No?" he asks. "Nothing there?"

"You know there isn't," I say, slouching even further into my chair.

"Let me talk about the original two, then," he says. "This year's Child One was abducted. Case remains open and unsolved. Even more bizarre, Child Two was abducted, too, though she somehow reappeared at her parents' house a few days later."

I lean forward. "What's the police report on the first kid? Any information at all?" I ask.

"There's nothing else. Kid basically vanished."

No, I think. *Nobody vanishes.* "A newborn baby doesn't wander off. Where'd this kid go?"

"This is from eight months ago. The Paris police have internally classified it as a cold case, though officially they say they're still investigating," Kevin says.

"Which means nothing," I reply.

"True."

"So this is it — the one we need to track. I mean, come on, it isn't just a coincidence that the first EM baby this year, in a boom year for EM babies, also happens to disappear."

"No," Kevin says. "That seems very unlikely to be a coincidence."

"Okay, then, do you have anything else for us to go on, or just *missing person*, end of story?"

"Sadly, that's it. The police have no active leads. Most missing infants turn up in the hands of some other family, some wannabe parents with a sob story that never overshadows the fact that they stole another family's kid, right? Is that what we're dealing with here?"

"Good question," I say. I grab the first page that Nurse Laffitte sent us, reading the initial entry. "Luis Sylvain. Born January thirteenth."

"That's the one," Kevin says. "Disappeared January nineteenth, a few days after he was sent home."

"Is he alive and well, just in the hands of the wrong people?" *And for that matter*, I think, *are the people who have him regular or EM?*

"No idea. Paris police don't know. I don't know."

"You're a world of help, bro," I say, tapping the red icon to hang up as I toss the phone onto the round table.

———

I'M NO POLICE DETECTIVE, but I know that A does not equal B. More specifically, the information known to the Parisian cops most certainly does not come close to what I know. Luis Sylvain is not a typical boy. He's an electromagician, and on top of that he was very likely created, not naturally made. So, while the Paris police think of him as a tragically missing little boy, I think of him like a brother. He's missing for a *reason*, and that reason is invariably because he's special, in the same way that *I* am special. And yet, weirdly, not. I mean, if someone can create an EM, that someone is doing so for a reason. And that's the reason Luis Sylvain is missing.

Percival must be having similar thoughts, because suddenly he says something that aligns perfectly. "What do we know?" he asks. "We know that Anton Bisset and his wife have something to do with what's going on. And they wanted us to stop asking questions and get lost, which is why she had the gun."

"So we need to get into their house," I say. "Find out what they're hiding."

"Maybe," Pers says, wheels turning in his head. "But if you were hiding a kid in your house, probably the last thing you'd do would be to let someone come *in*, right? I mean, you never know when a baby is going to cry, so having us that close would be asking for trouble."

"Okay, then what? Maybe they're just middlemen. Maybe Orkan Zidane and his stupid Prime Order took the kid. So we should search his building."

Percival tilts his head. "Which is where?"

"We sat there, right in his building, looking out the window. I could see the Eiffel Tower."

"So, yeah, that narrows it down to approximately all of Paris," Percival says. And damn it, he's right.

"All right, then we're screwed," I say. "We have nothing."

Pers shakes his head, flopping locks of blond hair back and forth. "Not exactly. We agree that the Bissets are in on this. We have to start with them."

"How? That old lady will shoot us."

"True, if she sees us. But I've been threatened at gunpoint before. I think we need to call your brother again."

"Why? What do you need?"

"What is it Kevin said he was good at? Data. As much data about the Bissets — and their house — as we can get."

————

MY BROTHER GIVES us everything he can find. One of the most likely to be helpful is also one of the more difficult to sift through — phone records. But if we can find a link between Bisset and the Prime Order, that would be something to work from, even if Anton tells us he's not in any order. "Check back to those January dates — the thirteenth through the nineteenth. Anything stand out?"

We're on speakerphone, so both Percival and I can hear Kevin clicking and typing. "I mean, there are phone records, but they look about the same as other months."

"Bank records?"

Kevin scoffs. "Do you think they sold the kid or something?"

"I don't know, just thinking out loud," I say.

More clicking. "I don't see any major deposits or withdrawals around that time."

"Man," Pers says. "I always assumed you were as straight-laced as they came. But you seem to have access to everything. Is this how you have so much money?"

Kevin grumbles. "Listen, Percival. I've been a computer programmer for more than two decades. I can get into systems because I know how they work. That doesn't make me a thief. Both our household finances and the finances of the EM community are completely spotless. Our parents handed Lyn and me a ridiculous inheritance, and I've busted my ass to keep it earning for us. I'm not skimming pennies off paychecks or anything stupid like that."

Percival throws up his hands, though Kevin can't see him. "Hey, chill, man. I wasn't accusing you. And even if you had done something under the table, I was just going to be impressed."

"Just because I can look at your bank account without you knowing about it, doesn't mean I'm taking money out."

Percival shoots me a look. "Your brother is taking this way too seriously," he says in my head.

"Wait a minute," Kevin says with a sudden rush. He clicks several more times, urgently.

"Care to clue us in?" I ask.

"Hold on." More clicking. "Yeah, that's strange."

"What's strange?"

"Something stands out, like a blip on the radar once I look at enough information. Going back over the past couple of years, it looks like the Bissets have been paying the same amount for electricity. It's billed every two months — I guess that's how they do it in France. But suddenly, in June of last year, their bill was *a lot* higher. Must have had a huge spike in electricity consumption. And then this year, it's remained high, every time."

"So... what?" I ask. "Are the Bissets EM junkies or something? They sure didn't seem like it."

"No idea," Kevin says.

"What's the name of the electric company?" Pers asks.

My brother clicks and taps some more. "It doesn't give a full name, just three letters. Em. Dee. Ee."

Percival snaps his fingers. "Is the D lowercase?"

"Yes," Kevin says. "Here, I can just search for it... There. It stands for *Ministère de l'Énergie*. Ministry of Energy, I'd say."

Percival is excited and I'm not sure why. "What? What is it?" I ask.

"The barricades — outside the Bissets' house. When I looked over the top, there were big black, shielded wires running into a partially open manhole."

"They're pumping electricity into the ground? Wouldn't that be backwards? Wouldn't they be getting their electricity *from* underground in the first place?"

"I have no idea, but those letters were on the barricades: *MdE*. Orange logo, right?"

"Yep, orange logo. Well, that sounds like a few too many coincidences for my liking," Kevin says.

"Great," I say. "So, Percival and I will go back and confront the Bissets about their electrical bill. I feel good about this."

Percival rolls not just his eyes but his entire head. "Lyn... We at least have to check it out. We don't exactly have anything else to go on, and like your brother says, it's a lot of coincidences."

I'm frustrated and annoyed. An electricity bill is the best thing we've got going for us, and my friend is dead. Still, I nod. What was it Zee said, some of the last words I ever heard her speak? *I feel strangely certain that everything is connected.* Yeah, me, too.

23

BLIND FAITH

I t's cold and completely dark when we arrive back at the edges of *Parc Montsouris*. Our cab driver does as we request and drops us off two blocks from the Bissets' house. Maybe Percival feels comfortable with all this midnight sleuthing, but for me it seems like I might as well have a spotlight on me. *Hey! Look over here! This girl is up to something she shouldn't be!*

The park is surrounded by a fence, which is generally no problem for an EM — we can just float over — but that will mean filling with power, which will mean glowing light blue, which will mean standing out even more than I already feel like I do. We need to find a place where no one will see us, and that's not at all easy. We end up walking almost the entire perimeter of the park until we find ourselves on the north side, near a train overpass, the best option we're going to get to avoid notice. I ready myself to fill with power and fly over the fence, when Percival points toward a wide-open entrance to the park not thirty feet from us. Immediately, I feel stupid. "I don't know how cut out I am for all this detective shit," I say.

Pers puts his hands on my shoulders. "It's easy. Just remember this. Most people aren't expecting the unexpected. Why would they?

Just do the simplest unusual thing you can, and you're probably good."

"I don't think any of that made any sense at all," I say. *The Simplest Unusual Thing. Good band name? Maybe. Good life plan? Doubtful.*

Percival leans down and gives me a quick kiss. "It will make sense. Promise." He grins, gleaming white. Then, after a quick glance in each direction, he leads me into the park.

We make our way toward the section of the park closest to the Bissets' house, which is easy enough when you have a map on your phone. From there, we just look. The lights are all out. The Bissets are older, so they're probably asleep, given that it's after midnight. Still, we stare at those dark windows for a good long time.

Hardly anyone is walking or driving on the street, so finally Pers comes up with what amounts to a plan. "We make sure the coast is clear, then we juice up and quickly fly over the street, directly into the middle of the barricades by their house. If the Bissets notice, well, I imagine we'll find out right away. Be prepared to run — or fly. If anyone *else* happens to notice, it's just a weird sparking light at a place where people already know the power company is working. The simplest unusual thing."

I sigh. He's serious about this as a life plan. "Then what?" I ask.

Percival blinks, shrugging. "Well, then we see where those wires go."

———

MOMENTS LATER, we're standing in the small rectangle formed by the energy company's barricades. They're easily over six feet tall, which means that essentially no one can see us, not even the Bissets if they happen to be both extremely crafty, watching us from dark windows, and extremely good at predicting the random millisecond when we'd appear in this place.

Pers grabs the manhole cover. "Damn, this thing is heavier than it looks."

"Too much for you, tough guy? Need me to tackle that?" I

shimmer blue, flowing with power. No human male, regular or EM, has ever liked this sort of banter.

Not surprisingly, Percival sighs. "I got it, jeez." He slides the cover along the rubberized electrical wires, but just at the last moment, it scrapes the pavement with a sound that echoes off the nearby buildings.

We freeze, breathlessly. Three or four seconds later, I realize that I'm actually counting the time in my head. I stand on tiptoes, looking toward the Bissets' house. "Still dark."

Pers nods. But still, I think we have a problem. With the manhole cover moved aside, I see a deep vertical shaft where the thick electrical wires from the Bissets' house run along one side, though the way down is otherwise clear and wide. The issue, however, is simpler: there's no ladder, no set of metal rungs, no way to climb down, and the descent looks to be a long one.

I huff. "Well, that sucks."

Percival looks at me, starting to glow. "Lyn, don't forget who you are." He lifts gently off the ground then lowers himself effortlessly down into the shaft, holding his elbows in front of him to slip through the opening and into the darkness below.

"That wasn't the least bit disturbing," I say before filling myself with power and following him down. Honestly, if I couldn't look past my feet and see his glow below me, I'm pretty sure I would chicken out, but he's there the whole time, so I keep going.

At the bottom, he continues glowing, but I see him walk to one side. I land near him, completely unwilling to release my power. Mostly because then it would be pitch black down in whatever slice of hell we've found ourselves. "What in the name of Rupert's Rumpus is this place?" I say. It was an old TV show I liked. Nerves bring out weird memories and even weirder ideas in me.

"I have no idea what a *Rupert's Rumpus* is," Percival says, "so I really can't answer that question. But, I do have a sliver of cell reception still." I realize that Pers is holding his phone in his bare hands, *while* he's glowing with power. I have to stop myself from asking him how such a thing could even be possible, but then I realize that his fingers and hands seem to be the one part of him not radiating blue-white light. *I will never figure out how to do that. At the very least, that's a 400 level course, and I'm still in elementary school.* He taps away on the phone, not the least bit amazed at the spectacle of what he's doing, searching, scrolling. After a minute, in the bright light of its screen, I see his eyes go wide. "Well, now. That's something special. Did you know there are miles of tunnels underneath Paris and some of them are lined with skulls and bones?"

I purse my lips, staring at him hard. "Do you think I would have followed you down here if I knew something like that?"

He nods, still swiping the screen. "Probably not. But it's true, apparently. There are catacombs — places you have to pay like twenty bucks to tour."

"So, we're in some underground tourist trap?" I ask.

Percival turns on his cellphone's flashlight and scans our surroundings. I have no idea what he thinks of the place, but I quickly assess what I see: low ceiling, crumbling walls, dust every-where, probably extremely dangerous, likelihood of a cave-in pretty high. "I'd say very few tourists have ever seen this part," he says, looking up at the expanse of vertical shaft above us. "Besides, how would they even get down here?"

"Good point," I say. "So, we're in a deep underground passageway that regular humans would have little hope of accessing, but EMs can get into easily, as we've just proven. Right?"

"Seems that way."

"Which just happens to be next to the house of the person we're investigating?"

"Also correct," he says, twisting around to look down one of the tunnels. "And there are quite definitely footprints in the dust going off in that direction. Though that hardly seems to be the most damning evidence."

"Oh?" I ask. "What would that be?"

He points his flashlight toward the upper corner of the passage-way. "The electrical cables also go the same way."

"Then away we go," I say, following Percival's blue glow into the well of black while the tiny hairs on the back of my neck stand at full attention.

———

I SUSPECT STRONGLY that walking through a labyrinth of tunnels underneath a foreign city would be a disturbing thing to do at any time of day, but the fact that my internal clock knows it's past midnight significantly ratchets up the tension I'm feeling. Even worse, at the third intersection we reach, the power lines go in two directions, so Percival has the wonderful idea to split up.

He takes the right path while I go left. "Keep talking to me," I say as we separate, unable to hide the stress in my voice.

"Nervous, dear?" he asks in a mocking tone.

"I can always float myself back up to the street and leave your ass alone down here."

"Just when we're getting somewhere? I seriously doubt you'd do that." His voice seems to echo from far away.

Sometimes, it just feels better to flow with power, but my light blue glow doesn't feel strong enough anymore, not for my comfort. I reach into the large pockets of my hoodie and pull out my gloves, slipping each on, then reach into the back pocket of my jeans for my cell phone. A moment later, its blazing flashlight comes to life.

I round another bend, still following my set of electric lines, but something else catches my eye. Words, painted in a rough hand on the irregular surface of the right wall. *Bout du Monde.*

Though I know almost nothing of the French language, I have existed on planet Earth for a couple of decades, and you bump into things now and then. The phrase tickles something in my mind, but the first word I can remember is *monde.* "That means *world,*" I say aloud to myself and the darkness, and the echoes of my own voice startle me. The strangeness of the sound reminds me of some old movie, most likely a terrible movie, at that, some cinematic garbage about a woman trapped in darkness, wondering if she'll ever see the light of day again. Oh wait, that's me, right now. And that breaks the logjam in my head, allowing me to remember the whole phrase. "*Bout du Monde*. The End of the World." My freak-out level hits a new high, until I chuckle at myself for such childish nerves, trying to calm down. *It's just graffiti*, I think.

Then I hear Percival scream.

24

THE END OF THE WORLD

I'm running, back the way I came, but that just makes the light from my phone's flashlight bob and weave in a disorienting way. *Did I miss the turn? No! Follow the power lines!* It's the only thing that keeps me certain I'm not lost.

But Percival is still shouting, and frustratingly, he seems to be getting farther away. "Lyn, a little help, please!"

"I'm *trying* to help you, but I don't know where you are," I shout back.

"Stickmen!" He's panting, and his voice is throbbing from the motion of running on the hard stone tunnel floor. "Two I think — came out of nowhere! Just running to stay alive at the moment! Some help would be nice!" He's sounding breathless.

Stickmen? In a tunnel underneath Paris near a guy's house who is quite definitely connected to the disappearance of a manufactured EM child? Some days I wonder why I get out of bed. *Also, what is the freaking deal with all these tunnels?* I see light up off to one side, away from the safety of the power lines. But it's flashing blue light, and I know it's Percival, blazing with power. *This is* not *how things end*. I run. Now I'm shining brightly with electricity, too.

Finally, I can see him clearly, because in these damned dark tunnels, Percival's light is just about the only thing I can see. Yet there's a problem. Between us, there's a crumbled section, the passage no wider than eighteen inches. No way I can get through that.

Pers backs up against the hole that separates us. "They're just about on me, Lyn!" He sounds terrified.

I throw myself at the other side of that hole, reaching toward him. *It's too far.* Bits of stone crumble down on me, making me wonder if the entire thing is about to collapse.

Percival turns, seeing my glow. He reaches out. I strain forward. It's not enough.

"This is not how things end!" I shout, cramming as much of myself into the small opening as I can. My fingers just barely brush Percival's... but I'm still wearing gloves. Growling in anger at my own stupidity, I flick my wrist sharply, once, twice, and the glove flies off, somewhere into the darkness. I reach out and find Percival's fingers once more...

...and he erupts with such a blaze of electromagic power that I am blinded, my eyes too used to the darkness. I can feel him drawing strength from me, our fingertips like a circuit I just cannot allow to be disconnected. Though the edges of the rough hole dig into the flesh of my arms and face, I force myself to press inward, to keep our fingers touching.

Power flows and flows, and then there is a distinct popping sound. "Hold on! One more!" Percival shouts. More flowing, then another pop. Finally, he releases everything and his fingers fall away from mine. I hear him flop down in the dark, exhausted. "What the hell?"

"Well, I'd definitely say we're on to something now," I say, sliding away from the rocky hole and dusting off.

Percival turns and I see just his face glowing on the other side. "Ya think? Come on, let's get back together. I think I'm done traipsing around down here solo."

"Probably a good idea." I scan the area with my phone's light. "However... problem."

"What's that?"

"Do you see power lines anywhere?" I ask.

I hear his feet scraping on the stone ground as he turns. "Ah, shit. When those damn things popped up, I just ran. Any way I could."

I have an idea. "That's fine, but you were looking up these tunnels — catacombs — on your phone. Was there a map?"

"I think so. Let me check." A few moments pass, and my overactive imagination begins to wonder a couple of things. First, has Pers left me? And second, whether he has or not, are we ever getting out of here? "Okay, well, the answer is yes and no. There are a *lot* of maps. Problem is that there are also a *lot* of tunnels. And I don't know where we started. And I definitely don't know where we've ended up."

"So, we have quite a few problems, then."

"Yep."

"Okay, let's try this. If I stand *facing* you and the hole between us, there is a passageway to my right, just a little bit behind me. If you face away from me and the hole, we'll both be looking in the same direction. Is there any path you can take on your right?"

"Um... yes!"

"Good. Hopefully that's a start. If we both walk down our right-hand tunnels — and *keep talking* to each other — maybe we can see if we get any closer. Sound like a plan?"

"It sounds better than the plan I have, which is nothing," he says. I can hear the grin in his voice, know that, off in the dark, he's showing off those perfect teeth. Right now, I very much want to see those perfect teeth again, up close and personal.

We walk and we talk, sometimes sounding like we're very close, and sometimes shouting to be heard. It all feels very much like the desperation I imagine people get before they figure out they're hopelessly trapped and bound to die, somewhere deep in the earth. Then, my flashlight — held in my one remaining gloved hand — catches something. A long, dark shadow. "Hold on a minute," I say.

Percival shouts back. "What is it, Lyn? Talk to me. Not more Stick-men, right?"

"No, sorry. Didn't mean to scare you. I think I see power lines."

"Oh!" Pers says, laughing. "Well, that would be a very good thing to find."

A very good thing, indeed, I think. I follow the lines, and quickly see them enter a wide chamber, much different from all the thin tunnels we've been in so far. "It's led me to some kind of room. And there are *things* here, like machinery."

"Maybe it's some kind of old city power plant system," he says. I can't tell if he's getting closer or farther away.

Scanning the room with my light, I'm suddenly very sure this isn't anything the city of Paris put together. Against the far wall, there is a gurney. Not the complex, mechanized kind like we saw in passing at Nurse Laffitte's hospital, but the simpler, manual kind, like you might see an EMT glide into the back of an ambulance. "Something is very wrong here, Percival. Can you get to me? There's a bed here. I have a very bad feeling about this place."

"Keep talking — I'm trying to get closer." I hear him grumble a curse directed at the maze of passageways.

Beside the bed, there's a tall machine with lots of knobs and buttons. In its center, there's a large monitor, but the screen is dark. Wires come out the top — the wires we had been following, I think. More thick power lines run to a series of three low, rectangular, boxy structures. They look like... "Coffins," I say aloud. "Oh my God, Pers. Get here fast!"

"Wait! I see power lines over here! I'm going to try to follow them to where you are!" Footsteps pound and echo somewhere behind me.

I don't want to do it, but I have to. I have to see what's inside the first box. Holding the blaring light of the phone in my gloved hand, I reach forward with my bare hand, seeing it tremble and glow with a dim blue light. *That's simply not going to be enough power for this moment*, I think, willing my electromagic to flow. Now the room is awash in the blue-white electrical shine of me. *Lightning in a bottle. Be lightning in a bottle.* I take a deep breath, then hold it as I flip open the lid of the box, expecting a Stickman to leap out at me.

What I see is infinitely more horrible, a vision I will carry with me for the rest of my life. I release every ounce of my power and fall down to my knees, immediately starting to heave with big, uncontrolled sobs.

The box truly was a coffin, but one littered with wires and electrodes. In the center, so tiny, yet so clearly visible, was the charred remains of a person. No. Not a person. A child. The littlest, most helpless child. "They killed him!" I shouted through wet gobs of tears. "They took him and they killed him!"

A moment later, something rushes up and grabs me. Not in a scary, rough way, but in the quick and smooth embrace of a lover. Percival is with me, holding me, telling me it's okay now, it's okay now. And I think, *no, it isn't. And it never will be again. Not for this little boy and not for a world that would let this happen.* In the depth of my sadness and uncontrolled anger, I know that revenge doesn't bring back the dead. I weep, burying my face into Percival's shoulder.

PART III

SPLIT INFINITY

25

THE CAVALRIES ARE COMING

You can be one of the most powerful humans on the planet, able to be struck by lightning a hundred times in a row, and turn that energy around into deadly bolts of electromagic, but you can also be a devastated little girl again. One that doesn't feel like she belongs anywhere, or that anything makes sense. One that feels nearly hopeless from the horrors of the world.

And in the middle of all that power and all that desperation, even you can be affected by the tiniest thing: turning on the lights.

Percival finds a wall switch near the room's entrance. Flicking it on, we're suddenly quite certain those power lines we'd been following are very real, and very active. The irregularly shaped chamber with the machinery and the coffin-like boxes suddenly is flooded with light, bright as day. I'm still sitting on the floor, but I've scuffed away from the box I opened, unable to bear its nearness anymore. After fumbling around in the dark, you'd think the overhead lights letting us see everything would be a good thing. The only problem is, I don't want to see everything. Not in this room. Not ever again. I start to get hysterical, unable to control myself any longer. "What are we gonna do, Pers? This, all this shit... And Zee, too, damn it!" I pound the floor with one hand.

"We're going straight to the cops," he says. "Simple as that. We follow the electrical lines, back out of here, up to the Bissets' house. Then we call the cops and let them see exactly what's down here. I mean, you can't get a more direct connection to a missing kid than we have here. Then the police will cut all of this off, confiscate all these machines, and throw the Bissets away for life. I hope they give 'em the electric chair."

When I reply, my voice sounds rough, gravelly. Exhausted. It's the absurdity of it all. Everything is absurd. I can't stifle the stupid, immature laugh that bubbles up at Percival's words. "You know, I was following your plan until that last part."

Suddenly he realizes what he's said. "Oh shit. If they gave the Bissets the electric chair, that would just make them super powerful. No, no, forget that. They'll just rot in jail for life. I don't even know if France has electric chairs."

I laugh again despite everything, what's happened, where we are. It's laughter and crying all rolled into one. "You're ridiculous, you know?"

Pers gives me a concerned smile as he kneels beside me, putting his arm over my shoulders. "Let's get out of here. We've seen enough." He manages to get me standing, moving.

We follow the power lines, walking as if we're in some strange funeral procession, which I suppose we are. We find the vertical shaft. It doesn't seem possible that it's so close... we wandered so far, so lost in the dark. As we lift ourselves, I'm thankful that I have enough power to even do that before I remember the superbolt of lightning. The power we stole from some woman named Michelle we'd never seen before. Finally, we stand on the street, beside the barricades, outside the house of the people I would very much like to see pay for what they have done.

Thirty seconds later, a flurry of police cars descends from every direction, screeching to a halt around us. Pers and I look at each other in confusion.

He's the first to realize the gravity of the situation. Though they may have to follow more rules than the armed bodyguards of the

Prime Order, these are still men with guns. "Put your hands up and act calm, Lyn. Those damn Bissets seem to have gotten the jump on us and called the cops before we got the chance. Which means they most likely have some sort of cover story."

I nod. "Great. That cover story most likely implicates us."

Parisian police officers burst from their vehicles, shouting at us in French. Neither of us know what they're saying, but, you know, standing still with our hands up remains the best plan.

"That's them! *Les voilà!*" a voice cries out, but it's a female voice. Not Anton Bisset, for sure, and though it sounds familiar, it's not Agnès Bisset either. I turn to see Madame Deschamps approaching quickly, sharply dressed in a matching crimson business jacket and skirt, with a pale white blouse contrasting the bright red. To her left are a couple of French EMs that look familiar from our visit to Deschamps headquarters, and to her right are the two EMs visiting from Singapore, people on the same quest for answers we've been pursuing. The five of them push through the ring of cops like they belong, while Deschamps says something to the police, an urgent, passionate series of words and phrases I completely don't understand. *Is she trying to get us arrested?* When she's done, the officer beside her looks away from us, and toward where the Bissets live. He gives a command to the nearby officers and they begin to converge on the house, then shouts something to me and Pers in a warning tone. "He's telling you not to go anywhere. They need to speak to you," Deschamps explains as she approaches.

"How did you know we'd be here?" I ask, confused.

Madame Deschamps gives me a knowing look. "Did you think you could come to my city, come see me with your concerns, and I would not keep track of you?"

Suddenly, I'm furious with her. "If you were *keeping track* of me, then why didn't you stop what happened to my friend?"

Her expression changes to one of regret, sympathy. "My dear, I may know where you are, and may be able to deduce things from that information, but sadly, I don't know everything."

Over Deschamps's shoulder, I see others coming forward: two

who look like EMs from Orkan's Prime Order, along with a couple of their regular human bodyguards, all of whom eye Deschamps's crew with distrust, and then another couple farther behind, harder to see. "Jeez, it's turning into a party here tonight," Percival quips. Something catches his eye, and he stretches to see over the others standing in the way. "Hayden? Uma?" He starts waving excitedly.

For a moment, I can't process what's happening. What is that, twelve, thirteen electromagicians together, in a public place, surrounded by cops? Fifteen if you count the Bissets. And Uma? Hayden? I twist to look between the others, trying to get a glimpse. Luckily the social distancing happening between the High Order group and those from the Prime Order is just enough for our New York friends to slip by, and in a moment, we're exchanging hugs. "Oh my God, you guys, what are you doing here?" I ask, tears welling in the corners of my eyes. I start to wonder how much I'm going to cry these days before shoving the thought down, pushing it away. It's not our friends showing up, or at least not *only* that; it's Zee, the dead kid, the damned Bissets, and, frankly, the entire nonsense between the two EM groups. It's draining.

"Hey, Lyn," Uma says, holding my shoulders and forcing me to look her in the eye. It just makes fresh tears fall. "We're here now. We'll figure it out together." She hugs me again.

"But... but, Zee is —"

She cuts me off. "We know. Kevin told us, before he sent us here to help out. I'm so, so sorry." Another hug, longer this time. I let it happen, pulling myself into her.

When Uma finally shifts away, I look toward Hayden, trying to return to some kind of normalcy with a sheepish grin and a lame joke. "If you're here, who's DJing this weekend?"

Hayden shrugs it off, smiling. "Eh, I got some kid to do it. His name is Josh, and he's relatively new, but he knows his stuff about music. Even introduced me to a couple of artists from Louisiana I'd never heard of before."

Pers grins. "You're listening to country now?"

"Very funny. Hardly. And I promise you, when I drop some of this disco/house mix shit on you next time, you *will* be dancing."

Uma interjects. "It *is* good. Still guys, we have other issues right now. Kevin told us as much as he could, but..." She glances furtively at the people and flashing lights surrounding us before continuing in a low voice. "I think we need an update." An unmarked car arrives on scene, though its flashing lights identify as yet another police vehicle. From it, a plainclothes officer in a dark suit steps out, walking purposefully toward the others.

Pers and I fill them in quickly, huddled together in a circle, from our arrival in Paris through our discoveries in the catacombs. I guess my descriptions of the electrified rectangular boxes and the infant inside one of them carry too far on the night air, because suddenly I realize Madame Deschamps has reappeared just a few feet away. "So, it is confirmed? You found the child?" I sigh and nod. "Then I will inform the police about this so that they can begin a search."

"What did you tell them already?" I ask, wondering how much trouble we're in.

"I said that you both are friends from America who decided you wanted to explore the catacombs, though I warned you it was illegal. And I told them you discovered that the Bissets were powering something down there, as well. Which is, of course, also illegal, and indicates that they have been breaking many more laws than you. Once I tell them it is related to the child, they will wish to question you, but I seriously doubt you will be punished for your actions." She begins to walk away, toward the policeman in the suit, who appears to be in charge.

I call out to her before she gets too far away. "It's some kind of machine," I say. "It... it sucks the life out of them." Just thinking about it threatens to send me into another downward spiral, so I turn my head, blinking away tears that are starting to form once more. My vision is momentarily blurry, wet droplets turning the surrounding lights into blinding flares of brightness. I wipe my eyes in an attempt to see clearly.

Then I see a man. There is a man standing across the street

watching us. The police activity has attracted a good amount of attention, but most of the people surrounding us are, to me, nameless
faces. This man isn't. He has scraggly wisps of grey hair poking out
from beneath a brimmed hat, and a beard that's equally disheveled.
"Look!" I whisper harshly. "Torden Detonde is standing right there!"

The others swivel their heads around, searching, looking, but I'm
already pushing past them. This is the man that tried to kill me. And
he's responsible for the deaths of countless others, including Uma's
brother, Zeb, and our friend, Robin. After Robin's death, we were all
devastated, but Mackenzie was most of all. Their budding romance
was snuffed out, just as now Zee herself has been snuffed out. I
realize with a sudden certainty that if Torden Detonde is here, in
Paris, with Zee dead, a child dead, and a mysterious amount of new
EMs being generated out of thin air, then he's related to it all.
Responsible. "You see him, right?" I ask Percival, hoping I'm not going
crazy.

"Yeah," he says. "Yeah, I do." He steels his chin, ready for whatever
comes next.

"Then come on," I say in a determined voice as I move toward the
street. "We need to grab him before he can slip away again."

Just then, two Parisian police officers jump in front of me, hands
out to restrict my movement, barking some quick and earnest words
in French. I'm having none of it, and try to shove past them, too, but
they hold me back. In that instant, I almost — almost! — zap them to
make them let go, but I catch myself. If they put me in jail for electrocuting two officers, or worse, shoot me, I'll never get Torden. And I'll
expose the others to a lot of questions that might be really, really hard
for them to answer, like how did we get down a ladderless well into
the catacombs in the first place. Still, I make another lunge to get
through the officers blocking my way, and once more they hold me
back. Across the street, I see something plain as day.

Torden is smiling at me.

Muttering curse words, I ram myself into the policemen,
desperate to get by, but they're bigger than me, stronger. They stand
their ground. I try once more, but suddenly another cop approaches

from behind, grabbing at my hands. I hear the tinkling metal of handcuffs coming out, then feel one snapped around my right wrist, too tight. The second handcuff snaps around my other wrist as they twist me around to face the Bissets' house. Pers and the others protest in a language many of the officers probably don't understand, and I'm pretty certain I'll be spending the rest of the night in a police holding cell. Pretty sure I've ruined the perfect moment to get Torden, force him to explain, and then make sure that he gets what's coming to him. There was that rock my brother threatened Torden with, back in New York — *the Touchstone of Something Something.* I don't remember the full name, but I know it takes away power, permanently. Maybe it would kill him, too. That would be fine with me. But for now, I've screwed up and I'm headed to jail. Shit.

Madame Deschamps approaches with a scowl on her face. She speaks in quick, sharp busts, admonishing the police. At first, they argue back, but when the suited plainclothes policeman steps forward, waving his hands dismissively, suddenly the uniformed officers relent. After a few words, they uncuff me.

I spin back toward the park. Though the rest of the crowd is still present, I'm not the least bit surprised to find that Torden Detonde is, once again, gone.

26

INFIGHTING

A t this point, surrounded by electromagicians from multiple continents and multiple sects, plus having been seen by Torden himself, the Paul and Stephanie Kramer ruse seems a little silly, so when the police ask me my name and story, I give it to them. Well, minus a whole lot of EM details. I even mention the other house we had, the explosion. I tell them the name of the deceased is Mackenzie Patmina. The officer jots notes on it all. He's most interested in the Bissets and the power lines running to where a dead kid was found in the catacombs, but hearing about *another* homicide seems to be noteworthy — and potentially related — information. Meanwhile, a team of rescue workers has been tasked with going underground to both confirm my story and retrieve the body. I don't envy their jobs at all.

As if there weren't enough EM gathered together on one street corner, Orkan Zidane arrives and confers with his group. I see him looking my way from time to time. Man, am I sick of being the center of attention.

Hours go by — three? four? — and not a lot changes. Then a radio crackles, and the boss man in his suit exchanges words with someone in French. When he's done, he leans to another officer, who in turn comes toward us. That guy then relays whatever's going on to the officer in charge of us. So that's what? Four levels of playing telephone before we even get to find out what's happening? I expect to hear that Godzilla has been anointed pope or something equally far removed from the original message.

"You are free to go," our holding officer says, heavily accented. "We have located the child's body, and it is as you describe." He says something else about not leaving town and being available for additional questioning, but I don't care about all that.

"Okay, but what about the Bissets?" I ask. "Have they been arrested?"

The officer shakes his head. "No, at least not yet. The house is empty. We will need to find them and question them. But of course, we see the power lines running from their house into the catacombs, so their connection to these things seems... undeniable."

I sigh. "Great, so do you have any idea where they might have gone?"

"This I am not permitted to speak about. Police policy. Please just let us do our work, *Mademoiselle*," he says, with a dismissive look that tells me we're done talking.

"Fine," I say in a huff, walking away. "Come on, Percival. We'll find them ourselves."

"*Please* let us do our work," the officer shouts as we walk away, toward the waiting group of EMs. "Oh! *Mademoiselle*, I nearly forgot!"

I look back, my dark mood plain on my face. "What is it?" I ask, expecting him to levee some other restriction on me, something else to piss me off.

"You mentioned the explosion, in the 16th arrondissement?" I vaguely recall our driver, Jean, mentioning the 16th was where our house was located, so I nod. Even thinking about having a driver in Paris seems like a memory from a thousand years ago. "We have attempted to confirm your story, but no body was recovered."

I blink. "I don't understand."

"Holy shit, Lyn," Pers says beside me, suddenly giddy.

I don't like sudden giddiness, especially in this situation. I wave a hand at Percival, clearly wanting him to cool it. Probably too stern, I know, but my mind is reeling. I take a breath. "What did you say? No body? What does that mean? Our friend Zee was *killed* in that explosion."

The officer shrugs. "Perhaps she was, but we have no evidence of it."

"Then... what? I mean, could you have, I don't know... *missed* her?"

"No," he says, shaking his head. "As you can imagine, an explosion in the city is not a common thing. It is a very big deal, and so it is very thoroughly investigated."

I try to respond, but have no words. Standing there, silently baffled, I try to rationalize what I've just heard. *No, this is wrong. This is false hope. Zee's dead. But... where's her body? If they checked the place carefully, they must have found something. And if they didn't...?* "Did somebody take her?" I ask aloud to no one.

Percival jumps on the idea. "You mean, like someone took us, just after, but then told us he had nothing to do with Zee?"

In a heartbeat, I'm totally on board with what Pers is saying, and that can mean only one thing. "I need to have a conversation with Orkan Zidane," I say, trying to contain my sudden rage.

Thankfully, he's only about thirty feet away.

———

"ORKAN!" I shout, stomping toward him. After my night, you'd think I'd be passed out from exhaustion, but suddenly I'm full of energy. Not EM energy, just the raw bile of being really, really pissed off. "You said you had nothing to do with her!"

Suddenly there are a whole lot of nervous electromagicians standing around, eyeing me and the police, back and forth. "Lyn," Orkan says in a voice that's trying and failing to calm me down. "I told you the truth. But can we talk about this somewhere else?"

"They said no body was found," I seethed. "How do you explain that?"

Genevieve Deschamps, who seems to have an almost visceral reaction against the simple act of standing next to Orkan Zidane, nonetheless slides between us. "Lyn, we should take all this someplace quiet. Then you can get your answers. I promise."

My gut says no. To hell with the police or people finding out EM business. This is my friend's *life* we're talking about. But even Hayden and Uma are looking at me with pleading eyes, and I relent. In an angry whisper, I level my demands. "Someplace nearby. Right now. Or else I'm telling my *whole* story to the police *and* making some calls to the media as well."

"Of course," Deschamps says. Behind her, Orkan nods his agreement.

———

AFTER A BRIEF DEBATE on whether we head to a High Order location or a Prime Order one — most likely sped up by my increasingly impatient demeanor — it's decided we go to neutral ground. And in Paris, that's most easily accommodated by one of the ten thousand cafes that dot nearly every corner of the city. Still, there are two problems. First, it's something like six o'clock in the morning and the sun hasn't yet made an appearance. And second, there are a dozen of us, while most cafes seat tables for two. Thankfully, the locals know where to go. Orkan and his group leave first, and while I'm reluctant to let the man out of my sight, I also have no desire to ride in a car with him. Instead, me, Pers, Hayden, and Uma follow Madame Deschamps and the rest of her group to their small, waiting van. Fitting us all inside is like loading up an EM clown car, but we aren't going far.

At the cafe, the somewhat anonymous members of both the High and Prime Orders — Deschamps's and Orkan's posse, for lack of a better explanation — shove chairs around and bicker with the owner of the place until he gives up and lets them do as they please. They pull together six tiny tables flanked by twelve chairs. Finally, we're all in the back corner of the place and every eye turns to me. I deflect their attention toward Orkan. "You magically appeared the moment our house was destroyed, and now the cops say Zee wasn't found inside. So, tell me: where is she?"

"I don't know," he says.

I leap out of my seat, but Uma, Hayden, and Pers rise to hold me back. "Hey now, Lyn," Percival says, leaning close. "You came here to hear what he has to say. Let him talk. Then, if he's full of shit, I'll help you kill him. Fair?"

"Me, too," says Hayden.

Uma nods in agreement. "Absolutely."

My only reply is a stern look that says they better not be kidding. About the killing Orkan part. When I sit back down, Pers gestures for the man to continue.

Rather than answer me directly, Orkan turns to Deschamps. "Have we ever kidnapped any member of your organization?" he asks her, calmly.

"You kidnapped *us*," Percival snaps.

Orkan sighs. "I told you. That wasn't a kidnapping. You were taken in for protective custody. We were trying to *save* you."

"And you just happened to know where we'd be and when there would be a problem?" Pers says in a mocking tone.

Once more, Orkan Zidane directs his comments to Madame Deschamps. "Ever since these two arrived, you've been tracking them, no?" She nods slowly. "Well, so have we. Having two new electromagicians in the city is noteworthy, particularly when they come with such renown. Stories travel quick and light, as they say."

"Renown?" I scoff. "What, because we uncovered what Torden was doing in New York?"

Orkan smirks and waggles his head. "Yes, that, but also something more."

Pers and I share a confused glance. "Care to clarify, friend?" Percival asks with an aloof tone. I know all too well that when Pers calls someone *friend* in that tone, he is most definitely not being friendly.

Turning to look me in the eye, Orkan begins a conversation that changes me. Changes everything I ever thought I knew about me, even the weirdo me that is an EM. "Lyn, across the centuries of the history of our kind, never has there been anyone who could tap into *another* electromagician's well of power. Yet you can."

I grimace at the thought. *What's this have to do with anything? Why is he talking about me?* Besides, I hate standing out. It makes me cringe. "That's not true! Percival's done it. Uma's done it, too."

Orkan smiles the exact kind of smile I hate the most: a knowing smile. "Yes, but have either of them ever done it *without you*?"

Of all the things we could be talking about, I'm definitely not expecting this. I don't know what to say, but I quickly scan my thoughts, my memories of the fight against Torden's Stickmen. "Yes! Percival, tell them! You did it yourself, just by touching hands with Mary Tate, in that warehouse! Remember?" I sound like I'm defending myself, and I guess I am, so that's another thing I hate. And besides, what did I do wrong? Tell people how to do something to save their lives and stop a madman? Why am I sitting here getting grilled about it?

"She's right," Percival says. Thank God someone hasn't gone insane. The group around us breaks into multiple small conversations, trying to sort this new information out.

Orkan raises one hand slightly from the small cafe table before him, silencing them all. "Has anyone else here ever accomplished this feat without Lyn Hopkins present? Tapping into the power of another electromagician, after hearing the rumors of this tale coming from New York? Any of the French in the room, or —" He nods toward the two EMs from Singapore, who are silently observing it all. "— from elsewhere?"

To a person, everyone shakes their head. *Everyone.* Including Percival, Hayden, and Uma. "What the —?" I mutter.

"My sentiments exactly," Orkan says. "What is going on? So I propose an experiment. With your permission, Lyn, I would like another electromagician — of your choosing, in this room — to attempt to connect with your power. Not *use* it, mind you, merely see if they can reach it."

"Sounds like a trap or a trick or something," I say.

"No trap, no trick," he replies. "You may even choose Percival for the test, if you like."

"I *do* like," I shoot back. Which I think means I just agreed to the test, and now I'm mad at myself. *Stupid.* "Shit. Fine. Pers will connect with my well of power. What does that prove? I already know it works."

"Yes, but then I wish for Percival to take any other EM of his choosing and step out of the building, to see if he can do it again."

"Whatever. Let's get this over with," I say, holding a hand out to Percival. He takes my hand and closes his eyes, which seems rather dramatic, but damn if everything isn't feeling overly dramatic, so what's the difference? I can feel his power through the touch, and I'm sure he can feel mine.

A moment later, Pers opens his eyes. "I can reach Lyn's power. I can tap into it if I want to, when we're in contact." If anyone would be able to confirm such a thing, it's Percival. God knows I don't let many other people touch me.

Orkan nods. "And now, Percival, please select someone else to take outside and test again."

To his credit, Pers sticks up for me and the lunacy of this business. "I've already been able to do it with another EM, and we were all the way across a wide room from Lyn at the time."

Tenting his hands before his face, Orkan contemplates the issue. "Let's change this part of the test slightly then. If you will select a partner, hold their hand and see if you can reach their power while you are in this room. Then, walk out of the cafe and keep walking for, let's say a block or two."

"Okay," Percival replies, before pointing a finger at Uma. "Do you mind being my fellow guinea pig?"

"Sure," she says, holding out her dark-skinned hand. Her expression is serious, and that has me worried.

Once they touch, they almost simultaneously tell Orkan that they can see each other's powers. "Then, please, continue the test as you get farther away."

Both rise, still holding hands like a boyfriend and girlfriend, which probably should make me feel at least a tinge of jealousy, except right now I feel embarrassed and annoyed. When they reach the door, Pers turns back. "I can still feel Uma's power." They push open the door and walk out into the street where the muted glow of sunrise is just barely starting to recolor the world. After a moment, they're out of sight, and then all the rest of us simply get to wait.

It feels like an hour goes by, but I'm sure that rationally it's more like three or four minutes. When the door opens again, Uma walks in without a word, making her way toward us and her seat. Percival enters pensively, coming our way with a detached look on his face.

"So?" Orkan asks.

"Near the end of the block," he says, bewildered.

"What happened there?"

"Her power — Uma's power — it just clicked off, light you'd turn off a light." Several of the EMs seated around me gasp.

My head spins. "So what? Who cares? We're *here* to find out who's making electromagician babies and attaching them to a machine that sucks the *life* out of them. Are none of you paying attention to that?" I slap one hand on the table, sending unused coffee spoons jingling and bouncing.

"Yes, of course, Lyn. But I think all of it is related," Orkan says.

"How?" I shout. "Other than being sent here by my stupid brother, what the hell do I have to with any of this?"

Orkan looks down at his hands, thinking a moment, before staring me in the eyes once more. "I think that someone wanted to lure you to Paris for a reason. I think they wanted to distract you and confuse you, send you all over hunting riddles. Make you suspicious of me and the Prime Order, and even Madame Deschamps and the High Order."

"Oh, that's what you *think*, huh?" I'm flailing now, mad and not seeing straight.

"Doesn't it seem to fit with everything that's happened, Lyn?" Orkan says emphatically.

I spin toward Deschamps. "And you, what do *you* think?"

She looks away, grimacing. "It is uncommon for Orkan and I to see eye-to-eye on anything. But here, I tend to agree. That is why all of us watched over you, why we rushed to find you. We are concerned that you've become a target."

"And who's targeting me?" It's a dumb question, I know, the moment it comes out of my mouth. There's only one answer.

"Torden Detonde," Madame Deschamps says. "That is why you must come back with me to our building — so we can protect you."

"No," Orkan interjects. "We can protect her much better than you. You know this, Lyn. You've seen our facility."

I sit there, slowly shaking my head, baffled by the day. No, the whole trip. Nah, forget that. I am simply baffled by life. Uncontrollably, I yawn, and suddenly my weariness bubbles up to the surface. I look at Deschamps. "You want me to hide in your fancy palace..." Then I turn to Orkan. "...And you want me to lock myself inside your prison. Well, forget it. I wouldn't do either of those things if they were my last option to stay alive. I fight for myself, with my friends, and for my friends." I glance at Percival, and he nods solemnly. "Ready?" I ask him.

"Any time, babe," he says, the hint of a pearly-white grin appearing.

"Then come on. The Kramers are going home."

27

GHOSTS

I'm alone, completely out of charge, and running for my life.

No, come on. No. I'm way too tired for this. Not now!

Glancing over my shoulder, I see nothing but darkness, but I can feel his presence getting closer. Torden. Always Torden. I hear something behind me crash, thundering footsteps. I zig and zag, but it seems like I'm in an endless open field of darkness. The only thing that's going to do me any good is to run and run and run, straight on until I escape or my heart bursts.

A loud sound breaks the silence, half roar, half human scream. Deep and throaty, with a rasp. I risk another quick glance and see it — Torden's Mega Golem, that collection of Stickmen parts sewn together into an unholy monstrosity. Each of its racing footsteps probably accounts for ten of mine. It'll be on me soon.

I swerve again, hoping the larger creature has less mobility than me. In that motion, I catch it out of the corner of my eye, so close that its multiple arms are swiping at me, and I almost stumble when I see what sits in the middle of its multiple Stickman heads: a human face. No, not a regular human, an ancient, grey-haired EM. Torden's own head has been sewn atop the Mega Golem. The creature opens its many mouths and roars again, Torden's eyes locked on me, his face grinning in its insanity.

I keep turning, basically doing a wide 360, getting behind the thing, seeking some kind of advantage. For a moment, it works, as the Mega Golem lumbers to turn and I'm able to put a little distance between us.

But the world is endless darkness, and I don't have endless stamina. At some point, I'll have to stand and fight, though alone that's likely to be my doom.

Ahead, I see two figures, barely noticeable grey forms in the blackness. *No, this isn't real*, I think. It's my parents, again. I run to them, breathlessly skidding to a halt just steps away.

Mom and Dad both have concerned looks on their faces, though they don't speak, don't hug me or touch me. Behind me, the Torden Mega Golem has recovered and made the turn, and now it's stomping toward us at a frightening pace. "Grab my hands, both of you!" I shout, reaching out. Somehow, the more I stretch my arms, the farther away my parents seem to be. "Hurry! We need to combine our powers to stop this thing!" I strain to touch their hands.

But they pull away. My own parents. I plead with them, I beg, but they won't reach out. Wordlessly, they shake their heads, pulling away their hands with an almost fearful look on their faces. The look you'd give to someone whose touch might infect you.

The Torden Mega Golem pounds to a stop just feet away, and I cringe. Tapping quickly into my power, I feel almost nothing, I'm so dry.

Torden's head, high above me, laughs. "And now you die, Lyn Hopkins!"

Desperate, I lunge toward my mother — my own *mother* — and she staggers quickly backward, causing me to sprawl out on the hard ground. *Why?* My mother's lips pull back from her teeth, a repulsed grimace. *Why?*

Torden laughs again. "You're disgusting to them, child. They don't want anything to do with you!" The Mega Golem bends forward, bringing all of its faces near to mine, the nameless Stickman heads and the abomination of Torden's wizened skull. "Why do you think they left you in the first place?"

"No," I say, though I don't believe myself. It makes too much sense. Why did my parents leave me alone? Because they didn't want me. Because I don't belong. Not with them, not with anyone. "Because I'm a freak?" I ask aloud.

The Torden Mega Golem sucks in air, stretching to its full height above me. "Exactly, my child," Torden says in a deep voice full of self-satisfaction. "Exactly."

With a swift movement, the many Stickman arms of the creature smash down on me and I am consumed, sponged dry of power, blackened, and gone.

———

STILL IN THE SAME BLACKNESS, I float, as if on air, as if on nothing. As if I am now nothing at all.

"What is it that man wants?" a faceless voice says to me.

A female voice.

"Zee?" I ask, confused and helpless. "Is that you? Where are you?"

"What does Torden want, Lyn? Ask yourself that."

"Zee! Come back to me! I need you!"

"It's easy if you try."

"I — I don't understand!" Blackness is all I can see, nothingness is all I can feel. Zee's voice is all I can hear.

"What does Torden Detonde want? Tell me."

"Um... power? I guess."

"Yes, of course. Power. You've known this. You've always known this."

"But he had power — he was in charge, back in New York, and it wasn't good enough."

"Not that. Think," Zee's voice says. But is it Zee? How could it be Zee? She's dead.

"They didn't find your body," I say aloud.

"Think, Lyn. About Torden."

"He had power, and he screwed it up! That's all I know."

"It's not all you know. What is he doing *here*?"

"Here? You mean in Paris? He's killing children! That's what he's doing!" I start to cry, dark tears in darkness.

"Why?"

"Because he's insane!" I spit. "Because he is the most horrible person alive!"

The voice of Zee stays silent, like it's waiting for me.

"Because he wants to use that damned machine on them and —"

"And?"

"And suck up their power!"

"Yes, exactly. Power."

I'm spinning and lost. I feel uncontrollable vertigo in the darkness, in my mind, in my life. "He needs their power. He said it extended his life."

"Yes. But now he needs more power."

"More than just sucking the life out of EMs?" I ask.

"Power to get power." Zee's voice seems farther away.

"I don't understand."

"Power to get power," she says again, but now her voice is faint.

"Come back! I don't understand! And I just want all this to end!"

But Zee's voice is gone, and I am left in a world without light or sound, spinning endlessly.

28

DIVIDE UNCONQUERED

I wake, knowing all of that bullshit was just a dream. That the Torden Mega Golem wasn't real. My parents weren't real. Zee wasn't real.

So why do I feel like I want to cry and die and hit someone and run away, all at the same time?

"Morning," Pers said, stretching as he sits up in bed next to me. He reaches out and gently strokes my shoulder. "How are you doing? Okay?"

For a moment, I'm frozen. Then I feel a shudder go through my body, like something unnatural is happening. I twist away from his touch. "Fine." I say gruffly. "I'm fine. I need a shower." I was too exhausted to take one when we got in around 7:30 in the morning, after we left everyone at the cafe, but that's far from the reason for me rushing off to the bathroom and locking the door behind me.

I can wash off the remaining dust and dirt from our night, but I can't wash away the strangeness inside me. Still, standing alone, crying in the shower, is easier than having to explain myself.

I WALK OUT WRAPPED in a towel and offer the bathroom to Percival, again mostly to have more time alone. He obliges, thankfully, and I get dressed deep in thought.

A little while later, we eat breakfast at a nearby cafe. I order something, eat it without really looking at it or tasting it. Percival tries to talk to me a couple of times, but I don't reply. I feel his confusion, and it just adds to all the turmoil in me. I want to say something, say *give me some time*, but instead, my mind does what it does, and when the words finally come out, they surprise both of us.

"I need to see Deschamps today," I mutter, breaking the silence.

Percival seems baffled, but recovers well. "Uh, sure. Let me just pay the bill and we can go." He starts to stand, reaching for his wallet.

"I need to see Deschamps today. Alone."

The word hits him like a blow. "Okay, that's, uh, okay. You can get there on your own?" he asks.

He's trying to be helpful, I know, but it's more protection, more coddling, more handouts. My expression darkens, and Percival pulls back with concern. "I'll be back by evening," I say, nothing more.

"Okay," he says. "Okay." His voice is cool, like the first hints of winter we feel in the air on our silent walk home.

———

UNDER AN HOUR LATER, I'm let into the Paris clan's hotel or office building or whatever the hell you want to call it, once more by Marcel Brodeur. He's stiff as ever, primly walking me down the same hallway we took when we first met the city's top EM. Well, the city's top High Order EM.

I even find her waiting in the same chair as before, sitting by herself with an open chair next to her. On the small, ornate table between the chairs, a gleaming silver teapot sits between two gold-rimmed glass cups. A tiny wisp of steam weaves its way gently upward from the teapot. All of this, I find supremely irritating. "You knew I was coming." Not a question. A fact.

"Yes."

"You're watching me? Like, round the clock?"

"No, not quite, but we are paying attention to your movements." Deschamps says all of this like we're talking about the weather, not stalking or illegal surveillance. "Won't you please sit down?"

"No," I say, crossing my arms. Out of the corner of my eye, I notice Brodeur slip away silently, like he has no desire to be present for what I do next. *Good idea.*

The older woman gives a gentle shrug. "You came a long way to stand there and ask me your questions."

"How do you know I have questions? Are you reading my mind, too? Wiretapping? What?"

Genevieve Deschamps rises slowly and elegantly to her full height, which is notably taller than me. "My dear, where you are concerned, I am two things. First, I am responsible for the safety and wellbeing of our local order of electromagicians. As such, you can fully expect me to keep track of any and all people with our gift who come into my city. You are no exception. And second, I am a peer and colleague of your brother's. I mean you no ill will, and in fact have been asked directly by Kevin to do what I can to keep you out of harm's way. However, what I am definitely not is some sort of counter-agent or criminal. If you would understand as much, it would be significantly easier for me to help you. Now. Won't you please sit down?" Deschamps gestures calmly toward the open chair. "The tea is freshly brewed and smells quite lovely." Out of nowhere, a man approaches wearing a black vest over a white shirt, bowtie, no jacket. If you were to search for *quintessential Parisian waiter*, I'm pretty sure you'd just see his picture. In fact, he resembles virtually every other waiter I've seen in Paris — from numerous cafes and restaurants, all the way to the guy who served us when Orkan fed us lunch. I try to hide my double-take as he stands behind the table, waiting to pour tea.

"Fine." I slump my shoulders, stepping forward and plopping myself crudely into the chair. "But how do you know I have questions?"

Madame Deschamps sits, politely crosses her legs, and looks at me with a warm smile. "My dear, why *else* would you be here?"

She has a point, though I'm in no mood to admit it. I pretend to be extraordinarily interested in the way our waiter pours my tea, then take an extra-long, careful first sip, trying to organize what I want to say. Instead, as usual, my mouth moves before my brain is ready. "Damn, that is good tea."

"I'm glad you are enjoying it." If nothing else, Deschamps is all class. She gives me silence, lets me sip tea, using her cup as her own sort of distraction, not staring at me, waiting for me to speak.

Finally, between random swallows of tea, I arrive at my first question. "Okay. High Order, Prime Order, no order at all. Which one is *right*?"

Deschamps places her teacup back on its saucer with a delicate clink and folds her hands in her lap. "I am sure I don't have to tell you that my answer to this question may be biased."

"Of course not. But give me your take, anyway."

She nods. "I suppose the oldest option would be to have no order whatsoever, but that left each of us to fend for ourselves. We had to hide who we were from the world of regular humans. Then, some of these individuals met up with others sharing the same ability. Some married, some became friends, others coalesced into social groups. From that, the High Order was born. Very smart electromagicians realized that together we could provide each other with community, safety, and peace. But we remained unknown to the rest of the world, by our own choice, codified into our laws. As time drew on, a small group of us dissented. They wanted integration with the regular world — recognition. But they inherently believed we would be shunned, and that we must be prepared for possible discrimination, even violence. This became the Prime Order. And though I do not believe arming us or hiring armed guards is wise, I do credit them for avoiding most conflict within our circles. They believe that those in the High Order should come over to the Prime Order of their own choice, at their own time, which has made the Prime Order's movement a slow one. The majority of us are quite happy where we are."

"You still didn't tell me which is right," I said.

"I think we are right, of course. The High Order. We should band together as a community, but avoid the endless conflict that integration with regulars would entail."

"And which one is Torden? I know he was High Order until my brother cast him out."

Deschamps purses her lips a moment, perhaps disliking my line of questions. "Torden Detonde has been, over time, all three, and none. He began in our community, as you know, but he could hardly be called a member in good standing, as you also know. When he ran from your brother, it is my understanding that he sought out the Prime Order, mostly because they refuse to punish anyone in their group. But quickly he found himself butting heads with those in charge, and he wanted to change many of the things they do. So he left, or they expelled him, I don't know. Ask Orkan Zidane about that. Now, I believe Torden is not a part of any order. Though that's not to say he operates completely alone."

"The Bissets told us they aren't in any order either."

"Yes, it makes sense," she said. "Clearly the Bissets and Torden are united in some way. Perhaps they like working as a sort of freelance organization, or perhaps their goal is even loftier: a third order of electromagicians."

"And he wants me, what? To join them? Or as one of his food sources." That choice of words even made me cringe.

Madame Genevieve Deschamps leans across the divide between us. "I believe Torden Detonde doesn't want you as an ally or a simple source of our power. I believe he wants to find a way to take from you the very ability that makes you unique."

I scoff. "As far as I'm concerned, he can have it. I'm tired of being the biggest freak at the circus sideshow."

"No," Deschamps says with deep conviction. "This we cannot allow. If Torden gained the ability to amplify his power just by touching another of us, he could do anything he wants. He could turn us all into slaves, batteries for his limitless power lust. And he could take on the regular human world in a way that may be unstoppable."

I droop in my seat, realizing I'm not getting out of this easily. No, it's going to be long and hard and difficult. Not to mention painful. "Why me?" It's a pitiful and lame question to ask, and most definitely rhetorical, but it slips out anyway.

"A better question is *how*," Deschamps asks. "How is it possible that Torden discovered this ability in you before you did yourself? He clearly was singling you out for something before everything happened in New York. Did you ever physically touch him? A hand-shake, a hug?"

I shiver. The thought of giving Torden Detonde a hug is repug-nant. "No, never. I avoided Torden's pavilion. And the times when I did go there, he was always seated on this big chair, like a throne. I never got very close."

"I see. Well, we know your special ability works in proximity, too, but if two electromagicians near you touched and discovered this power, they would not easily be able to determine what made it occur, unless they were specifically tracking your movements, which would mean they already knew it was you. A catch-22, as it were. Assuming Torden never laid a hand on you."

Laid a hand on you, I repeated in my mind. Something about that. *Laid a hand upon you.* "Wait! He did. He did touch me, just once. I was walking in Manhattan alone, after dark, and some man was following me. It was him, but I didn't know it, so I tried to hide in an alley, but he found me anyway. When he approached, I stumbled over some-thing, and he grabbed my arm. I even gave him a little electric shock, thinking he was a mugger or something."

"That would have been the moment," Madame Deschamps says, slowly nodding her head. "If you used your magic while physically connected to him, Torden would have felt this ability within you. And then, with his lust for power, you would have become his most sought-after prize."

"Then why not just capture me, right then and there?"

"It's hard to say. Probably because of your family, your parents and brother, and their history with the High Order. Because of his place in the High Order, which afforded him the ability to carry out his schemes easily. He needed a way to lure you, without disrupting everything he'd built up. And with you living in the same city, I suppose he thought he'd have time. Even he couldn't guess that what you'd do next would disrupt his entire world."

I'm floored. But still, it's so typical for me. *Find a nice, older man, they said. Someone stable, with a good job. Yeah, sure. I'll take the crazy old wizard building golems in his basement, who wants to use me for spare parts and a backup charge.*

Freakin story of my life.

I BEGRUDGINGLY ACCEPT an offer from Deschamps for her driver to take me home, but I'm wary of them knowing exactly where we live, so I have the guy drop me at Sacre Coeur, the big white church on the hill where I saw Torden the first time. It's a major tourist destination, so getting there through the crowds is a slow process. Still, those same crowds quickly make it difficult for the driver to see which way I go when I leave the car. Besides, I take several wrong streets first, keeping track on my phone until I finally find my way to Madame Martin's apartments. The kind old woman herself lets me in, making me realize she must have been watching the door. *Who else is watching this door? Probably spies from both orders, meaning my twisty route home was all for nothing.* Climbing the stairs, I'm so busy kicking myself that it takes me a moment to notice the sounds I hear from within our flat: voices.

I wait in the stairwell, listening. I hear Percival's voice, muffled to the point where the words aren't clear, but recognizable by tone. I hear a woman briefly speak, then several people laughing. Suspicion and fear and concern and even a tiny tinge of jealousy spark me, and I twist the knob, throwing the door open.

There, by the small table, are Pers, Uma, and Hayden, each with glasses in hand. Uma has the chair, while Percival stands leaning against a wall. Hayden has managed to make a second seat out of an end table. They all look at me in surprise, though Percival is the first to shake it off. "Lyn! You're back," he says, his tone jovial but just a bit forced. *Maybe he thought I'd never come back*, I think. "Come. Have a drink with us." He grabs a fourth glass from a shelf over the table and extends it toward me. Though we're in France, land of wine, the bottle between them on the table looks clear and potent.

My momentary tangle of emotions outside the door turns to embarrassment, and my face flushes red. "Okay, sure," I say, mostly so they'll stop looking at me. As Percival starts to fill the glass, I pretend to need to check something in the bathroom. "Be right there." Click the door closed softly, I stare at myself in the bathroom mirror. *These are your friends. Stop freaking out and worrying about orders and powers and things you can't control. Get it together!* I look about as far from *together* as I feel, but I run the water, splash some on my face, and dry off with a hand towel. When I return, Percival hands me a glass liberally filled with a powerful smelling clear liquor. "What is it?"

"French gin," he says.

I take a whiff and feel my nose burning. "Did you mix it with anything?"

Hayden grins in a way that tells me he's already had a couple of drinks like the one in my hand. "We sorta forgot that part."

"It's not bad. You get used to it quickly," Uma says, trying to look reassuring.

I eye the liquid suspiciously, but after everything that's happened in Paris, if there is one thing I think I deserve, it's a stiff drink. I shrug and take a big gulp. Too big, because a moment later, I'm coughing uncontrollably from the burning sensation that now fills my throat, searing down into my belly.

Percival claps me on the back, gently. "Hey, hey, Lyn! Take it slowly! This stuff is potent."

Through my coughs, I manage a raspy reply. "That's what I was hoping for." I raise my glass, though very little remains within. "To those we have lost!" I say, trying more than anyone will ever know not to let my voice crack or give off how I truly feel. The others lift their drinks, too, and now suddenly we're all very serious.

Four stone-faced electromagicians smash their glasses together way too hard, shouting *Cheers!* before gulping down the kind of liquid fire we all hope will make the memories less painful.

———

HOURS LATER, the bottle is empty, and all four of us have a glassy look in our eyes that says sleep is necessary. Percival tells Hayden and Uma they can crash with us for the night, but one look around the small flat has them making apologies and heading for the door.

"Madame Deschamps has rooms for us," Uma says with a bit of slur to her words. "We'll jusss go back there."

"Okay," Percival says, grinning rows of white teeth. His hair has flopped into his face, covering most of his eyes. And it's not in some sexy, disheveled way. It's more like he's beyond the point of caring if he can see or not. "Night, guys."

I wave a goodnight, a halfhearted smile on my face, as they close the door behind them. Percival turns to look at me, still smiling in a goofy, half-awake kind of way. As I stand from the table, he comes to me, wrapping his arms around me. "Hey," he says. "Everything okay?"

"Yeah, sure," I say, fidgeting in his grasp. "I just need to use the bathroom."

When I come out, Percival is gently snoring on the bed. There's plenty of space beside him, but I decide instead to turn off all the lights and sit by the table. Even as high up as we are, the flickers and flashes of lights in the city make patterns of movement on the walls and ceiling. I watch those for a long, long time, trying to make sense of them as if they are my swirling thoughts.

29

DIGGING IN THE DIRT

Percival nudges me awake with the sun already high in the sky. "Hey. Good morning. How are you?"

I nearly slip out of the chair before catching myself. I don't have a headache, but it feels like I might soon. My mouth is the desert, and I wipe a hard crust of rock salt out of the corner of my eye. Let this be a reminder, folks: hydrate. "Fine," I say, too quickly, too rough. "What time is it?"

He checks his phone. "Almost eleven."

I groan, trying to stand and feeling the twisty knots in my back from sleeping in the chair. "I need a shower. Then food. And water."

————

WE GO to the nearest cafe and eat in silence. Percival knows something is wrong. I know something is wrong. But sometimes, not talking about it easier. Not better. I know, I know. Just easier. Do I judge you?

Walking back to the flat with no specific plan for what to do and no conversation to make a plan, my phone rings. It's Kevin.

"Hi, Lyn. Are you all okay? Safe? I heard from Genevieve Deschamps that there was a lot going on last night."

"We're fine." My voice breaks, coming out shaky, mostly because I haven't used it much so far today.

"Good. Well, listen. I've been looking more into the whole business of the Bissets using excess power and that got me thinking — are there any other places where power usage in the city has drastically changed in the past year?"

He pauses, waiting for acknowledgment or applause or something. I just grunt. "Hm."

"Anyway, look. I want you to see something. It's a map — well, a map with overlays. I can send it to you, but I'd rather walk you through it, so I'll send it to Percival's phone and we can keep talking while you look at it there, good?"

"You're the boss," I say flatly. Passive aggressive much? Both of our phones buzz a moment later. Percival taps his a couple of times, then turns it to show me a gridded diagram of streets. I put Kevin on speakerphone. "We see it."

"Okay, good," Kevin says. "It's Paris, of course. But more important are the colors overlaying the map — see those?"

Percival pinches the screen to zoom all the way out and we recognize the loosely oval shape of the city with gradients of red and yellow on top. "Yeah. What do they mean?"

Kevin gives a nervous chuckle, a sound I'm familiar with from him. It means he's really excited about something. "I crunched a ton of numbers. Well, to be honest, my computer did, but I had to *get* all the numbers, and they weren't that easy to come by. Anyway, I grabbed all the data I could from that power company, *MdE*, for about the last three years. Records on every property in Paris — commercial and residential — and their electricity consumption during that time frame."

"Okay, *and*?" I say, impatiently.

My brother huffs. He doesn't like being interrupted, and even less so when what he has to say excites him. "Lyn, I was able to *acquire*" — he says the word in a deliberate way that makes me realize he really means *hack and steal* — "multiple terabytes of data that includes every account in the city of Paris. Do you have any idea how many accounts that is? Then I parsed that data to sort and rank it according to my careful specifications, tweaking it several times until it produced something useful. Finally, I was able to create this heat map to make everything understandable, even to a layperson such as yourself. So, do you want to give me five seconds of your time to explain it and maybe a tiny bit of kudos?"

"Settle down, big bro," I say. "I didn't mean to shit on your hard work. Keep going." My words come out with a tinge of anger, because, you know, the last thing you want to do when you're already confused and angry is acquiesce to someone else's feelings. Even if that someone is trying to help you. Human nature can be a really stupid thing.

I hear Kevin breathe a heavy sigh, but thankfully he continues without more argument. "The darkest red spots are places where there are unusually high electricity consumption over the last eighteen months. You can zoom in on the map to see exactly what I mean, but it boils down to this: three places in Paris are red hot based on my criteria. The first is the Bissets' house. That right there pretty much makes me believe my number crunching is accurate."

"Whoa," Percival says, swiping to find the hotspot where Anton Bisset and his charming, gun-toting, child-killing wife live. "Excellent sleuthing, dude." He swipes again, randomly, scanning across the map of Paris for other similar blobs of red. "Where are the others?"

"Before I go on, I have to say that this work is data analysis and can have flaws. By my calculations, there is a seven point oh four —"

"Sorry, Kevin," I interrupt, hearing him audibly grumble. "We get it. This isn't perfect, but it's more for us to go by than anything else we have right now. Thanks." There are times when the words *thanks* and *sorry* feel painful coming out of your mouth. This is one of them. But you say them anyway, right? "Where are the other two spots?"

"Sure, right. I'm just saying that there are three *really* hot spots. That may or may not be important. If you check out the other two and find nothing, then we have to go to the next layer, and that layer has a few more options to investigate."

"How many more?" Percival asks.

"Three hundred and seventeen."

Percival lets loose a pained *oooh*. "Then I hope we find what we're looking for in one of these other top spots."

"Agreed," Kevin says. "The second spot is on the Left Bank, same as the Bissets, so I figured that would be the one to check out first."

"*Left Bank?*" Percival asks, echoing my own unspoken question. "What does that mean?"

Kevin answers quickly, explaining but wanting to move on. "With any river, you face in the direction of its flow. The right bank is to your right, the left bank is to your left. In Paris, the Seine flows to the west toward the English Channel, so, facing west, the southern portion of the city is the Left Bank, while the northern portion is the Right Bank. It's just that Paris is one of the few cities that uses these terms regularly. Got it?"

"Roger, sir," Percival says with a silly grin, something neither Kevin nor I am in the mood for at the moment.

Kevin simply ignores him. "Both of the other two primary hotspots are churches. The one on the Left Bank is called *Église du Val-de-Grâce de Paris*, and the one on the Right Bank is called *Église Saint-Eustache*. Val-de-Grace Church and St. Eustache Church. Both are under some kind of major, multi-year renovations at this time, so I would imagine that hiding some errant power lines would be possible. Also, I was wondering why they were both churches, and that made me think about who's paying the bills. With the Bissets' house, it was the Bissets. Easy enough, though running the lines out of the house involved a risk. I imagine they have a friend working high up in the *MdE*, but haven't confirmed that. Anyway, with the other two places being churches where major construction projects are underway, my guess is that they thought higher electricity bills would be easily attributed to the work done, and therefore essentially ignored. That's just a theory at the moment, of course. Most importantly, the reason Val-de-Grace Church on the

Left Bank stands out is this: it's sitting above another section of catacombs."

Involuntarily, I shudder. *I can't take another dead body in a dark tunnel. Please, no more of that,* I think.

"Well," Percival says. "I think we know where we're going tonight."

"Yes. And good luck," Kevin says, not helping anything at all by treating us like some sort of dark ops spy task force, when we are the least qualified people for that job on the planet. "Take Hayden and Uma with you, okay?"

"Sir, yes sir!" Percival says, and this time I actually punch him as I tap the button to end the call.

Percival looks at me like he's hurt, but it isn't from the punch. "You didn't even say goodbye. To your own brother." His mouth hangs open in disbelief.

Sarcastically, I wave at the disconnected phone. "Bye, Kev!"

———

TALKING WITH OUR FRIENDS, I realize I made the best choice not staying with Madame Deschamps and her Paris community. Everywhere Hayden goes, everywhere Uma goes, someone else is conveniently there, conveniently watching. In particular, those two EMs from Singapore seem to be on constant alert. It's a good thing we want to wait until nightfall, because it takes forever for Hayden and Uma to sneak away without having six or eight other EMs from various countries follow them. Dinner on the town is the only thing that doesn't immediately draw unwanted attention. Still, we all know they're likely followed, so when they meet up with us, we make sure to have a long and extremely boring dinner sitting out in the open at a street-side table. We sip our wine slowly and tell each other stories with forced smiles, trying not to look sideways too often. Finally, with the sun fully down, we walk back toward our flat. Montmartre has notoriously twisty little streets, winding up and down the hills, with alleys along the sides. It's not hard to turn a corner and be quickly out of eyeshot of someone who might be following behind, so we pay close attention — while seeming not to — until we know we're on a street totally alone and in the dark.

And then we use our EM power to quickly float ourselves up onto the roof of a nearby building, four or five stories high.

From there, we look back down to the street, waiting for signs of life. Of someone trailing us. At first, there's nothing, but finally, after a full minute or more, a man in dark clothing rounds the bend and stops, seemingly confused. He scans back and forth, and we know he's looking for us. When he finally throws up his hands and turns around, we all fall to the rooftop, stifling laugher with into our hands.

"*Au revoir, mon ami!*" Hayden says, maybe too loud. Uma shushes him, and Hayden shrugs, still laughing.

"Since when do you speak French?" Percival asks.

"High school. Three years' worth of classes."

"So, you're fluent then?"

Hayden scoffs. "I think you just heard the sum total of what I remember. Don't get carried away with my knowledge of the French language."

"Fine," Percival says, slapping him on the back. "Still, you're better than the rest of us, so you're in charge of any translations, if we need them."

"Wonderful," Hayden says, his shoulders sagging.

Keeping an eye on surrounding windows and the streets below, we do a few quick flights to other rooftops before dropping back down to street level in a narrow alley. From there, we walk casually back out onto one of the bigger streets, just as a large group of people is streaming past, hiding our sudden appearance. The Metro is two blocks away, and then its thirty minutes or so on the train to our destination. Hopefully the odds of running into an EM spy in that timeframe are low.

———

THE DOME of *Église du Val-de-Grâce de Paris* is heavily covered in scaffolding when we arrive, which is probably good, as it confirms the church is being renovated and gives us a focal point for our search. Given the time of day, I doubt we're going to be able to just buy a ticket to the crypts to see what's inside. The doors are all dark and locked. But we don't really need street-level doors.

We circle the large church, looking for anything suspicious. To the east of the building, there's a wide-open lawn with rows of trees, so we use those to find a nice hidden place, and then we simply launch ourselves up into the scaffolding surrounding the dome. From there, we follow walkways and stairs set up for construction workers, making our way down to a flat section of roof that surrounds the dome. It doesn't take long to locate an unlocked roof access doorway and slip inside.

We tiptoe and whisper, looking all over the church, keeping an eye out for thick power lines, but knowing those may not be the only suspicious signs. Still, in less than 45 minutes, we meet up in the middle of the dim transept. "Anything?" Percival asks.

"I think you would have known if we found something," Uma chides. "There doesn't appear to be any way to get down to the catacombs from here, not even in the crypts."

"Okay, so then what? Call it a bust?"

"Seems that way," Hayden says.

Then everyone turns to me, like I'm in charge, and I just nod agreement so they'll cut it out. We fly ourselves back up to the gallery, make our way out the rooftop access door, then float down to the lawn behind the church where we started. Suddenly my phone starts buzzing, at the exact moment my toes hit the grass, and needless to say, the vibration scares the shit out of me. I grab for my phone quickly, seeing that it's Kevin as I swipe it open. "What?"

He must hear the breathless tone to my voice. "Are you okay? You sound spooked."

"I *am* spooked. By you. We just got out of the first church when my pocket started vibrating. Very bad timing."

"Heh, sorry," he says, not sounding too sorry. "But I have something else for you, especially now that you've cleared Val-de-Grace. Put me on speaker, if you can."

"Okay, just don't, like, *shout* or anything. We're on church property still." I put a hand over the phone and mouth *It's Kevin* to the others, then I push the speakerphone button as the others gather around me.

"Listen, everyone. Your next stop is St. Eustache Church. I just want to let you know what you may be getting yourselves into."

"If it's anything like this place," Percival says, "it'll be a lot of empty, dark spaces with no sign of Torden Detonde."

"True," Kevin says. "But there is one big difference. I just did some online sleuthing and discovered that renovations on St. Eustache have been on hold for almost three years. Supposedly there are structural concerns that require a major investigative review, and that's taking a lot of time. The portion of the building under renovation is relatively small, so I guess the church is just operating around it. Still, there's been no real movement in three years."

"But your data still shows a power spike from the past year and a half?" I mutter.

"Yep," Kevin says.

Hayden, Uma, Percival, and I exchange glances, pretty certain what that means. Then something unexpected happens: Uma nods, with a solemn look on her face. "Let's do this," she says. Of course it's Uma; Torden is responsible for her brother's death. I nod back as Hayden and Percival do the same.

"We're going now, Kevin," I say. "If you don't hear from us soon, uh…" What? What did I need him to do in New York City if I never made it back there myself? Even the city where I've spent my entire life doesn't seem to hold much for me. *Maybe I belong nowhere*, I think. "If you don't hear from me, then I guess, um… give my regards to Broadway."

30

ONE WRONG STEP

The ornate structure of St. Eustache Church pops up suddenly in front of our taxi as we drive down Rue de Turbigo, a stretch of road that begins as a relatively wide avenue then turns into a thin curve tucked between a little cafe and the church itself.

From our vantage, as we step out of the car, the building starts at a narrow point, then grows wider and higher, with a round clock atop its nearest squat tower. "It doesn't look all that big," Hayden says, squinting up at the clock. "This shouldn't take too long, huh? I mean, we can give it a quick look around, then be back in time for a few more *Tales from Percival's Past* over a glass or two of French gin, am I right? Pers?"

Percival doesn't answer. To our left, he has wandered off into a wide square, his gaze fixed to something high in the distance. "You might want to look at it from this angle," he calls back to us. Moments later, we stare at the massive façade of the church, all arched windows and flying buttresses. Its size is even more awe inspiring given our first impression, which apparently was nothing more than a tiny side chapel. "Let's walk the perimeter first," Percival says, swirling one finger around in a circle.

At the far side of the building, we start to see signs of renovations — or at least the place where renovations should be happening, had they not been put on hold for several years. On the opposite side from where we were dropped off, the church is tucked against another tiny road, Rue du Jour. Here, what appears to be a major entrance is fully smothered in skeletal metal scaffolding, with tatters of plastic sheeting flapping idly in the chilly, light breeze. I have no doubt the plastic was, at one time, intended to cover up the unsightliness of the scaffolding. Now, the plastic is what gives the place that distinct, bombed-out, post-apocalyptic hellscape look.

Something makes me freeze. I stand still, waiting, and once again, the others look to me for guidance. I don't move or speak, not for a moment or two, just feeling.

"Lyn?" Hayden begins, before Uma shushes him. All eyes remain on me.

Finally, it clicks. The strange sensation hovering lightly over my skin. The slight thrum reverberating up through my feet, coming from the ground. *There it is. I found you.* "Do you feel it?" I ask the others.

Uma leans toward me, eyes half closed. "Feel it?" She's trying.

The two guys simply look around. I don't know if their senses are tuned enough. Or maybe I'm making shit up. But I don't think so. I think it's there.

Uma speaks, slowly, a little unsurely. "Something's... vibrating?"

I lock eyes with her, the passion of the moment apparent. "Yes! What else?"

Fully closing her eyes, Uma stretches out with her other senses. "My skin. It's tingling."

"What are you all talking about?" Percival says. "I don't feel anything."

"Me neither," adds Hayden.

Uma doesn't move, trying to absorb more. "It's there. It's *definitely* there."

I nod. We all suspected this was the place. Now we — or at least

Uma and I — know for sure. "We can feel the power being used here. It's not like someone blasting music or a jackhammer tearing into the street; it's hardly there. But when you feel it, you know it."

"And what exactly is *it*?" Percival asks.

"I don't know," I say. "Not exactly. But I know this is where we're supposed to go. Torden Detonde is somewhere nearby, doing something that he very much should not be doing. The Bissets, too, I would imagine, and possibly others. We're all in danger — serious danger. We'll need to be careful, and we'll need to approach with a plan."

"Okay, then," Hayden says. "What's the plan?"

I turn to Uma, who is just opening her eyes. "Where would you say the feeling is coming from?" I ask, not because I don't know, but because I want confirmation.

"Below," she says. "Somewhere below us."

"I agree." I gesture for the guys to lean in. "I think we should go in pairs and come in from different directions, Percival with me, and Hayden with Uma. That way each team has someone who can feel the source, aim for it. We'll take the back of the building, and you take the front. Even though we're pretty sure everything we sense is bubbling up from below ground, let's start at the top of the church just to be sure we're not walking into a trap or missing something we shouldn't. Good?" Heads nod in agreement. "One wrong step and..." I don't bother finishing. Everyone knows. Torden has shown he's not above killing to get what he wants. "Let's all duck around the corner there and zip up to the roof at that tall spot — I think it's a bell tower. From there, we can split up and make our way inside and down. Once we hone in on the source, I'm sure we'll all be back together, most likely in the crypts or some other passages below ground. In the meantime, Uma and I will be in direct contact. No broadcast chatter got it?"

"Got it," Hayden says. Pers gives a thumbs up. As always, our special EM way of communicating is either one-on-one or an open broadcast to the world. It would be great if we could do a group chat, but nobody's brain has invented that functionality yet. Maybe Torden has a machine to do it. If so, I'll thank him right after I beat the shit out of him. I'm normally no fist fighter, but I think I can easily take the old man. And if I can't, well, I'm certain Percival can. It's all gonna depend on how many guards he has — people like the Bissets, or an army of Stickmen. Maybe he has new Mega Golems, since I blew up his first one. But I'm hoping, irrational though it may be, that we just find *him*, all alone in some stupid little laboratory.

Nervously checking up and down the road, we wait until it seems there's truly nothing happening nearby, then we fill ourselves with power and fly quickly to the top of the bell tower. It has a square, flat roof surrounded by a low wall on all sides, and we drop ourselves into the middle, barely making a sound. From the tower, I can't help but look around, and suddenly I'm sad. I try to shake it off, ignore it, but it stays with me. It's the *view*. Sacre Coeur, the big white church, sits atop a hill in the distance to one side, while the Eiffel Tower dominates the view in the other direction. *What would it be like just to be regular? Just to be in Paris to see the sights, eat the food, drink the wine?*

"Lyn?" Percival asks quietly, trying to jog me out of a mood he can see I'm in but probably wouldn't understand.

"Yeah, ready," I snap, looking away from it all. I quickly scan the dark, angled roofline of the main church structure beside us, snapping my fingers and pointing when I find something useful. "See there? There's a way near the corner, and if I know anything about Medieval architecture, then I'd bet there's another door just like it on the opposite side. Percival and I will take the one facing us, while you two check the front side, around that way."

Hayden puts his hand up like a kid in elementary school. "Um, do you know things about Medieval architecture?"

"Of course not," I say.

"Perfect," he replies.

"Just follow me, Hayden," Uma says before floating over the edge of the bell tower and down to a narrow sort of walkway that surrounds the giant roof of the church. Hayden gives us a silly salute before he starts to glow light blue and goes after her.

Finally, it's just Percival and me, alone on the bell tower. He comes to me, standing face to face and putting his hands on my arms. Involuntarily, I tense. "Hey, it's just me. You know, this sort of reminds me of that first time, back on the tower in Jersey. Remember?"

I remember, but at the moment, it's the farthest thing from my mind. "Yeah," I say, my voice neutral, my posture still uptight.

"Lyn, what's going on? I feel like, I don't know, ever since that night when the house was blown up, things have gotten *different* between us. Complicated."

"What do you mean?" I ask, stalling. I don't want to talk about, especially not on the roof of a bell tower in the middle of Paris. Maybe not ever.

Percival's hands hold me a little more urgently, and he pulls me closer. "I feel like you're pulling away from me, and I don't want you to do that. I know that this entire trip has been one disaster after another, but I want you to remember who has been by your side the whole time. *On* your side the whole time."

My shoulders droop. He has a point. "Look, Pers. I'm sorry. I guess everything's getting to me and I'm just not feeling connected right now. It's not just you. *Believe* me that it's not just you."

"What do you mean?"

"I mean *everything* — this city, New York City, the High Order, the Prime Order, Deschamps, Orkan, my brother, Torden and his people, hell, *regular* people for that matter."

"Slow down, you're losing me," he says, and I'm not even sure he understands the double meaning, but I do, and it feels like something hitting me in the chest, making it so I can't breathe.

We're at the door on the front side, ready to go in, Uma's voice says in my head. *You guys ready?*

I sigh aloud before replying, realizing the moment after I do it that Percival is taking it as a sign of frustration at him. He can't hear Uma's voice in my head. *Hold on*, I say gruffly to Uma before looking up at Pers. "They're in position now. We need to get down to the door."

Percival releases his grip on my arms like he's letting me go forever, stepping back slowly. "Okay, then. Whatever you want."

I stand there, seeing the hurt in his eyes a moment longer, feeling emotions swirl. But I can't. Not now. I quickly turn, fill with power, and send myself in an arc down to the walkway surrounding the main roof. For a second, I wonder if Percival will follow, but then he's there, alighting gently next to me. With my heart pounding in my throat, I reach to open the door. *Ready*, I send to Uma. *Go now.*

On opposite sides of the roofline, Uma and I throw open our respective doors. Both are unlocked, which is great, though not hugely unexpected given that it's unlikely anyone else is breaking into giant cathedrals by coming down from the sky. Still, the moment I step in, I notice a small electrode attached to the edge of the door sill, mirroring one on the door I've just pushed open. There aren't any blinking lights or blazing sirens, not yet, but I know what we've just done all the same. "They have an alarm."

"Let me see," Percival says, following me into the building. He scans the sides of the door frame until he sees something he likes. "Got it. Easy." Percival touches one finger to a wire running beside the door and it emits a short but powerful burst of electromagic.

"What just happened?" I ask.

Even in the near-dark, I can see Percival grinning. "Wired alarm system. Old school. I just shorted the whole damn thing out, or at least knocked out the part that handles this door."

"All right, well, I'm gonna have Uma and Hayden zap their end, just in case."

"Good idea."

I relay the info to Uma and a moment later get confirmation that it's done. With that behind us, we start to investigate our surroundings. The first thing I notice is the temperature. Outside, the nighttime fall air was blustery and cold, but in the church, especially up high, it's noticeably warmer, especially because we're in a pretty small space. That's because we're inside, but not *inside*, meaning we're not in one of the public areas of the church. We're in some high narrow hallway that runs the length of the roofline, but it's so dark inside, I can't see a thing. Almost simultaneously, Percival and I begin to glow with power, using ourselves once more as dim flashlights. In the gloom, I see the passage run off to my left in a straight line for some distance, while on my right, there is a short bend ending in an arched doorway. Percival shrugs and points toward the door, so I tell Uma to look for a similar door on their end, trying to find a way down.

Turns out, the passage is easy: just beyond the arched doorway, a narrow spiral staircase begins, the kind of thing that would cause heart palpitations for people scared of heights or claustrophobic. Luckily, we're neither, and we scramble quickly down to the next level. There, in just a few steps, we're presented with an awe-inspiring sight; the cavernous interior space of the cathedral splays out before us, with massive stained glass windows reaching up to the roofline above, and the enormous public ceremonial space of the church below. On the floor many stories below us, rows and rows of brown, wooden chairs look like a company of army ants arranged for battle in the dim light.

Though we can see into the main public space of the church through open archways, we're still in a private hallway that lines the long side of the church. Percival asks the obvious question. "Should we check out *all* the spaces up here, just to be sure?"

I pause, checking once more for the source of the power I feel. It's not off toward the alter of the church — my left — it's below us, down and right, so I shake my head. "No, we need to go lower." I see Hayden and Uma framed in a dark opening across the expanse between us, and I wave to get their attention, then use one finger to make a spiraling downward gesture. Hayden flashes a thumbs up.

The next section of staircase is still quite narrow, but this one seems to go on forever, much longer than the first segment we descended from the roof. Finally, we step out onto the main floor of the church at almost the same moment as Uma appears from the stairwell across from us. "This is the end of the road for our side. It doesn't go down any further," she says, and her words break the silence like cymbals crashing, brash and jarring. We all freeze, as if ninjas or federal agents or a thousand Stickmen will suddenly jump out of the darkness, drawn by the sound of her voice.

When the echoes die down, I start to breathe again. Beside me, Percival gestures for the others to come to our side. "There's crypt access over here," he whispers. Even that seems to bounce off the walls, not a crash and bang, but instead the hissing of many snakes, slithering into the distance.

Once more, we spiral downward, but this time the stairs are wide and easy. The air grows noticeably cooler as we descend underground, and, for Uma and me at least, the vibrating thrum of something powerful seems to draw ever closer. "It's definitely down here," Uma says, and I nod agreement. At the base of the stairs, there's a wide room that would likely be in utter darkness if it weren't for the light blue glow of four EMs standing within. The rear wall of the room is hidden completely in scaffolding, once more covered in plastic sheeting, though the plastic here is pristine, not tattered from the winds.

Hayden approaches the scaffolding cautiously. "Guys, this seems like a dead end."

"Let me take a look," Percival says, filled with confidence.

"Well, unless you can walk through walls..."

Before Hayden can even finish the thought, Percival is holding back a flap of plastic. A narrow but suddenly obvious passageway lies behind it. "Through here."

Hayden's jaw falls open. "How the —?"

Smiling, Percival slaps Hayden on the back. "Don't sweat it, buddy. I kinda have experience finding my way around where I don't belong."

"Should I even ask?"

"Nope." Percival ducks past the plastic, crouching to get under a cross bar of the scaffolding, and then he's out of sight. The rest of us hurry after, with me going last. Down a short corridor, we come to an ancient-looking wooden door. It's unlocked, so we pass through without issue. The next door, however, is different. It's a flat, metal, industrial-looking thing with an inset lock, and appears to be recently installed. Plastered on its surface is a big red sign that reads *DANGER. Casque de sécurité obligatoire.* Given the black-and-white image of a man in a hard hat next to the words, no translation is necessary. "Anybody happen to have a key?" Percival asks.

"Very funny," Uma replies.

"Worth a shot," he says. "Good thing I know several ways to open a locked door."

"Several?" I ask. "If you know more than one, is there a quiet version?"

"Depends on what you mean by quiet. There are ways that produce less noise that others."

"Try one of those, then."

Grabbing his wallet from his back pocket, Percival pulls out a credit card. Even I'm familiar with the old credit card trick to open simple locks, but this door looks too substantial for such a basic method. Then I notice Percival slide a thin compartment from within the credit card, revealing a set of tools I can only assume are lock picks. He glances at Hayden. "Again, don't ask." As someone who doesn't routinely break the law — that is, if you can overlook me entering a cathedral without permission in the middle of the night in Paris — I'm shocked how quickly and easily Percival is able to unlock the door. It doesn't even look like it takes skill; it's mostly just him holding one tool still in his right hand and quickly jiggling another tool in his left.

"Holy shit, dude, that was awesome!" Hayden says. "Where'd you learn to pick a lock like that?"

Percival plays it cool, turning slowly around with one finger to his lips. "Technically, I raked the lock, not picked, but who cares, right? It's open." He tucks everything away in his wallet, then slowly pulls the door open. Ahead lies nothing but darkness. Even our EM glow isn't doing much to penetrate the gloom, so Uma taps her phone until its flashlight blazes on. We can see a tunnel-like hallway, but that's about all we can see. "Ladies first?" Percival says jokingly.

"Sure, send us to the slaughter," Uma retorts, but she steps into the hallway anyway, her light guiding the way. Ten or so steps in, she pauses. "Look at this, guys." She tilts the light upward to highlight thick black power lines running along the ceiling.

"Bingo," Percival says. "Do you still sense we're going in the right direction?"

Uma tilts her head, like a dog listening to sounds people can't hear. "Definitely." She continues into the darkness.

At the far end, the space opens to an irregularly shaped room, and here none of us even have to ask which way to go next. On our right, a large hole sits gaping in the stone wall. Someone has chiseled or sledgehammered or blasted their way through. "Where does it go?" I ask, as Uma walks closer with her light. In its glow, we see a distinct change in the color of the space beyond the ragged hole. No longer is it the light tan of the church's stone foundation; the space beyond is flat grey — concrete, and dug out in a rounded formation. "Is that the Metro?"

Uma considers the question. "I doubt it's a main line, but maybe a side passage? Like where they'd handle emergencies or move a broken-down train?" She steps through the hole gingerly, following the power lines overhead. There, she turns back to me. "Come in here, Lyn. You have to feel it here."

As I scramble into the grey tunnel, I see there are tracks on the floor, so it's definitely something to do with the subway. The passage goes off to our left and right in darkness, but the electrical lines we've been following go left, so that's our direction. Still, even if they weren't there, I'd know which way to go. I feel the vibration humming in my entire body, drawing me toward it like a moth to flame. Percival and Hayden come last, and as they each enter the subway tunnel, I see their eyes light up. "You all feel it now, too?" I ask.

"Oh yeah," Percival says, pointing left. "It's that way."

As if responding to his words, the thrumming suddenly stops. Uma gasps, and I nearly do, too. "What happened? Where did it go?" she asks.

I wrinkle up my face with anger, annoyance, and determination. "I don't know, but I know where it was. Come on."

The others follow behind as I trudge off into the dark, but soon

Uma is beside me with her light. We trace the power lines together. Not far from where we began, the subway tracks abruptly end, where a large barricade has been placed to stop any train that might think of overshooting its parking space. Just past the barricade, the passageway terminates, but we see two options: plain metal doors, one on the left, and one straight ahead.

"It's like a game show," Hayden says with a chuckle. "Which door do you pick? Behind one is a million dollars. Behind the other..."

"Dead ahead," I say. "That's where it was coming from, I'm sure of it."

"Same here," says Uma.

As for the door, we don't even bother to try it, we just gesture for Percival to work his magic, and he does so with a prideful, happy expression. *At least someone feels like they're doing something useful down here*, I think. Once unlocked, he holds it open for the rest of us, curling one arm in welcome like the doorman at a posh hotel. Hayden steps in first, followed by Uma, then me. Percival enters last, and there's the slight hissing sound of a hydraulic arm retracting as the door closes automatically behind him. When it's done, the silence — even a sort of psychological silence — is deafening. *What happened to that buzz of power? Why did it shut down?* I think.

A moment later, I wish I never had such a thought, as there's a loud *click* that echoes off the concrete walls. Before we can react, the hum of machinery starts again, low at first but quickly rising to a teeth-rattling throb, coming from all directions.

I realize a moment too late that I'm frozen, and worse, I can't tap into my electromagic power. The light blue glow that had been emanating from each of us is gone, and we four stand there in the dark, unable to move or do a thing.

Without warning, electric lights pop on overhead, and I try to blink away the stark brightness. My eyes, ignoring me, remain open and immediately begin to water. *I can't even blink*, I think. *What have we stepped into?*

Even looking around is impossible, so I can only see what's directly in front of me. Still, it's enough. Bare copper wires line virtually every inch of the wall in this round room, circling us completely up to about a height of ten feet. Beyond that, stark, simple concrete walls continue upward as if we're inside a missile silo or some other tall shaft. But it's the wires surrounding us that are the source of the throbbing vibration, their deep bass note dominating our hearing and blocking out all other sounds.

That is, except one: the laughter of an old man, coming down from somewhere unseen above.

31

THE SCIENCE OF MAGIC

"Lyn, Lyn, Lyn," the distant voice of Torden Detonde says, echoing down to us. "It's so good to see you again. I must thank you for coming to visit, especially so far from home."

I want to say *Shut up, you old piece of dirt! Turn off this damn machine and let's you and me have a conversation. You want something from me and I want something from you — your head on a platter.* But I can't say a thing. My tongue and lips are as frozen as the rest of me. For a moment, I wonder if my heart has also been stilled, and if so, how long I have left. Then I feel a faint rhythm deep in my chest. Whatever's happening, at least it's not going to kill me. I mean, not immediately.

"I understand you've already met my friends, Anton and Agnès Bisset," Torden says. Two voices call out *hello* like this is a chipper little meet-and-greet. "And of course, you are already quite familiar with the fourth member of our group, Rand Haldor." Rand, Torden's long-time second-in-command from New York, doesn't say a word, but I can feel his radiating hatred. "So, there are four of us, and there are four of you. How wonderfully symmetrical things have ended up. That will make the process easier."

I want to scream, but only a muffled gurgle escapes my frozen lips. Then I remember something from when I was little. I used to like watching this show where a ventriloquist named Hal performed on TV, but I had no idea what a ventriloquist was. As far as I knew, the fluffy puppet named Topper Smiley that Hal held was alive and talking. That is until one day when Kevin walked in and took a little piece of my childhood away. "If you look close, you can see his lips moving," Kevin said. I still didn't get it. Of *course* I could see Topper Smiley's mouth move. He was *talking*. But Kevin plopped down on the couch next to me, waiting. When Topper Smiley spoke again, he pointed. "See there — look at the corner of Hal's mouth." And I saw it, the little twitch of his lips, the slight bobbing of the muscles in his neck. The illusion was forever ruined; Topper Smiley was just a puppet, a thing. I'd been falling for a lie. Now, stuck in Torden's trap, I decide to try my hand at the trick.

No, not throwing my voice or any sort of voodoo like that — just speaking without moving my mouth. Trying to push air out with my diaphragm. "Or en oo aah ur." All right, so my first attempt is basically gibberish, but the fact that *any* sound comes out at all gives me hope.

Torden calls down to me. "Ho, ho! Are you trying to *tell* me something, dear Lyn?" He laughs again, and the others join in.

To the degree I can, I grit my teeth. Forcing air up from inside, I push it out, doing my best to form words. "Oor en yoo ass urd."

The laughter above pauses a moment, then I hear a male voice — Rand, I think — speak up. "I believe she is trying to say, *Torden, you bastard.*" Once more, they all laugh.

"Lyn," Torden calls down. "Save your energy. It won't do you any good."

"Ut oo oo unt wih uh?" I ask.

"I'm sorry, dear girl, I really can't understand you," he says.

Once more Rand translates. I don't know how I feel about Rand being the one person that can understand me, but it isn't good. "I think she said, *what do you want with us?*"

"Oh," Torden says, all smiles and sunshine. "Well, that is a fabulous question, and I'm so glad you asked, Lyn. Or should I call you *Lightning*?"

"Uh oo," I say, and no one needs to translate that.

"So feisty, even till the end. I admire that, I really do. But, this *is* the end, Lyn, for you and all your friends. Look around you," Torden says. "Ah, apologies, you can't. Well, look in front of you. You'll see the coils of wire wrapping around this entire room; those are critical. To clarify all of this, it's important for you to understand that, while we call the ability we all share *electromagic*, it might be better termed something else, something more scientific. I've played with a few other names, but for now I call it *EEMS* — *enhanced electrical manipulation and storage*. I've even developed a ranking system to indicate the relative power of an individual, based on their capabilities with electricity as well as their personal Quotient. That is, their personal ability to take a set amount of electrical energy and stretch its utility as long as possible. Some of my rankings are subjective, because of course I haven't had the time or ability to test everyone personally yet, but I think my estimates are a good start."

A new mechanical sound whirs high above us, and there are low clicks and clacks. Whatever's up there sounds like it's moving. Coming down toward us. I struggle against the force holding me, but I'm completely frozen. *Damn it!*

"Uma, you are an EEMS level six. Don't be too discouraged by that. The numbers go from one at the lowest to ten at the top, and five is indicative of your average individual. You are, therefore, a step ahead of average, which is good."

Because I entered the room first, everyone else is off to my left, but Uma is slightly behind the rest, so I can't see even a glimpse of her in my peripheral vision. Still, I hear her wordless grunt that's invariably an indication of what Torden can do with his rating system.

"Hayden," Torden continues, "you are also a six, though Percival, I believe you are a five, possibly even a four. I know I haven't directly tested you, but your abilities just fail to impress me."

Instinctually, I can feel Percival seethe next to me, and I bet he's very much hoping he can personally demonstrate his capabilities for Torden.

"Then at last we have Lyn. Sister to the new *leader* in New York, child of a pair of famous — or perhaps infamous — electromagicians. It will come as little surprise that you top the scale. You are an EEMS level ten. And you are also my prized possession. Now, back to the current situation. I asked you to notice the bare wires surrounding the room. Of course, we've all seen electromagicians who become addicted to conventional electricity — tapping the juice from wall sockets, and such. We call these people EM junkies, because the energy they consume taints their bodies, ruining them. So of course, while I work with manmade electricity in these wires, it is only useful as a tool, not sustenance. The real source of power here is, of course, you. You all are standing in a room that has been outfitted as one giant solenoid, built by me, specifically to do exactly what it is doing now: holding you in place, with no ability to move or use power, until I am finished doing what needs to be done. Oh, and don't bother struggling to ask me what my plans are, I'll go ahead and tell you."

I try to use electromagic communication to talk to Percival, but nothing happens. It seems that every aspect of our magic has been shut down. *Think, Lyn, think. How can we get out of this? If I could only knock out the power to the room...* It's an idea much easier said than done, in my current situation.

"My plan is very simple. There are four of you, and there are four of us. Each one of you will feed one of us with your power, filling us and extending our lives. I have developed a machine that is ten times more efficient than any golem — what you call a Stickman — at pulling electromagic from a host and funneling it to a recipient. That machine is here, just above your heads, though I imagine none of you can see it. But here's the truly wonderful thing about my latest creation: with my new machine, we each now have the option to consume your power all at once, like a single, great big feast, or we can do it slowly over months, perhaps even years, a steady, consistent power source that we can savor."

Monster! I try to shout, but it comes out more like "On-Er!" *What the hell?* I think. *Months? Years? Trapped here, being sucked dry of energy like a vampire's victim slowly drained of blood.* I'm not one to contemplate suicide, but compared to being a years-long buffet dinner for one of these ancient assholes, it's looking like a solid option. The new mechanical sound above us thumps loudly, then goes silent, and all I can do is picture Torden's machine waiting like a vulture in the sky, high overhead.

Though I still can't see him based on the angle, I hear Torden clap his hands once, then rub his palms together briskly. "How shall we begin? Ah, of course. Ladies first. Madame Agnès Bisset, would you do the honors of selecting? Oh, and, you all know that Hopkins is for me."

"Aiy? Aiy ee?" I ask in my guttural nonsense language.

"Why you, Lyn? Are you asking *why* I am keeping you for myself? Hm? It's simple, dear. Even more simple than the fact that you top my ratings scale. I know what you can *do*, and I will be performing *special* procedures to ensure that your unique ability to tap into and combine multiple sources of power becomes a skill that I will soon possess. You know, I feel very lucky. Back in New York, my only option to deal with you was to have a golem take your power. One big surge and everything would be done. That would have been a real shame, losing out on your special gift. But *now*? Now I can use my machine to slowly tap your power while I work to devise a process that will make *your* unique ability become *my* unique ability."

I rage, incoherent sounds boiling out of my throat and bouncing off the surrounding walls.

Torden *tsks* me. "Make as much noise as you like, dear. We're underground, well off church property, in a subsystem unused by the Paris Metro for many years. No one is going to hear you. No one is coming to rescue you." Once more the quartet above laughs, and I vow to myself that if I ever have the ability, I will smack the laughter out of each and every one of them. "So, Agnès? Who will it be?"

"The tall, dark-haired boy," she says, like she's picking a lobster for dinner. She means Hayden.

"An excellent choice," Torden says.

Above us, his machine once more makes its mechanical whirring sound, growing louder as it lowers itself toward us. Toward Hayden, with the goal of using him as Agnès Bisset's very own charging station.

I hear another wordless howl and realize it isn't me this time. The sound coming from my friend Hayden is full of anger and sadness and fear and despair.

32

FLICK OF THE SWITCH

Hayden continues to bellow a throaty sound, the best he can do without the use of his tongue or facial muscles. He's paralyzed, and not just with fear. He's stuck, wrapped in the invisible hands of Torden's thrumming machine; we all are. I try to move, try to help him, but I can't budge, not even a millimeter.

From above, Torden's machine grows closer. I know that movement is impossible, and I know that my magic appears to be gone, but I have to try something. I pull, deep from within me, harder than I've ever pulled in my life, trying to force electromagic to erupt from my body. I pull with such strength that I begin to wonder what will happen if I succeed. Will I tear myself apart, ripped to pieces by the power of my own magic? Still, I try.

I can just barely see Hayden to my left, so it's only at the last minute that I see the tube-like structure sliding down around him. I pull desperately from within, feeling nothing. Never in my life have I felt like a regular human, not that I remember. Now, at the worst possible time, that seems like all I am.

The tube continues downward and in just moments, Hayden is fully encapsulated by it. Everything becomes still. Seconds later, lights flicker and blink, and the machine around Hayden makes a series of start-stop pulses, like it's testing something. From within the tube, I hear Hayden making wordless whimpering sounds.

Be strong, Hayden, I think. I pull once more, reaching farther inside, like I'm trying to reach from the bottom of my well of power and pull all of it up at once. Nothing happens.

"All systems are operational and ready," Rand says. I can't see any of the four — Rand, Torden, and the Bissets — but their words echo down the smooth cylindrical concrete tube we're in, to my ears, plain as day.

"Good," Torden replies, his words low, not meant for us. "Agnès, sit here, put your hands on these couplings and lean your head back against the rest. Your body may tense a bit with the process, and I wouldn't want you to knock your head."

"Thank you," she says, and I want to scream. They're all acting like they've packed a picnic lunch and are politely sitting down on a blanket in the park to eat. But the meal is not a baguette and cheese, it's my friend, Hayden.

"Do you prefer one large influx of energy, or would you like to consume only a portion now? We can set a schedule for future transfers, if you like." My mind reels. Am I in a movie? An altered reality? Torden sounds like some lottery official asking the big winner if they want the lump sum of cash or the installment plan.

"Well, as you know, I have been ill recently. I think it would be best if I got the full dose right now."

"As you wish, Agnès." Torden sounds so tender, accommodating. I scream, all noise.

Something clicks and the machine holding Hayden begins whirring again, rising steadily in volume. Lights on the side blink in random patterns I don't understand.

Within the tube, Hayden's whimpering has stopped, but we still hear him. He isn't shouting gibberish or even yelling in pain. He's coughing and gasping, irregular staccato sounds. I'm certain he's dying.

With everything I have, I thrust my will down into the deepest reaches of my body and soul. If my actions were physical, it would be like reaching through my chest, through the center of my heart, and wrapping my fingers around my spine, trying to pull it out. Rage sounds echo off the walls, and I realize it's not just me; Uma and Hayden and shouting wordlessly as well. We're all trying to rip ourselves free of Torden's grasp so we can do something, anything to help our friend.

Hayden's gasping breaths grow even more ragged, more irregular.

I curl my mental fingers around something, the center of all that is me, and I pull, but that something feels as frozen as my body. It won't move. I can't move it.

Hayden spits out a loud wet sound that reminds me of a sponge dropped on a kitchen counter. *Sponge. Just like the Stickmen. Just like this machine.*

I pull and pull and pull and pull on the dark something within me.

But it won't move.

Nothing will move.

Until finally, the machine around Hayden sputters to silence, then slowly glides upward.

Out of the corner of my eye, I can see him standing there, just where he was. But now Hayden is withered and darkened, sooty black and coal grey. Even his clothes appear burnt.

I release the useless thing inside me, because it's too late. I'm too late. I've failed another friend. I hear muffled sobbing from Uma behind me, a gurgling, heartfelt pain coming from Percival's throat.

This isn't like Zee, I tell myself, eyes unable to move but still taking in the husk of Hayden on the fringe of my vision. *There's no mystery about it. His body is right there.*

Torden's machine clicks back into its place unseen above us, but there is constant sound all around me. Percival, Uma, and I are wailing and crying, the best we can with our bodies paralyzed.

I hear Torden above, in a low voice. "How does that feel?" He must be talking to Agnès Bisset, the woman who just took away the life force of my friend.

"*C'est magnifique,*" the woman replies, with a sensual sort of sigh that tells me she *enjoyed* what she just did.

I promise you. For every ounce of bliss that just brought you, I will inflict a pound of pain. You will regret this moment, all of you. I struggle to move, desperate to get free. I scream again.

Suddenly, someone echoes my scream from above. But unlike my muted rage, the second sound is a high-pitched, primal yell, a hellish banshee cry.

A moment later, there is a loud crash as all the power goes out and I flop to the floor in complete darkness, slamming my knee into the concrete surface. The sharp spike of pain is enough to tell me I'm free, finally.

I raise an unseen hand in front of my face, then tug at my power, as bluish-white arcs of electricity bounce between my fingers.

Now we begin, I think.

33

RISE AGAIN

The screaming above continues, but now I can actually lift my head to see. Given the power has been cut, I am surprised that I can make out anything, but there is some kind of light up there, illuminating things just enough. The concrete shaft we're in goes up several stories, with Torden's damned machine hanging near the top like a malignant tumor. Midway up on my right, there is a rectangular gap cut into the wall, like an observation deck. From there, the yellow glow of a backup light emanates, punctuated randomly by flashes of blue. Once or twice a bolt of electromagic reaches out to strike the far wall.

The lower-pitched shouting of the men above adds to the overall cacophony of sound, and I realize that I need to move. I don't know who or what disrupted Torden's little party, but I need to help them. I fill myself with electromagic, looking over my shoulder at the others. "We need to get up there!"

Percival nods, suddenly bursting with an electric glow. "Ready," he says. Beside him, Uma wipes away tears, but she nods as well as her body begins to shine with power. Off to one side, Hayden's wasted body lies in a crumpled heap, but I can't look at him now. I have to finish this. There will be time for mourning later. Or at least that's what I tell myself, knowing that it may be others mourning us all.

I leap, using magic to thrust my body toward the observation window, and a moment later drop into a firefight. Uma and Percival fly in the window just after me. We're in a wide room lit harshly by battery-powered floodlights mounted near the ceiling. It's bright enough to see a bank of machines to one side, little lights blinking randomly, with wires attaching them to a laptop on a desk on right, and what looks to be a dentist's chair on the left. Though no dentist I know would have nearly so many wires and electrical attachments on their exam chair. I see damage in the form of a large ragged hole in the middle of one of the machines, and smoke billows upward to gather at the ceiling, warning that soon our supply of breathable air may be cut short.

Still, all of that is just background noise. What really matters is what I see in the middle of the room, and it both fills and breaks my heart at the same time. Though her hair is matted and dirty, and her clothes look like oily rags, I can hardly believe my eyes that Zee is standing right in front of me, a long fireman's axe in one hand, and electromagic bursting from the other. She's being circled by Torden, Rand, and the Bissets, who, at the moment, have their backs to us. I think Zee notices us, but she's being coy, hoping to keep the attention of the four elder electromagicians facing her.

In the space of a heartbeat, a million thoughts flood my mind. *Zee! She's alive! Where has she been? She's so filthy? What happened to her? How did she avoid the explosion? How did she get here?* Behind her I notice power lines sparking where they've been severed at about head height. That, combined with the hole in the machine and the axe in Mackenzie's hand, tells me the tale of what just happened. *She ruined Torden's little plans and set us free! That's my girl!* I glance over at Percival and Uma. "Magic's not the way here, guys. They'll just suck up our power."

Pers grins, curling one hand into a fist and pounding into the palm of his other hand. "Then I say we use good old fashioned physical brutality on these geezers."

"That's a plan if ever I've heard one," Uma says.

As one, we rush forward. Percival, with his longer strides, gets there first, grabbing Rand by the shoulder and spinning him around. The look of shock on Rand's face is definitely worth the price of admission, though it doesn't last long. It's quickly replaced by a crumpled, semi-conscious look as Pers clocks him right in the side of the head with his balled fist. Rand collapses to the floor. One down.

Simultaneously, Uma and I arrive on the scene. Uma slams into the back of Anton Bisset, sending him crashing into a concrete wall. His reaction time is slow, and I'm pretty sure I hear bones breaking from the impact. Given his head hit first, that could be his jaw, or maybe even his skull. Either way, good.

I feel the profound, fulfilling sense of justice served as I tackle Torden and drive him to the harsh cement. "I hope your two-hundred-year-old body is ready for a beat down, you son of a bitch!" Torden and I slide as one across the floor, with him taking the brunt of the force. Plus, I get in a solid punch or two to the back of his head before our momentum stops, and I see streaks of blood painting the bare grey beneath us. Desperately, he writhes below me, and though I am many, many decades younger, the guy is surprisingly strong. He throws me off, and I roll into a crouch.

To the side, there is a blaze of bluish-white as Agnès Bisset fills with power, but of course it doesn't worry me. *Fire me up, lady. I dare you!* She doesn't. Instead she uses her power to zip her body out the door. She's gone in under a second, leaving the rest of us behind.

Torden struggles to his feet, but Rand and Anton Bisset have thrown in the towel. Rand is sprawled out on the floor, and if he's not completely knocked out, he's damn close. Anton is folded up against the wall, his hands holding whatever bones were broken in his face.

"Give it up, Torden," Percival says. "You're done."

"You!" Torden seethes. "You stupid... *children!* You have no idea what you're doing, no idea what powers we control."

Zee takes up a position behind Torden, axe at the ready in her hands, blocking the door. Uma, Percival, and I form a wall on the other side, blocking the observation window. "There's no way out,

Torden," I say, standing and brushing myself off. "And now I'm gonna take you back to my brother and let him ensure you get the justice you deserve."

Torden's eyes flare at the comment, and I know I've struck a nerve, maybe even scared him a little. "Like hell," he says.

I recall the punishment Kevin threatened Torden with — that thing that can take away an electromagician's power. Its full name escapes me, but I remember part of the name and that's enough. "The High Order has a certain Japanese *touchstone* all ready for you, old man. As Kevin would say, *Ubi concordia, ibi victoria.*" *Where there is unity, there is victory.* I glance at each of my friends in turn, stopping on Zee. She echoes my smile, and I see that even her teeth are grimy-looking. "Well, it's nice to see you again, Ms. Patmina. What have you been up to recently?"

"Oh, you know," she says, pretending to fuss with her hair. I can't believe how good it is to hear her voice. "Just enjoying Parisian life. I think I might get a summer home here."

"It looks like you've been sleeping under a bridge," Pers says with a chuckle.

Zee dips her chin with a knowing smirk. "You have no idea, my friend. No idea."

"Seriously, Zee," I say. "What the hell? Where have you been? What have you been doing?"

"Ever since someone tried to blow me up, I figured it would be best if I stayed hidden. Make whoever it was think he succeeded. Try to help you all as best I could, while remaining out of sight."

"That note," I say, eyes lighting up. "*Watch over the children.* That was you?"

"Yep."

"Why? How could you know?"

Zee shrugs. "A hunch, mainly. We came here to investigate the rash of EM babies. Then someone tried to kill me. Those two things had to be related. I didn't want you and Pers so intent on avenging me that you forgot why we were here — and why we were in danger — in the first place." Zee looks at me, then away, quickly. I've seen her do this before; it means she has something emotional to say and doesn't really want to say it. "I was there, you know, Lyn. At Sacre Coeur, when you tried to talk to me. I heard you. And I almost talked back to you. Until I saw Torden. After that, I spent a lot of time following him. I've seen him come down into these tunnels countless times. But this will be the last." She holds the axe menacingly above the old man.

Torden squirms, a rat in a trap, and I tense, thinking he's going to try to rush past one of us, get free. Then I hear the click, coming from the doorway behind Zee. "Enough of this," a thickly accented woman's voice says. Agnès Bisset. Zee slides to one side and we can all see the problem: Agnès may be a wrinkled old lady, but she's now holding the same black gun we saw her with before, the one she threatened us with at her house.

Suddenly, all our feelings of victory and joy flitter away like embers from a dying campfire. My shoulders fall, just as I watch Torden stand tall and smile. *I really hate that man*, I think.

Percival lets out a heavy sigh, shaking his head, though his eyes never leave the gun in Agnès Bisset's hand. "Jesus, do you take that thing everywhere?"

Torden begins to slowly laugh, a sound so smug and self-centered that it feels like an ice pick shoved in my ears. "Well, now. Where were we?"

34

BEST LAID PLANS

Torden Detonde is strutting. Positively strutting. Rand Haldor and Anton Bisset drag themselves off the floor, but they're no concern. It's Agnès Bisset and the gun in her hand that command our attention. If she was simply a regular human, one quick zap would take care of her before she could pull the trigger, but she isn't and so we're screwed.

"Mackenzie, Mackenzie, Mackenzie," Torden says with *tsk* and a little laugh. "You have been very naughty, my girl. You've damaged my machine and cut off power. But those are just *things*, and *things* can be *fixed*. Though I am sad that I didn't properly kill you the first time."

"So, you admit it?" Zee spits out in anger. "You tried to blow me up. You know, if Granny over there wasn't holding that gun, I'd plant this axe in the middle of your forehead."

"Oh, that is precisely why I did it, dear. It was the only sensible thing to do." He speaks like it's all completely sane. Like he's sane. "You represent a risk. I knew it would be nearly impossible to get Lyn away from *both* you and Percival, so I figured the job could be done one person at a time. Since you are the stronger of the two, I chose you first."

"What do you mean, stronger?" Zee asks.

"You're EEMS level eight, by my estimate," Torden says, and I realize Zee wasn't present for that whole wacko description of his electromagician rating scale. She looks baffled.

"It's just some mental bullshit he came up with, Zee," I say. "Ignore the old man. He may be senile."

"Clever and humorous to the very end, eh, Ms. Hopkins? Nonetheless, Mackenzie, you represented the greater risk. I sought to eliminate that risk, but you survived. I won't make the same mistake twice. But, tell me. How did you manage to get out? You should have been sleeping?"

I'm not sure if Zee tells the tale because she has no choice at the point of a gun, or wants to dig at Torden for having his plans screwed up. I'm hoping it's the latter. "I got a warning, just in time. A male EM voice snapped into my head, scaring the shit out of me. He said he didn't have time to explain, but the building was rigged to explode and I had to get out immediately. At first I told him to piss off, because I was trying to sleep, but then he said something that got me moving."

"And what was that?" Torden asks with a joyless grin.

"He knew my name. He said, *Mackenzie Patmina, if you don't fly out the window of that house in the next thirty seconds, you will be enjoying the endless sleep of the dead. I won't warn you again.* So I figured, either it was a prank and I'd look like a fool zipping myself out the window, or it was real, and I'd be saving my life. The downside of potentially looking like a fool was far outweighed by the prospect of dying, so I took off. A moment later, I shot myself out the back window and before I even reached the top of the next row of houses, our place blew up. The flames were at least ten feet tall, shooting from a hole in the roof right above where I would've been sleeping. Whoever it was, I guess he's not a big fan of *you*. I'll have to thank him when I meet him."

Torden's false smile puffs out, like a wisp of smoke from a candle blown away by a sudden breeze. "Unfortunately for you, Ms. Patmina, that day will never come." He looks sharply toward Agnès Bisset. "Shoot her. Now."

"Wait!" I shout, diving to get between Zee and the gun, though I know bullets will kill me just as easily as they will kill her. Mind racing, I try to stall for time, think of what we can possibly do to get out of this mess. "Don't you want to tell us all *why*? Don't you want to tell us all *how*?"

"Why? How?" Torden asks, shaking his head. "What are you going on about?"

"The children," I say. "The babies. The whole reason any of us are here in Paris in the first place. How did you turn regular human babies into electromagicians? And why? We should all, Zee included, at least get to know that." It's an obvious stall, but it's just the kind of thing Torden Detonde may not be able to resist — the opportunity to pontificate and look like a genius. I just hope he doesn't see it for what it truly is, an attempt to stop him from killing my friend, if only for a moment more. *Think, Lyn, think!*

He looks at me unblinking, and I'm certain he's going to wave his wrinkled hand and have Zee shot. Then a slow, satisfied grin spreads across his face, not the warm and inviting smile of a child or a friend, but something that looks more like weathered paper tearing in half, ripped by unseen stresses, revealing yellowed rows of teeth below. *If only electromagic could kill you, you ancient bastard. I would destroy you right here and now.*

"Well," Torden says. "Well." For a moment, I think that's all he's going to say, until his tone changes suddenly. He's now the master, the teacher, enlightening and informing us, the foolish young. "I've always had a natural inclination toward the ways of science, and with many decades more of life with which to learn, I would dare say that my knowledge and skills — in multiple scientific disciplines, mind you — far exceed most of the well-known experts of our time. For many years, I sought to determine the factors that make us different from regular humans, and, thankfully, using some of the most modern computer equipment, I discovered something incredible. As you probably know, our genetic configuration is housed in our DNA. But what you may not know is that we each have distinct qualities. Not a lot, mind you; despite the radical differences humans think they possess, whether race or ethnicity or gender, or even qualities like height and build, the truth is that every human on Earth is within about one tenth of one percent when it comes to their genetic make-up. Meanwhile, the chimpanzee, our closest living relative, is separated from humans by a little over one full percent of their DNA."

Percival mockingly raises his hand. "Excuse me, but I don't think we signed up for this class, so if you'll excuse me and my friends, we'll just be on our way." He steps toward the door, but a quick wave of Agnès's gun stops him in his tracks.

Torden clears his throat, annoyed at the interruption. "As I was about to say, I have discovered the genetic difference between EMs and regulars, and it is slight but critical. In fact, the DNA of an electromagician falls inside the normal range of genetic possibilities within which all humans exist."

"And just how is it that you figured this out and no real scientist ever has?" Uma says.

Torden's expression hardens in an instant, and he lurches toward Uma. "Be thankful that I am ignoring your snide comment, child. As for your foolish question, tell me why any *regular* human researcher would be looking for *electromagician* DNA? See how ridiculous you sound now? Or did you forget that they don't even know we exist? Yet."

The last word hangs ominously, and I think back to what Orkan Zidane told me about the Prime Order and their desire to reveal themselves to the world of regulars: *There is no need for us to hide in the shadows any longer.* "Okay, Torden. You figured out what made us unique. Then what? How'd you change the babies?" I almost ask *why* as well, but seeing the weirdo dentist chair connected to a bank of machines and a laptop has me pretty convinced I already know that answer.

Once more, Torden lets his ego take over. "Well, first it's important to note that I had been working on my machine for years." He gestures toward the ruined device along the far wall. "Luckily this is only one of several prototypes, so while Mackenzie's handiwork does put a damper on the here and now, it hardly derails my work for long. I have many people working with me, on many different prototypes around the world. This isn't even the nicest one. But you, Lyn Hopkins, you should be thankful for my machine. Without it, I would have simply had one of my golems bleed you dry of power, all at once. Now, with my machine and its capability to parse electromagic in installments, you can live on. At least until I determine how to clone your abilities into me, that is. In any event, once I knew the genetic markers in our DNA, it gave me a simple idea: could I manipulate a regular human to become an electromagician? I could, of course, find some adult regular to experiment on, but that would be messy at best. Instead, I felt that I could try to alter a newborn. Newborns are already undergoing a massive process of growth, cell production, and change, so what better subject for my experiment?" The fact that he expresses exactly zero remorse or concern for the *subject* of his experiments, especially when that subject is a helpless infant, tells you all you need to know about Torden Detonde, asshole extraordinaire. "I worked with my colleague, Anton Bisset, here, to first acquire perinatal stem cells from actual EMs giving birth in the hospital, and then to inject those stem cells into other infants to see what happens. The results are truly amazing. I imagine Nurse Lafitte performed her little test for you, showed you how we can tell if an infant is one of us or not?" I nod. "Good. Well, very quickly we had success with our process."

I steel myself, needing to say the next thing, but wanting to do it without emotion. Torden didn't deserve to see my emotion. Still, the image of what I saw in the catacombs comes rushing back to me. The charred little body. "But then you took the first child and killed him." I clench my jaw, unable to say anything more.

"Yes, yes," Torden says, waving a hand dismissively. "That was most unfortunate. We didn't get any measurable charge from the boy. But it was also educational, you see. My current theory is that the child was too young. Perhaps children need to grow to maturity before they can be harvested, or perhaps they just need to discover their own ability before the machine can use them. Eventually, I'll know for sure, since as you know, I have quite a large number of future candidates."

Torden's words are stabbing into me like daggers: *science, theory, subject, experiment*. But the worst word of them all is *harvest*. Torden Detonde and the others with him are creating a generation of electro-magicians whose sole purpose is to extend the lives of the elderly. My hands ball into fists, and the beginnings of a plan form in my head. Not a good plan, and certainly not a foolproof one, but a plan. We've already proven that physically we can take them all down, so the only thing stopping us is the old woman Agnès and her gun. How good of a shot could she possibly be? How quickly can she fire? If I can make her miss with the first shot, or even just take the bullet in a nonlethal place, I can drop her. Then the other geriatrics are in for a rude awakening. *Pers*, I buzz in his mind.

Yeah, he responds.

If we move fast, I think we can get the gun from her hands before she does too much damage. It's our only shot.

There's a healthy pause before he replies again, and even his in-my-head voice sounds weary, resolved. *Let me take her out. You just be sure to dive behind something. Preferably something she can shoot instead of you, like maybe Torden.*

It's my plan, so I'll do it, I tell him. *Just be sure to keep the others from getting away. Promise me.*

Lyn, I said I'll take out the gun.

Percival, stop it. I didn't tell you my plan to argue about it.

And as if she can hear our words, Agnès Bisset fumbles her free hand into a pocket of the frumpy sweater she's wearing, pulling out a second gun that matches the one she's holding. "Here," she says to her husband, passing it over.

Shit, Pervical says in my head.

I don't even bother to respond, because there's simply nothing else to say. The plan was likely to get me hurt or killed, but it was the best idea I had. It just came too late. I'm always too late.

Uma must realize that the silence has gone on too long, because suddenly she pipes up. "Okay, then there's just one more thing I don't understand."

Torden smirks smugly. "And what is that?"

"Of all the places in the *world*, how'd you get away with doing all this *here*? In Paris. I mean, sure, there are pockets of the High Order all over the world, but here you've got more than just them to worry about. Here, you've got the *Prime* Order, too."

"Simple," he says with a chuckle. "The Prime Order knew what I was doing all along."

35

CIRCUIT BREAKER

They knew, I think. In fact, that's all I can think. *They knew and they lied about it. No, worse. He knew. Orkan. And he lied right to my face.* "Lies..." I mutter.

Torden keys on what I've said. "Yes, Lyn. Lies. The entire world is made up of lies. You just need to decide two things: which ones you choose to believe, and which ones you cannot allow. The rest are immaterial. So. Do you believe in the High Order? Or the Prime Order? Or are you like me, unable to tolerate either?"

"I'm nothing like you," I say through clenched teeth. "You're a murderer. You killed Robin, and Hayden, and even a helpless child."

Leaning close, Torden's nose is inches from mine. "Lyn Hopkins, I am so very much looking forward to taking all that you possess. As for murder, I don't plan to kill you. I plan something much worse, to *use* you for a long, long time. Besides, I must tell you, after the first few dozen times, murder really loses its steam. It's hard to get too worked up about it." I stammer to reply, but Torden turns away, toward Agnès Bisset. "Enough fooling around. Shoot Mackenzie Patmina already and let's be done with it."

"No!" I shout, but Anton Bisset is right behind me, pointing his gun at my head. I'm frozen. *There must be something I can do... I can't watch Zee die twice.*

The old woman, standing in the open doorway, lifts the gun with a devilish grin, aiming at Zee's head, while Zee's eyes dart around the room, knowing there's nowhere to run or hide. I see a wet shine on her cheek and know she's crying. Together, she and Agnès are like those damned theater masks — comedy and tragedy, one smiling and one weeping.

Until suddenly the smile on Agnès Bisset's face disappears. She looks like someone just ran over her cat, and for several moments we're all confused, Torden, Rand, and Anton, too. "Madame Bisset, if you please," Torden says impatiently.

Then a head pops up, just behind Agnès, adorned with goggles and a black hood. Dark forms push past the woman, barging into the room, quickly forming a circle around the bunch of us. One takes the gun from Agnès's hand, and another, brandishing a much, much larger gun than either of the Bissets, goes to Anton and quickly disarms him.

"Uh, did someone order a team of commandos?" Percival says. Instinctively, we put our hands up. There are easily half a dozen people, all in black, each with what looks like a military-grade rifle, their laser scopes lighting up a random, moving pattern of red dots on the walls, machines, and across each of us. "Or maybe ninjas?"

"Everybody line up against this wall!" one of the armed men shouts. "Keep your hands out of your pockets and no one gets hurt." From the corner of my eye, I see Torden fill with electromagic, the slight blue tint around him a dead giveaway to me, but maybe unnoticeable to the men surrounding us. Or at least that's what I think at first. The shouting man points directly at Torden. "And none of that! We know what you can do. These black suits dissipate electrical energy. However, if you choose to attack us, we will fight back and it will be with lethal force. We are well aware that you are *not* bulletproof."

The light blue aura around Torden quickly fades, as does his expression. "I can only imagine who sent you," he says with disgust. Another person enters the room, tall and wiry thin, ducking to get through the entryway. "As I suspected. Orkan Zidane. Well, you can call off your dogs now. Or have you forgotten the Prime Order doesn't interfere, doesn't dole out justice."

"Ordinarily, you would be correct," Orkan says. "But these are, apparently, not ordinary times."

"*You*," I say. "You lied to us. You knew what Torden was doing. That's how it was so easy to find us — both when we explored the catacombs below the Bissets' house and now. You knew where we were going long before we did."

Orkan levels a cool look toward me. "I acted according to my best judgment, and the best judgment of my society, Lyn. Plus, I was only aware of *some* of Torden's activities. The genetic manipulation of regulars into electromagicians, while unusual, was not truly harming anyone. I was unaware of his plan to cultivate those individuals for his own gain, though even that, too, is not necessarily an actionable offense by Prime Order guidelines."

"Not *actionable*?" I shout. "Are you out of your mind?"

Zee interrupts. "That's the voice. You're the one who told me to escape before the explosion."

"I am," Orkan says, with the slightest of bows.

"Well, you better look through that window over there and see what this man has done to our friend," Zee demands. "It's about time someone came along and stopped this maniac."

"He killed Hayden," Uma says, her voice catching.

"I was *defending* myself from these people. They came here. They attacked *me*," Torden shouts.

"Bullshit!" Percival yells back.

Orkan raises both hands to regain order. All around us, the armed men look antsy. "Everyone settle down. I will assess what's going on here."

"You'll *assess*?" Torden scoffs. "You? You've interfered now *twice*," Torden says. "Once with Mackenzie, and again here. How can you truly call yourself Prime Order, the free and open society, when you keep stepping in where you aren't wanted?"

"Call it a favor," Orkan says cryptically, his eyes fixed on Torden.

"Ah!" Torden says, suddenly smiling and full of glee. "A *favor*. Well, that explains a lot, doesn't it? In fact, that explains *everything*. Your so-called Prime Order thinks itself so perfect, so worthy for all of us to join, and yet, when it comes down to it, you're just a good-old-boys' club, willing to force your will upon us with your little army here. You're no better than the High Order, after all. Did you even bother to tell Lyn *any* of the truth?"

Orkan's face darkens and he stares at Torden with open hostility. "I advise you to stop talking."

"Oh, you do, do you?" Torden laughs. "Or what? You'll shoot me? Just for speaking my mind? Go ahead! See how many electromagicians come over to your side after that! Your society will wither up and die if you lay a hand on me. I'm doing *nothing* to threaten you. Unless the truth is a threat."

"What truth?" I ask, confused. "What are you talking about?"

"I said be quiet," Orkan barks.

"I will *not*," Torden shouts defiantly. "Tell her, Orkan! Tell her who told you to interfere here! Don't you think she deserves to know?"

Orkan dips his chin, staring at the ground, silent.

"Tell her!" Torden shouts, and his anger stirs the armed men to action. The two nearest him snap their weapons up to aim at him, one at his midsection, one at his head. They look to Orkan for direction, seemingly all too willing to pull the trigger.

I can't believe I'm doing it when my hand reaches out hand pushes away one of those guns. I'm saving Torden Detonde's life, and if ever there was proof that I have no idea what I was doing, this is it. The man with the gun shoves me away violently, slamming me into the wall.

"Enough!" Orkan says, and suddenly all is still. "Enough. I have attempted to manage this situation, but all of you keep making things worse. You want to know who told me to interfere? Fine. I'll tell you, though Torden, you already well know." Orkan walks over to me, reaching out one hand. I pull back, afraid of another rough handling, but his hand settles gently on my shoulder. "It was your parents, Lyn. They asked me to intervene."

"What?" I say. "That — that's impossible. My parents are dead."

Orkan shakes his head slowly. "They aren't. Marianne and Jeremy Hopkins are alive and well. They founded the Prime Order, with me, decades ago, and now they live in Geneva, the central hub of our society."

"Shut up!" I scream, pulling my hands up to my ears, a childish gesture. "Stop lying to me!"

"It's no lie, Lyn."

Beside me, Torden begins to cackle a laugh. "Don't believe him, girl? Ask your *brother*."

"Brother? Kevin? He knows. My — they — I — " I don't have words, can't make sense of it. Only one thing rises in my mind, the same words I had so recently thought related to Orkan, but now realize apply to *everyone*: the Prime Order, the High Order, Orkan, Torden, Kevin, and even my own parents. *They lied to me. They all lied to me. For my entire life, everyone has lied.*

I never remember feeling truly included in any group, any gathering, in my life. Not truly. Tolerated. Allowed. But not *accepted*. Not *belonging*. Still, I've never felt such a sense of wrongness before. A sense that nothing is what it seems, no one is who they say they are, and I utterly and completely am not a part of anything. I don't belong. Not in any order, and not in some dark underground tunnel in Paris, foolishly playing the part of a helpless pawn, unaware of the hands that keep shifting my position on the chess board.

I hate it.

I want nothing to do with it, or with anyone.

I can't even look Uma, or Percival, or Zee in the eye, for fear of another betrayal, another situation where I thought I knew the truth only to have the blinds thrown back and my sad reality revealed.

I have to get out.

I have to get out.

Before anyone can react, I burst with power, pushing myself force-fully past the armed men and out the door, down the long dark hall-way, and up up up. Moments later, I shoot into the bright morning sun, not caring if a million people see me, a human-shaped meteor rising into the autumn sky.

36

BLINKING LIGHT

I wake in silence and darkness, at a place where the bed is wide, reasonably plush, and comfortable. Beside me, a small, orange light blinks on the bedside table. I ignore it.

I get up, take a long, hot shower, and dress, then check my phone with an ungloved hand. Percival was right, at least about one thing: it does get easier with time. I don't destroy phones anymore, at least not by accident. I tap the weather app and scroll. *Storms expected in two hours, lasting about four. That'll do.*

At the wide windows, I grab the dangling plastic rod and use it to open the curtains, revealing bright, late morning sunshine. I'm on my own; there's no need to get up at the crack of dawn. I'll keep my own schedule, thank you very much.

Below my window is a wide asphalt parking lot, maybe a third full of cars in various sizes and colors. On the far side, a large sign dominates the view. It's intended to look like rough-cut timber, though I suspect it's fiberglass or something else likely to withstand the apocalypse. *Wispy Springs Ski Resort, Antler Valley, West Virginia.* Above the supposedly carved sign, there's a billboard with a giant photo of smiling skiers clad in all sorts of bright colors. Well, there's no skiing happening today, given that it's already 88 degrees at eleven in the morning. In the distance, green goes up and up in pointed rows, the mountain range that would be littered with those same happy skiers if this were December, but it's early June; I've been on one long, extended charge hunt for nine months.

I sit on the wooden bench that runs under the window and grab for my hiking boots, lacing them up carefully. The ski lift is running so it'll get me and any other summer adventurers up to the top, but from there I need to branch out. Find my own private space before the lightning comes down. Because I want that charge, need it. I'm still an electromagician, even if I have no Order, no group, no tribe.

Yeah, I'll head back to New York when I'm ready, and I'll even head back to the family home, living with Kevin. But I don't have to talk to him. If he wants to lie to me for my entire life, then he doesn't get to know what I'm doing any more. One good thing, at least for him, though: it's weaned me of using Kevin's credit card. I use my own now, burning through dear old Mom and Dad's money as I please. Serves them right for abandoning me. Still, I know Kevin can see my charges. How else would my phone be blinking to tell me there's voice mail? He's figured out that I blocked his number on my personal phone, so he calls the places I stay instead. I've blocked pretty much everyone by now.

Just above the ridge line of the mountains, the clouds are growing dense and darkening. *Here we go.*

I'm about to head out, but the damned blinking light irks me, and I know that if I come back to the room later and it's still blinking, I'm gonna be pissed. So I push down the speakerphone button and hear the phone emit a brash, electronic dial tone, then I stab at the voice-mail button. The machine clicks as it starts playing back recordings.

"Hey girl," Zee's voice says, and I'm pleasantly surprised to hear her first. "I'm worried about you. Give me a call, okay?" *Short and sweet. Thanks, Zee.*

The phone clicks again. "Lyn, it's Kevin. Look, I'm sorry. I can explain everything if you'd just talk to me. It's been a long time now. Can't we just talk about this? I mean —"

I thumb the Next button, and the machine spews some garbled tones as it advances. Modern technology, this is not. It clicks once more.

"Hi, Lyn. It's me," Percival's voice says. "I'm, well, not quite sure what to say, but I wanted to say *something*. I can't presume to know all that you're going through, but I'm here, if you need me. If you want to be with me, still." I'm about to push Next again because frankly I cannot deal with all this maudlin shit right now, but Pers catches himself and changes his tone of voice. "Anyway, enough of that. I just wanted to tell you that, when you're ready, even if it takes a long time, you can give me a call. Nothing serious. Whatever you want. No pressure. Okay?" There's a long pause in the recording, and I have no idea what Percival might have been doing during that pause, but listening to it, I realize I'm not breathing. I suck in fresh air as he finally continues. "All right, that's all for now. I know you're still charge hunting, so good luck. Go ride that lightning, Lyn. Talk to you soon, I hope. Bye."

The phone clicks again and goes silent, but I stand there looking at the machine for a long time. "Bye," I say to the echoes of Percival's voice in the empty room at last, grabbing my backpack and opening the door. Immediately the warm air hits me, and I feel the dampness it carries. The trees nearby start to wave rhythmically in the growing breeze.

All my life, I was on the fringe of a tiny group of people with electromagic power. Then I found out they were part of something bigger, the High Order. Mystical mumbo-jumbo, that is. In Paris, I learned of the Prime Order, a faction started by my own parents when they left me to be raised by my brother. Well, I don't care what any of them want, and I don't care about any of their rules. I can't help but think that life was simpler and better when I knew nothing of all these damned groups and all their stupid ideas on what's right and wrong.

It's time now to live in the one place where I actually belong — inside my own skin. And that means doing things for me, not following some ancient set of rules, or some pseudo-enlightened desire to integrate with the regular world. No, I just plan to eat, sleep, and do the one thing that fills me up more than anything else.

Time to go get struck by lightning.

THE END

of

TWICE

Lightning Hopkins
Book 2

NEWSLETTER

Sign Up for Keith Soares's New Releases Newsletter

Get release news and free books, including private giveaways and preview chapters. To join, just visit KeithSoares.com and select the option at the top of the page to get two free books, or go directly to the newsletter sign up form.

facebook.com/KeithSoaresAuthor
twitter.com/ksoares

ABOUT THE AUTHOR

Keith Soares

For 22 years, Keith Soares ran an interactive game, web, and app development agency working with clients like National Geographic, PBS, Verizon, HarperCollins, and the Smithsonian Institution. As a team leader dealing with agency deadlines and late nights waiting on code updates, he converted some of the inevitable downtime into creative time and started writing science fiction and fantasy novels in 2013.

In 2020, Keith left the agency world behind to become a full-time author, trading computer code for plot outlines. He lives in Alexandria, Virginia, with his wife and two daughters, who are all avid readers.

If you've enjoyed this book, I hope you'll consider leaving a very brief review with the store where you purchased it. Thanks.

www.ingramcontent.com/pod-product-compliance
Lightning Source LLC
Chambersburg PA
CBHW031718170626
46808CB00005B/1791